Praise for ~~R~~ ... ~~FFEY~~

"Guffey is my kind of crazy. He understands that the universe is preposterous, life is improbable, and chaos rules: get used to it."
—Pat Cadigan, author of *Mindplayers*

"Robert Guffey's writing has impressed, entertained, and enlightened me pretty much since I first met him. My suggestion? If he wrote it, read it."
—Jack Womack, author of *Random Acts of Senseless Violence*

"Along with Cormac McCarthy, Guffey is my favorite modern fiction writer."
—Gary D. Rhodes, author of *The Perils of Moviegoing in America*

"Guffey . . . combines the technique of a good investigative reporter with that of a (well published) fine storyteller."
—Victor Peppard, *The Mailer Review*

"The Weird is [Guffey's] territory. He finds cracks in the reality machine, crawls inside, and shines his light on incredible happenings piled on top of mad happenings. He's sane. That helps. Iron-rock sane. He's insatiably curious. That works, too. He has the basic instinct of a true journalist: he knows what he doesn't know, and he admits it, and then he crawls, wriggles, scratches, digs until he makes the unknown into something real we can see, no matter how strange it turns out to be."
—*New Dawn Magazine*

[Guffey's] work, full of vast and somewhat offbeat scholarship, is. . . imbued with a Southern Californian sensibility that reminds one both of the trippy work of Philip K. Dick and the Sunshine State Noir of Tarantino (circa *Pulp Fiction*). His writing is emotionally warmer, and he has a deep affection for his oddball characters. I could see the director Paul Thomas Anderson adapting it for the screen."
—Craig L. Gidney, author of *Skin Deep Magic*

Also by Robert Guffey

Collections
Spies and Saucers

Non-fiction
Chameleo
Cryptoscatology: Conspiracy Theory as Art Form

UNTIL
THE LAST
DOG DIES

ROBERT
GUFFEY

NIGHT SHADE BOOKS **NEW YORK**

Night Shade books may be purchased in bulk at special discounts for sales promotion, corporate gifts, fund-raising, or educational purposes. Special editions can also be created to specifications. For details, contact the Special Sales Department, Night Shade Books, 307 West 36th Street, 11th Floor, New York, NY 10018 or info@skyhorsepublishing.com.

Night Shade Books® is a registered trademark of Skyhorse Publishing, Inc.®, a Delaware corporation.

Visit our website at www.nightshadebooks.com.

10 9 8 7 6 5 4 3 2 1

Library of Congress Cataloging-in-Publication Data

Names: Guffey, Robert, author.
Title: Until the last dog dies / by Robert Guffey.
Description: New York : Night Shade Books, 2017.
Identifiers: LCCN 2017006597 | ISBN 9781597809184 (pbk. : alk. paper)
Subjects: LCSH: Comedians--Fiction. | Epidemics--Fiction. |
Humanity--Fiction. | Regression (Civilization)--Fiction. | Satire. |
GSAFD: Fantasy fiction. | LCGFT: Apocalyptic fiction.
Classification: LCC PS3607.U472 U58 2017 | DDC 813/.6--dc23
LC record available at https://lccn.loc.gov/2017006597

Cover artwork and design by Keith Negley

Printed in the United States of America

NOV 29 2017

To Mom and Dad,
for getting the joke

"He who follows the crow will be led to the corpses of dogs."
—ancient Arabian proverb

"I never met a blind man who wasn't a son of a bitch."
—W.C. Fields

UNTIL THE LAST DOG DIES

CHAPTER 1

The Insect Queen of Venus and Other Strangeness

(September 19, 2014)

I took to the stage wearing a simple t-shirt and blue jeans. It was all part of the strategy. It was best to be as average, as invisible as possible before you opened your mouth and let the jokes fly. That way the audience wouldn't build up any preconceived notions about you until you began your patter. You let your humor speak for you.

The air was so clear it was obscene. Years ago a law had been passed banning smoking in clubs, and I still knew comedians who bitched about it—including me. I can't explain this. I don't smoke. I hate smoke. I already obsessed over my health as it was, forever wondering if I was coming down with terminal lung cancer due to the carcinogens in the California air.

Back in the old days, when I was just a little kid (the youngest smartass to brave open mike night armed with an endless supply of fart jokes), I was always trying to convince Lenny, the owner of the club, to put up fans near the bottom of the stage, to at least blow the smoke in the opposite direction, but I was new at the time and he never listened to my suggestions. I suppose I could've just quit, but Lenny was one of the few club owners who'd actually pay for my act. So I just had to grin and bear it (literally).

Ah, the irony of it all: As I was spitting out jokes I was sucking in death. I often thought of that Charlie Chaplin quote: "The clown is so close to death that only a knife-edge separates him from it, and sometimes he goes over the border, but always he returns again." Or as Heather likes to say, "You're never bored when you're a masochist." Perhaps that's why I missed the smoke.

It was a typical Friday night at the tail end of summer. The place was packed. Most of the audience was drunk, which only worked to my advantage. Even though I'd been doing this for many years I still had to deal with the butterflies in my stomach. Some nights I actually thought I was going to throw up . . . until I started talking, that is, and then my brain switched to auto-pilot and nothing existed except the laughter. I've talked to the guys who have been doing this half their lives, and according to them it never changes. Everyone goes through the nervousness, no matter how experienced or established they are. It never gets any easier. I guess I could've figured that out on my own, but when you watch those guys on TV you never think about how much turmoil is brewing right underneath the surface. Comedians are very angry people; most of the time they don't even know what they're angry at, and yet none of that subliminal rage leaks through your TV screen, no matter how large or sophisticated the entertainment system.

I began my act like I usually did: with silence. Not a lot, just enough to keep the audience off-balance. I'd been heavily influenced by Andy Kaufman's stage performances. I liked to make the audience just a bit uncomfortable. At the beginning of my act my nervousness was actually an advantage; I didn't try to hide it. In fact, I tried to accentuate it: stuttering a bit, dropping in a few "ers" and "uhs" here and there, maintaining an open-eyed stare like a little kid caught in the headlights. For some reason this seemed to help. The audience didn't like false arrogance and bravado. They were more sympathetic to someone who seemed just a bit nervous, as nervous as they themselves would be in the same situation. The truth is I don't really know if this is why the act worked. It just did. In the end who can explain such things?

"Uh, hello," I said, waving slightly as I pondered my next move. Reading the crowd is an essential skill for any comedian. In my experience there's an inverse ratio between the size of the crowd and their tolerance for my usual free-form, experimental humor. The larger the crowd the more conservative my jokes become. It happens almost naturally. On a hot night like this drunks are in no mood for biting, incisive political satire. They want dumb impressions and one-liners and racist jokes and they damn well better get it. I don't care what anybody says: standup comedy is the most dangerous avocation on Earth, more so than mountain climbing or defusing Cambodian landmines. One wrong slip of the tongue and you might find yourself hanging from the rafters of the club by a piece of hemp rope.

I waited a beat, then launched into my opening tirade: "Y'know what's been pissing me off lately? These activist types who stand outside Trader Joe's or the Post Office with those little petitions in their hands and toss insane questions in your face like, 'Do you have time for the environment?' Or: 'Do you have time to save the whales?' Could you be *more* fucking annoying?

It's impossible to answer that question without looking like a total dick. It's like 'Have you stopped beating your wife?' The question's purposely designed to guilt trip you. So one day—I swear to God, this really happened—one day I'm leavin' Trader Joe's and this acne-ridden teenage boy is standing there with a clipboard in his hand, and he looks at me with a total straight face and says, 'Do you have time for teen rape?' Well, without even thinking about it I said . . . 'Are you gonna hold her down or am I?'" The audience gasped, not sure whether they should be offended or not; they burst into laughter only a second later. "So I said, 'Have a nice day!' and walked away. The kid seemed a tad stunned. Well . . . that's what the asshole gets for asking a leading question. Don't try to manipulate me, you prissy son of a bitch."

Then I talked about my family, what it was like growing up with an Irish father and a Chinese mother. ("Every time my mother breastfed me I was hungry again an hour later.") My father was the perfect subject for humor. He was a complete paradox. Though he was a card-carrying racist, he married a Chinese woman. ("He ordered her through an ad in the back of *Soldier of Fortune* magazine. They had a special deal that day. Buy a chink and get a life-long subscription.") Growing up with my father wasn't easy. He was disappointed that his only son seemed genetically incapable of hitting homeruns and holding forth on the grand significance of football. He figured I must've been, in his words, "some kinda pillow-biter." ("Did you hear what Pat Robertson said the other day? He said God caused the hurricanes in Florida to punish Disney World for sponsoring a Gay Pride Day. Imagine that—homosexuals attract hurricanes! I think I've figured out how to end the drought in Ethiopia. Just ship all the gays over there! Fuck, when the military figures out they can use gays to control the weather they'll roll out a fuckin' red carpet for 'em.") Despite our many differences, however, I haven't been able to escape his influence. I admit that I've inherited a tinge of my father's racism. ("But I'm trying to make up for it. I'm writing a screenplay about the Ku Klux Klan. It's called *Boyz in the Hood*. You think that title's been taken?")

As the laughter grew I stared out into the audience. The room was so dark and hazy it was difficult to see anyone. You couldn't really know what they were thinking until you heard the laughter—or didn't. This has happened too, of course, but I don't like to talk about it. None of us do. When you hear silence, the trick is to simply keep going. . . .

"Hey, I just heard on the news that a guy got caught performing necrophilia in a funeral home here in California. It turns out they can't charge this guy with anything because necrophilia isn't illegal in California. Now, wait a minute, hold on here. You're telling me that if you smoke a friggin' doobie you can get thrown into the slammer for up to ten years but if you stick your dick in a dead guy you get to walk scott free? Of course, if you get caught smokin' a joint *while* having sex with a corpse, *then* they can charge you with something. Huh? Is something slightly off-kilter here or what?"

I then launched into a routine I had developed while forced to hear a slew of amateur L.A. poets yammering their pretentious stuff and nonsense over the course of a thousand and one open mike nights at clubs and coffee shops all around Southern California. I called the routine "My Girlfriend's a Coke Whore." As with most of my material, it was mostly autobiographical. (Thank Yahweh/Ba'al/Osiris/etc., I was no longer with the delightful female who had inspired the bit.) The routine consisted of me reciting a "poem" with a straight face while my fellow comedian, Danny Oswald, sat at a piano behind me belting out responses to my existential agony in the form of song. Despite being the whitest white guy in this dimension or any other, Danny could do a pretty damn good Louis Armstrong impersonation, which is why I asked him to help me out in the first place. Here's how the routine went:

Me (my hands shaking slightly as I read from a crumpled piece of paper, my golden and immortal poem): "My girlfriend is a coke whore. The other day I found a condom in her cunt. It was not mine."

Danny (while singing in his throaty, bluesy voice and allowing his nimble fingers to dance gracefully across the ivories): *"You gotta give everybody a chance."*

Me: "I don't love coke . . . but I love her. I hate loving her because when I see her blowing another man, it breaks my heart."

Danny: *"You can do anything if only you believe."*

Me: "When I see her the next day I ask, 'How could you do this to me?' She looks at me and then gets on her knees and I remember what a beautiful person she is."

Danny: *"The love between a man and woman is so pure."*

Me: "But she only does this so I let her into my apartment, and then she steals from me. She stole my cell phone, she stole my toaster."

Danny: *"White toast golden brown on both sides, not any-more."*

Me: "And later I asked why she did that, and she kissed me, and I was weak, and I made love to her. The moment I came she said, 'You fuckin' faggot!' and I put my pants on, and I left her apartment."

Danny: *"The fire in a woman can make a man go crazy."*

Me: "But the very next day, the *very* next day, I catch her getting fucked from behind while she's sucking some other guy's balls. And when she saw me she spit the balls out of her mouth and said, 'You fuckin' faggot!'"

Danny: *"Oh shit, I can't help you with that."*

Me: "For weeks after that I could not talk to her and could not maintain an erection. I bought pills off television and through mail order from Mexico, but those balls in her mouth, those balls in her mouth."

Danny: *"Life has its sweetness but its bitterness too."*

Me: "A couple of days later she showed up at my apartment with her new boyfriend. She asked to borrow money, then said, 'Sorry about that faggot thing.' 'Which one?' I said. 'All three of them,' she said. I gave her a fifty dollar bill, and she spit her gum out in it, and put it in her bra."

Danny: *"What the fuck . . . what the fuck . . . you got me there . . . I'm stumped. . . ."*

Me: "A few weeks later she called and wanted me to bail her out of jail. I told her I would as long as she agreed to get treatment. On the way back home in the car she asked me for gum."

Danny: *"Ugh . . . god damn it . . . not the gum thing again . . . what's with that gum thing. . . ."*

Me: "She started treatment, and the effects were immediately apparent. During my visits to her I noticed shaking, chills, and irritability. I told her she looked beautiful, and she asked me to stay with her forever."

Danny: *"Forever's a long time . . . talk to your lawyer. . . ."*

Me: "But when she was giving me a blowjob I could barely keep my erection because her technique had deteriorated. And I just couldn't be . . . with someone . . . who didn't understand me."

Danny: *"Blue . . . blue . . . blue . . . balls. . . ."*

Me: "I realized that cocaine opened up a part of her psyche that made her a mouth-fuck genius, so I went out and scored her sixty dollars' worth."

Danny: *"On the corner of 8th and Junipero talk to a guy named Ronnie . . . he's black. . . ."*

Me: "But instead of sucking my cock she escaped the treatment center and ended up blowing a bum for what turned out to be a bag of baking soda."

Danny: *"Baking soda's fantastic 'cause it keeps everything fresh. . . ."*

Me: "That's when I realized that I just can't be with her anymore. No matter how much I love her, it can never work out between us. Nor can I ever be rid of the pain of my love."

Danny: *"Can you please now explain that gum thing to me. . . ."*

The laughter swelled. We did a solid ten-minute set, leaving the audience primed for Karen Griffin, an angry black lesbian who told a lot of jokes about . . . well, angry black lesbians. What else? I prayed Karen came back in one piece. Danny and I strolled back to the bar where one of the comedians who'd gone on before us, Heather Wheeler, was drinking a beer. Danny and Heather Wheeler were, like me, disgusted with the current state of standup comedy. Most of the time we'd end up right here at the bar, eating peanuts, getting drunk, and grumbling about how flaccid and vacuous most comedians were—the successful ones, at any rate. Many nights we fantasized about ramming a stake through Dane Cook's thieving heart and planting his head on a barber pole. I'd even worked out a five-minute routine around exactly that premise.

Of course, all the mainstream comedians claimed we were just bitter, and maybe that was true. I'd been in and out of standup for years. If a major network had offered me a part in a lame sitcom at that time would I have had the balls to turn it down? I don't know, I'd like to think so. When you haven't eaten anything but Saltine crackers and Campbell's chicken noodle soup for a month you're less inclined to be self-righteous. On the other hand I knew a lot of friends of mine—talented young comedians—who had been plucked out of obscurity from the alternative night clubs, plopped down in the middle of a major network who immediately cast them in another mindless sit-com that tanked in two weeks and ruined their reputations, leaving them floating in some mist-filled limbo where they were no longer "alternative" or "mainstream." They'd sold their souls for a pile of fairy gold that turned to dust within seconds of grasping hold of it. I didn't want to end up that way.

Which is why I mainly stuck to the alternative L.A. clubs like Largo, the Cyclops, and Prospero's. I couldn't stand the mainstream nightspots like the Improv or The Comedy Store, where all the comedians were either cute Jewish guys or beach-blond jocks who apparently found great philosophical relevance in the poor quality of airplane food or the unreliability of park-ing meters, nothing even in the general *vicinity* of obscene or cutting edge or controversial. Hell, I don't really blame them. Life's much simpler in the mainstream. I mean, hey, don't get me started on that time the black Muslim began heckling me from the front row. I took off my glasses and told him to come up on stage and tell me what he thought about me to my face. Ninety-nine percent of the time hecklers are just cowards who will slump down in their seats when challenged. On this partic-ular occasion, however, I just happened to tap into that rare one percent of the population. Danny tells me my jokes were even funnier with a broken nose and lips the size of Encino. If so I'll do without the extra laughs, thank you.

Danny's a weird guy, a real shut-in. The only time he ever leaves his room is to go to the clubs. He lives in a small apart-ment with his dad, who's a retired mechanic. I don't know how he got the brain he did, but of all the comedians I know he's the one most deserving of success. He's kind of like a cross between Jackie Mason and Andy Kaufman, both wise and insane at the same time. He's the gentlest soul you'll ever meet, though it's difficult to talk to him because he's constantly in character. He has a hard time relating to people off-stage. That's a common occupational hazard, I think.

He got goofed on a lot as kid. Hell, which one of us didn't? Danny claimed it was because of his last name. As a result he became obsessed with the JFK assassination. He's fashioned a lot of jokes around it, more than you can possibly imagine. The one I remember the most is a little two-liner that goes: "Did you know that Oliver Stone is making a sequel to *JFK*? It's called *KFC*, about the assassination of Col. Sanders." He says it with such a straight face you almost believe it might be true.

"You killed again," Heather said as we slid into the seats on either side of her.

I shrugged. I rapped my knuckles on the bar to get the bartender's attention, then held up one finger. I don't know why, but a beer tasted best right after a performance. "I think I sucked. I always think that."

"Cut the bullshit," Heather said. "You know you were good. You think they were laughing out of politeness?"

"I could've been better."

"You could always be better," Heather said, tossing a peanut in the air and catching it on the tip of her tongue. She had a talented tongue. It was her best feature, in fact. "You could always be worse too," she added. "You could be dead." Heather was thirty-two, three years older than me. She wasn't an attractive woman, she was just kind of average. She had mousy brown hair, hardly wore make-up and had a scrawny, underfed body. Nevertheless she had a way of shaping the space around her as if it belonged only to her, a way of moving across the room that announced to everybody in no uncertain terms: "I know exactly who I am, I don't care what you think about me, and get the *hell* out of my way." She had Attitude, with a capital A, and that more than made up for her plainness. Her looks grew on you after awhile. She had a beautiful smile, wide and bright and enticing. I think she'd had sex with about twelve different comedians on the L.A. nightclub circuit (none of them Danny or me) and in every case the relationship ended with *her* dumping *him,* not the other way around. I often wondered what it would be like to be her boyfriend, but I was also afraid of being eaten alive. One night when I'd had one too many drinks I made an awkward, fumbling pass at her that ended with Heather physically removing my hand from her left breast while suggesting various alternative placements for it like the garbage disposal or the inside of the microwave oven. It was kind of embarrassing. The night ended with me slinking out of her apartment while she visited the toilet. The next morning I called to apologize, but she quickly changed the subject. Neither of us had mentioned the incident since then.

"What if I am dead?" I said. "What if we're all dead and this is Heaven?"

"Gee, wouldn't that be Hell?" Heather said. She tossed another peanut into the air. This time it bounced off the side of her mouth and landed somewhere on the floor. "Shit!" she said and peered angrily at the floor, as if intent on retrieving the peanut and strangling it for its impudence.

"*The Peanut That Got Away,*" Danny said into his beer. "Starring Hardy Kruger and Alec McCowen. Rank Pictures, Great Britain, 1957."

Another obscure reference. Sometimes I didn't know what the hell he was talking about.

I spun around on my stool and watched Karen Griffin performing for a few moments. She was telling a joke about political correctness: "You know, I've come to the conclusion that us queers should just get back in the fuckin' closet. The world seemed less weird that way, don't you agree?" The audience laughed and clapped. She was really winning them over. "I mean, have you ever heard of this children's book *Heather Has Two Mommies*? It's about two lesbians who raise a kid. I'm totally against that, man. I mean, shit, dykes can't raise kids. After all, it says so in the Old Testament. Genesis I:I: 'Dykes can't raise kids.' It's right there on page one! Just the other day I saw a sequel called *Heather Has TWELVE Mommies*. Now, this is getting way out of hand. It was a pop-up book! I opened it up and these turkey basters flew out and almost hit me in the head. Shit, nearly knocked me out cold, man."

She had the audience in stitches. "She's getting more laughs than I did," I said to no one in particular.

"Of course," Heather said. "The audience is afraid she's going to kill them if they don't laugh."

Griffin did look scary. She insisted on wearing this skin-tight black body suit on stage, and her kinky hair was spiked out in all possible directions; the top of her head looked like the jumping jacks I used to play with as a kid. Even more scary were her eyes. She suffered from some weird condition that enabled her to bulge her eyes out of her head until they appeared to be as big as cue balls; this was both nauseating and funny at the same time. Her skin was as black as the depths of the Cayman Trench and her body impossibly lithe, as if she spent the majority of her time swimming deep underwater. She looked like the offspring of a mutant aquatic spider from another planet that had attacked and raped a human being on some lonesome road late one night out in the middle of nowhere. I would never say this to her face, of course.

Heather might. I don't think they were too fond of each other. I never knew why.

"I think it has more to do with the fact that she's god damn funny," Danny said, responding to Heather's snide remark. He turned around, planted his elbows on the bar behind him, and watched Griffin ripping into some poor heckler in the front row. "I want to marry her."

Both Heather and I stared at him in shock. Danny very rarely made any reference to women whatsoever, except perhaps in a comedic way. I wasn't even certain he'd ever been on a date, though any guy on a stage tends to attract groupies, no matter how unappealing he is.

"Are you high?" I said.

"No," Danny said very seriously, "I think I love her." It was hard to tell when he was joking or not. He brushed his hair back with his hands, then smoothed out his flannel shirt. "After her set I've decided I'm going to ask her out on a date."

"She's a *dyke*," Heather said. She had this bemused look on her face that was rather hilarious.

"I know," Danny said. "That just makes her all the more intriguing."

Heather glanced up at the ceiling and rolled her eyes.

"He's got to be pulling our legs," I said to Heather.

"Don't you bet on it, kiddo," she said, tossing yet another peanut into the air. This one dropped right down her throat. She almost choked on it. For a moment I thought I was going to have to perform the Heimlich Maneuver. I began slapping her on the back as she coughed and sputtered like a backfiring car. Fortunately, just as Griffin was finishing her set, Heather got her coughing under control. When I turned to look at Danny he was already walking toward the stage. Heather and I watched him approach Griffin as she stepped off the side of the stage, while behind her Lenny grabbed the mike and began doing his usual patter in between acts. We saw Danny lean toward her ear in order to be heard over the noise. After talking to her for no more than twenty seconds, Griffin flashed a wide ivory-white smile (the first time I'd seen anything even remotely resembling a smile on anything even remotely resembling her face) at which point she extended her elbow (I thought, My God, she's going to disable his floating rib with a quick jab in the side!) and allowed Danny to slip his arm through hers. They strolled off toward the backstage area arm in arm, looking like long-separated sweethearts.

Heather and I remained silent for quite a while. I felt like a witness to a rare religious miracle.

At last I muttered, "That must've been staged."

"I don't think so," Heather said, turning her back on Lenny's patter and addressing her beer mug once again.

"Excuse me, what're you talking about? You think *Danny* has the ability to sweet talk the Insect Queen of Venus into a candlelit dinner within twenty fucking seconds?"

"Yes."

I sighed and knocked back a swig of beer. "God damn it, you're probably right. The universe really does work like that, doesn't it?"

"It's an odd-shaped world full of odd-shaped folk."

"Why don't *I* have that ability? I mean, I'm a professional comedic linguistic technician. Words are my stock in trade, fachrissakes! I should be able to flap my lips and make women roll over and play dead, right?"

Heather shook her head. "It's gotta be in your genes. You're good enough to make people laugh, but you're not persuasive." She began waving her finger in the air as if she were about to make a brilliant philosophical point. "Now Hitler . . . Hitler, on the other hand, was the exact opposite." She took another sip of her beer. "He was persuasive, but he couldn't make people laugh."

"How do you know?"

She shrugged. "I dunno, have *you* ever seen footage of Hitler crackin' out witty one-liners, making all those wide-eyed German boys in their sexy S.S. uniforms bust a gut over jokes about sauerkraut or Volkswagens? No, you just see him waving his fist around, complaining about Jews and taxes and things like that."

"Maybe they just never show the footage of him being funny."

"So you think they're hiding it? The Jewish media is suppressing evidence of Hitler's scary talents, is that it?"

"I wouldn't put it past them."

"Are you kidding?"

"Yes."

As Heather finished her beer Danny and Griffin emerged from the back of the club with their jackets on, looking like they were primed for a night on the town. Griffin was beaming like a little girl in love for the first time, falling all over Danny as if she couldn't bear not to be in physical contact with him for more than two seconds.

They strolled right up to us. Danny said, "Well, we're heading on over to Ye Rustic Inn for a few drinks. You want to join us?"

Ye Rustic Inn was a funky little bar in Los Feliz where some of us hung out after our gigs were finished, swapping jokes and offering constructive (and/or deconstructive) criticism on each other's performances. I was about to accept Danny's offer to join them, just to observe the synergy between an angry black lesbian and a neurotic white shut-in, when Griffin suddenly leaned over Danny's shoulder and said, "Look, I don't want to be rude, but why don't you just keep your ass planted where it is, okay? I want Danny all to myself." She slid her hands down Danny's chest and ran the tip of her tongue over his ear lobe.

Somewhat taken aback, I replied, "Well, hell, I didn't want to go anywhere with you two anyway."

"And I have to wash my hair tonight," Heather said, not even turning around to face them. She was watching them in the mirror behind the bar.

Danny said, "Well, uh, I'll see you guys later then . . . I guess," as Griffin dragged him toward the exit.

When the doors closed behind them I turned to Heather and said, "Well, how do you like that? Can you believe that?"

"Yes." Heather paid the bartender for her beer.

"You're certainly taking this in stride."

She shrugged. "It doesn't affect me."

"Doesn't affec—? Are you crazy? This affects everyone in the world. The mantle of the Earth is shifting, the galactic center dissolving, the universe retracting at a faster pace than ever before due to the mere *possibility* that Griffin and Danny might procreate tonight and spawn who knows what kind of evil homunculi. Can you even begin to comprehend how this might alter the gene pool?"

"Let's hope they stick to the shallow end of the gene pool, far enough away from us more highly evolved primates to not derail us from our upward spiralling path." She rose from her stool.

"Hey, where're you going so early?"

She sighed. "Home, I guess, then to bed."

"Yeah, it's been a long night, hasn't it? I'm not doing much of anything either. You know . . . thought I'd go back to my little rabbit hole, maybe heat up a can of Campbell's chicken

soup, the kind with 33% more chicken in it, sprinkle some Saltine crackers on top . . . you know, watch the snow on my black
and white TV I bought at a yard sale, then retire to my mattress
on the floor for a restless, lonely night's sleep."

Heather and I stared at each other for a few seconds, me
with an affable smile on my boyish face, she with a totally
unreadable, stoic expression. So forceful was the orgone energy
in the room at that moment I could feel the sexual tension
exploding out of our bodies like forks of lightning, interlocking,
spinning, dancing an electrical dance. I knew I had her within
my grasp. I just needed to close the deal with a few smooth,
well-spoken words.

Before I could open my mouth, however, Heather said,
"Well, hope you have fun, then," and left the club.

I watched the doors swinging shut . . . back and forth,
back and forth . . . then returned my attention to my glass
of beer. Out of the corner of my eye I could see the bartender
snickering over my rejection, so I glared at him insanely like
Mohamed Atta staring at the Twin Towers right before blowing
them to smithereens. He decided to clean the opposite end of
the bar, leaving me alone with my pain. I dropped a peanut
into the glass, watched it break the surface tension, studied the
resultant ripples that spread out quickly in concentric circles.
I sighed and thought: Most people call me bi-sexual, because
whenever I try to have sex with them they say, "Bye-bye, bye-
bye!" I giggled into the beer and figured I might as well add that
to my repertoire. Yeah, might as well.

Later that night, as I was sitting at home eating a bowl of
Campbell's chicken soup with Saltine crackers sprinkled on
top, I heard a strange news report on the radio (the snow made
watching TV impossible). A major university had just released
the results of a five-year-long scientific study; the scientists

involved had come to the conclusion that the deterioration of the ozone was due not to the burning of fossil fuels, but to the methane in cow farts. I glanced at the calendar to make sure it wasn't April Fool's Day. Nope, it was the middle of September. It was a serious report! Imagine the amount of tax-payer's dollars that had been used to fund such a thing. Why didn't the scientists just break down laughing halfway through the first day? That would've ended the whole charade right there. More disturbing still was the fact that the newscaster didn't erupt into wild guffaws while reporting the silly thing. I often wondered if most of the human race wasn't suffering from some kind of strange disease, an anti-evolutionary trait that prevented them from detecting the mad humor that surrounded them each and every day.

Little did I know that this would prove to be more than just idle fancy.

CHAPTER 2

The Last Gasp of a Narcissist ·

(September 22, 2014)

Two nights later I played a different club, Prospero's in West Hollywood. The crowd was smaller, the weather cooler. I went on at eight p.m., right after the M.C. described me as "a cross between Aristotle and Groucho Marx, except not as dead. Please give a big round of applause for the one and only . . . Elliot Greeley!"

I loved performing at Prospero's. The atmosphere was so much more relaxed. I could always expect an intelligent crowd. They allowed me to do what I liked best, which was to just let my mind wander in a kind of stream-of-consciousness rant, relating strange incidents that might have happened to me only hours before going on stage. Every sentence didn't have to end with a punchline. Some of my best performances had been at Prospero's.

Tonight I put two wooden stools on the stage. On the top of one stool I placed an old cassette recorder I'd found at a thrift store in Long Beach. I hit play, then strolled over to the other end of the stage, picked up the microphone,—no emotion in my face whatsoever—sat down, and began chatting just as the tape kicked in. On the right side of the stage my recorded voice attempted to tell a sad story in a way that was funny—but in a pathetic sort of way; meanwhile, on the left side of the stage, I told the story seriously, without once cracking even the wisp of a smile.

I don't want to bring you down or anything but, uh, when I was eighteen I tried to commit suicide? I've been seeing an analyst about it for three years. He says I suffer from delusions of persecution, but I'm sure he's just saying that to destroy me. So far the only *real* thing we've learned is that I have an uncontrollable urge to run through red lights because I was born Caesarian.

Anyway, one night when my parents were out of the house I decided to . . . y'know, off myself or whatever. So I pop about a hundred pills . . . actually, it was a hundred and one pills because I figured I *just* might need that extra pill. So, you know, I'm just kickin' it, watchin' some TV, trippin' out on this whole

When I was in high school I tried to kill myself. I was depressed, y'see, so my parents sent me to a therapist because they were afraid. The therapist didn't do shit. He sat there and stared at me, scribbling shit down in his notebook, while I talked and talked and talked. Just like I'm doing now. Nothing ever got accomplished. Every time I left that office, I was more depressed than when I came in.

One time the two of us debated the various drawbacks and virtues of suicide. He quoted G. K. Chesterton at me: "Suicide is the last gasp of a narcissist." I quoted James Branch Cabell back at him: "The optimist proclaims that we live in the best of all possible worlds; and the pessimist fears this is true." He death thing, when I think, "Hm . . . maybe this wasn't such a hot idea after all." So I call my girl-friend Tina.

Let me tell you, Tina was the most beautiful, loyal girl in the world. She'd do anything for me. But her parents controlled her every move. Her mom would monitor the phone to make sure I wasn't calling too much. So tonight Tina's mom decides to answer the phone. . . .

God, she was a terror. The weirdest thing about her? The mom? She was born with no fuckin' vagina. This is true. She didn't get one until after she was married. The doctors had to scoop one out with a fuckin' Baskin and Robbins uten-sil when she was eighteen or somethin'. Even more strange is the fact that her husband Phil knew all this and married her anyway. Imagine marrying a psychotic Barbie doll. The worst of both worlds—all nagging, no shagging.

Her parents hated me. First they were scared I was gonna get her pregnant, then they blamed

didn't know what to say to that one. He had a lot of degrees hanging on his wall, but he didn't know crap about human beings.

So, anyway, I wanted to stop seeing the son of a bitch, y'know? My parents wouldn't let me. They forced me to go. Twice a week, for three years. By the time I was eighteen I couldn't stand it anymore. The bas-tard was so depressing, I just decided to end it all.

I went into my room, turned on the television—maybe *The Simpsons*? I don't know. I poured out all the pills my therapist had given me to "cure" my depres-sion. All they'd done was make it fuckin' worse, y'know? So I figured I'd give those little blue fuckers the chance to end my funk. Forever.

I drank them all down with fruit juice. What was I think-ing? Was I trying to be fuckin' healthy? It doesn't make any sense, I know. I'm just tellin' you what happened, okay?

I just sat there thinkin' about the Coyote in those old Road Runner cartoons. The Coyote me when she turned bi-sexual on 'em. Can you believe that? Mom's got no fuckin' vagina, so they adopt this kid, she hits puberty, decides she likes rubbing fuzzies with the chick down the street, and it's *my* fault? "You're a bad influence. You turned my daughter into a lesbian." Right. House, M.D. had to slit you open with a shoehorn and you're questioning *my* sexuality? I told 'em, Go find a kid with no cunt if you're so concerned. I'm sure there must be some floatin' around out there. Just flip through the back of the *L.A. Weekly.* Special pregnancy-free children. No assembly required. No freakin' maintenance.

Where the fuck was I? Oh, yeah! So her mom answers the phone and goes, "Hello?"

Now, at this point I'm in a panic because I'm almost dead and I've lost all capacity for speech. So I think I said something like, "Hhhhrrrmmmmhuher!"

Her mom goes, "Oh, just a minute. Tina! It's Elliot!" Five

never falls until he looks down, right? You know. You know what I mean. That's what I did. I looked down. I looked down and saw the endless pit of cold hellish darkness I knew I'd sink into if I let myself fall asleep right then and there. So I called my girlfriend. Her name was Tina. She wasn't much to look at, she'd cheated on me about five dozen times, but what the hell. She said she loved me. Why not believe it? Hell, what was the alternative?

Well . . . the pills, I guess. But they were turning out not to be too much of an alternative. I guess I drank way too much fruit juice. Twenty-two ounces of Prune Juice Medley can wreak havoc with your digestive system, particularly when you mix it with pharmaceutical grade speed. I called Tina, and her mom answered the phone. I couldn't understand what she was saying. I couldn't understand anything. I couldn't talk. I remember crying, wanting somebody to erase the past hour, but that was impossible. I was lying flat on the floor, trying to mumble into or ten or sixteen minutes go by. Finally Tina answers the phone: "Hello?"

"Hhhhrrrmmmmhuher!"

"What? You've taken a hundred pills?"

"Hhhhrrm!"

"A hundred and *one* pills? Oh my God! Just stay there. I'll call for help." She hangs up, runs around the room twelve times fast in a circle, stops, and goes, "AAAAAAAA!"

Her mom peeks into the room. "What's wrong, dear?"

"Hhhhrrrmmmhuher!"

"What? Elliot's taken a hundred pills?"

"Hhhrrrm!"

"He's taken a hundred and *one* pills? Oh my God!"

So they manage to call the paramedics. The ambulance arrives at my house driven by the Keystone Kops. Yeah. This is true. Harpo Marx is on the roof playing with the siren, Woody Allen's in the back, fretting. It's crazy. It's a real party.

So we make it to the hospital where they pull my stomach out the receiver . . . but it seemed to be crawling away from me. The whole damn world seemed to be crawling away from me.

I woke up in the hospital, two fat nurses hovering over me, forcing liquid charcoal down my esophagus. I gagged and threw up tar three or four times. Then they shoved these white plastic tubes down there and pumped my stomach. Imagine half of a vacuum being lodged way way down into the middle of your fuckin' chest and you can't spit it up, no matter how hard you try. I felt claustrophobic, like the walls of the whole damn world were closing in on me. I wanted to die again . . . just as long as the pain would stop right then and there. Just stop. Please . . . just stop.

It didn't. I was awake for the whole ordeal, and I was still awake hours later when my father came into my hospital room and cussed me out so loud the nurse had to drag him away. He called me a faggot and said I wasn't fit to be his son. My mother just patted him on the shoulder through my mouth and wring it out like a dish towel until there's not a trace of poison left inside. They even manage to find an old sock monkey I'd been searching for for a long time. Eventually someone decides to notify my parents, right? My father strolls into the hospital room in this business suit, this briefcase dangling from his hand. He goes [sighing]: "Okay . . . what have you done *now*?" I'm thinking, "Boy, Dad, inspire the will to live."

A few months later Tina leaves me for this cheerleader, my mom dies of brain cancer, and my dad orders me to go to work to pay for the hospital bills. The last I heard Tina's mother was renting out her artificial vagina to pick up some extra cash. I guess you can do whatever the hell you want with it as long as you bring it back in the shape you found it. And, uh, I became a comedian, of course. But other than that everything turned out fine. I mean, I haven't tried to kill myself again in the

and quietly asked him to forgive me. "Be like the Jesus," she'd say to him, "be like the Jesus."

I had to share a room with a girl who was recovering from a heroin overdose. She was just a couple of years older than me. I remember having a fantasy of us falling in love with each other. We never spoke to each other. She never even noticed me. She just kept staring at the corner of the ceiling, mumbling jingles from old commercials. I tried to join in at one point, when I recognized one, but she acted as if I wasn't even there. I was a ghost to her, beneath her notice. I think I fell in love with that girl; I never even knew her name. I wonder if she's still alive now.

Tina managed to visit me once, with some pimply-faced dude in tow. He became her new boyfriend a couple of weeks after I was let out of the hospital. She broke up with me on the same day I had to go back to my therapist and tell him why I tried to commit suicide. And I told him. I told him it was the

past . . . three hours or so. So
what's new with you?

last gasp of a narcissist. . . . So
what's new with you?

"So what's new with you?" The cassette's last sentence hung out there in the silence. I had timed it perfectly. The taped story came to an end at the exact moment that I put down the microphone and stared at the audience. I held that stare for a while, said nothing else, then placed the microphone gently on the stool and strolled off into the wings.

Later, I came out again and took the exact opposite approach, launching into mainstream mode. You know, routines with real jokes in them. Imagine that. I proceeded to riff with the audience, now and then weaving in my set jokes. I got a good reaction that night, but not a *great* reaction. I sensed a strange lack of enthusiasm on the part of the audience, as if some of them were just going through the motions. I wondered if I'd unbalanced them too much with that first act. I found that a little hard to believe. I mean, this was a real cutting-edge dive. Usually the people in the audience were total freaks. They liked stuff that was off the wall. Tonight, I had no idea what they liked.

You rarely get sympathetic laughter in standup comedy, no matter where you are. If they think you're funny they laugh, and if they think otherwise they let you know very quickly. To encounter this unreadable flat affect in the faces of some of the audience members was disturbing. At one point I even tried to make a joke about it, wondering aloud if a group of tourists had been bussed in from the Village of the Damned expressly to catch my act. They didn't seem to catch the reference. Obscure pop culture references are always hit and miss anyway, so I just shrugged it off—or tried to.

After I finished my set I headed backstage, feeling like a G.I. who'd been under siege all night by Viet Cong snipers, emerging from the rice paddies at dawn to make his way back to base in order to tell the tale to his friends. I heard Ivan, the owner, call my name. He patted me on the back and said, "You did a great job out there, man. Bizarre, but great."

"Yeah, *I* thought so. But didn't you notice something weird about the audience?"

Ivan bit his lower lip, pulled his long brown hair back into a ponytail. What with his bushy moustache and beard, his unkempt sideburns, and his tye-dye shirt, he looked like he'd just stepped out of a PBS documentary about Haight-Ashbury. He was an aging hippie, though you wouldn't know it from his fat bank account. He owned a number of nightclubs around town, but Prospero's was his main love. As a former standup comedian himself, he'd taken up the crusade of saving experimental comedy from total extinction.

"Now that you mention it," he said, "the clientele's been dipping off lately. People who usually come in at least once a week never come in at all anymore. And the ones who do come in seem . . . I don't know, different somehow."

"What do you mean different?"

Ivan shrugged. "I don't know, not quite as hyped up as they usually are. *You* know. This place is usually hoppin' with the hippest dudes in town. But lately, I don't know . . . instead of artists and writers and actors, we seem to be attracting accountants and bank tellers. Real fuckin' squares."

"Where are they all coming from?"

"No, man, I don't mean we're getting *actual* accountants and bank tellers, I mean the artists and the writers and the actors are all *behaving* like accountants and bank tellers. They've turned into real stiffs. It's like *The Walking Dead* out there some nights. Hardly anyone ignores the no-smoking ban anymore. That's a load of worry off my shoulders, of course, but still . . . it's kind of depressing. I thought Southern California was the last bastion of rebellion. Instead they're all rollin' over like Ted Cruz at a hog callin' contest. What with all the pollution that's pumped into the sky from all the fancy foreign cars cloggin' up all the freeways, what the hell do they care *what* we suck into our lungs in our own free time?"

"It's not pollution that's the problem," I said, "it's cow farts."

Ivan tilted his head and just stared at me for a second. "What the fuck're you smokin', man?"

"Nothing, nothing. Listen, I'm gonna head on over to the bar, okay?"

"Fine, have whatever you want. Uh, say, that Ted Cruz simile was pretty good, wasn't it? Maybe you can use that in your act."

"Maybe. Catch you later, Ivan." I patted him on his bony shoulder and made a bee-line for the bar. I was surprised to find Danny sitting on one of the stools, knocking back a glass of red wine. I'd never seen him drinking anything other than beer. "What the hell?" I said, sliding onto the stool beside him. "Did the beer tap run dry or something?"

Danny launched into his dead-on Bela Lugosi imperson-ation. "I don't drink . . . *wine*." He broke character. "Oh, well. I guess I can't use that line anymore, can I?" He took a sip from the glass.

I gestured for Marion, the bartender, to get me a glass of beer. Marion was a beautiful redhead in her early twenties, pos-sibly the last person on Earth a depressed guy wanted to look at while he was getting smashed. Someone should pass a law that all bartenders can only be old burly guys with nicknames like "Bull" or "Popeye."

"So why the sudden wine fetish?" I said.

Danny shrugged. "Karen introduced me to its subtle, refined qualities. It's good for the heart, you know."

It took a few moments to figure out who Karen was. "Hey, you mean Griffin? Since when did she become Karen?"

"Since Friday night."

"Oh my God." I lowered my head into my hands. "I can't believe it. This is impossible. On the first date?" Danny nodded. "Incredible, just incredible." Marion placed a glass of beer in front of me. I downed two large gulps, then wiped the foam from my lips with the back of my forearm. My usual table manners were the first casualty of my shock. "How did you manage it?"

Danny snapped his fingers. "It was as easy as 3.141."

The image of Griffin's spiked hair rolling around on a bed as she sucked on Danny's face was difficult to eject from my mind long enough to hold a rational conversation with him. I grabbed his forearm. "Please. You've got to give me all the details."

He shook his head. "I respect her too much for that."

I dismissed his comment with a wave of my hand. "You didn't get anywhere with her."

He shrugged. He didn't care whether I believed him or not. That convinced me all the more. I grabbed his wrist and squeezed it in desperation. "Please, you have to tell me how you did it."

He took another sip of wine, then said, "Mirroring."

"Excuse me?"

"A technique of Neuro-Linguistic Programming."

It was like he'd suddenly begun speaking another language. "What the hell're you talking about?"

He leaned close to me and said, "I've been reading this book that these former Pentagon guys wrote that tells you how to deal with people in the business world."

"What is this, some hypnosis book?"

Danny shook his head again and reached into his inside jacket pocket. He pulled out a small mass market paperback entitled *The Warrior's Edge*, the cover of which depicted a man in a business suit cocking back a bow and arrow. The suit looked just like the one my father wore to the hospital when I was eighteen.

"It's amazing," Danny said. "You can get people to do what you want just by mirroring their body movements."

I took the book from him and flipped through it. "So did you see the advertisement for this in the back of an old comic book between the sea monkey ads and the trick shaving foam?"

"I'm telling you it works." He glanced around the room, then pointed at a hot blonde chick who was sitting at a small table with some young surfer dude, probably her boyfriend. They were both laughing at the comedian on stage, a guy named Jack Varner who was doing a routine about radioactive Mormons in Utah. "I bet I can get that blonde to come over here by the time Jack's done with his set without me saying a word."

"Oh, you'll use semaphore or something."

He held his hand in the air like a boy scout. "I promise not to attract her attention in any way."

"You're on. What're we betting?"

"If I lose I have to spill the beans about what happened between me and Karen on Friday night."

"Perfect. And if I lose?"

Danny shrugged. "You have to buy me a beer at Ye Rustic Inn sometime."

I slapped my hand on the table top. "Which I probably would've done anyway! It's almost a win-win situation for me." I brushed my hands together eagerly. "Oh, I can't wait to hear those sordid little details. Maybe I'll work 'em into my act."

"You have my permission to do so. Now shh. This takes some concentration." Danny turned sideways on his stool as if he were watching Varner's performance, but out of the corner of his eye he was observing the blonde, studying her every movement. Slowly, he began to position his body in such a way that it was an exact mirror-image of her own. Whenever she changed position, he changed position as well. At some point Danny even seemed to have altered his breathing patterns to match hers. Sometimes it seemed as if the blonde had unconsciously begun to mimic *Danny's* gestures, but I knew that was impossible. As Varner's performance continued I noticed the blonde glancing over at us every few minutes or so, staring at Danny with a puzzled look on her face. I checked my watch. It was almost nine p.m. I knew Varner would be done within a few minutes. My initial skepticism had given way to nervous apprehension. Silently I urged Varner to hurry up and be done with it.

Just as Varner launched into his big finale, an amazing impression of Vladimir Putin doing whip-its during a G8 conference, the blonde glanced over at us one last time, whispered something to her boyfriend, then got up from her chair and began walking toward us.

Oh my God, I can't believe this, I thought.

She sauntered right up to Danny and said, "Do I know you from somewhere?"

"Well, I've performed here quite a bit," Danny said. "Perhaps you've seen me on stage."

"Oh, are you a comedian?" she asked, smiling, obviously very impressed.

Danny shrugged as if it were no big deal. "Oh, yeah. . . ."

The woman frowned. "But this is the first time I've ever been here. I couldn't have seen you on stage."

"Maybe it was at another nightclub around town."

"Maybe, but I don't think so. You seem much more familiar than that." She bit her lower lip for a moment, as if deep in thought, then threw her hands in the air and said, "Oh well, maybe I'm just being crazy again. Are you performing later on tonight?"

"Yeah, I'll be going on in about twenty minutes," Danny said. "Maybe you'd like to join me for a drink afterwards."

"Oh . . . I'm kind of with someone at the moment," she said, gesturing toward her boyfriend, who kept throwing us hard looks.

"Bring him along," Danny said. "Just as long as he doesn't get in our way."

The woman laughed. "Well, I'll ask him, I guess."

"Uh . . . so how'd you like *my* performance?" I said.

As if noticing me for the first time, she glanced at me briefly and said, "You were okay," then turned back to Danny. "Do you perform here often?"

"At least once a week."

"Well . . . maybe I'll bump into you again sometime. Bye." She gave us a little wave and returned to her seat just as Varner left the stage.

Danny sipped his wine with a big smirk on his face. I stared at him in shock. "What the fuck? How did you do that?" He pointed at the book, which I picked up off the bar and flipped through once again. "Does this teach you how to be the fucking Shadow or something?" I broke into my stereotypical black voice. "Who knows what evil lurks in the hearts of men? The Shadow do!"

"No, it teaches you how to tap into your inner potential."

"What happened to you? A couple of days ago you were a total shut-in, now you're a god damn self-help guru. What made you pick up this book in the first place?"

Danny balled his hand into a fist. "I have to learn how to play hardball if I'm going to go head to head with these studio execs."

"What studio execs? What're you talking about?"

"I just signed a two-year development deal with HBO. They're going to try every trick in the book to cheat me, I *know* it. They think they can manipulate me like a puppet on a string, but they've got a big surprise coming."

"Wait a minute, wait a minute, you signed with HBO? When the hell did that happen?"

"Last week."

"I didn't even know you were in negotiations. Why didn't you tell me?"

"I'm telling you now." His voice suddenly took on a hard, brusque tone I'd never heard before—at least not from Danny. He wouldn't look at me. He kept his eyes focused on the glass of wine.

"Okay, so you're telling me now. That doesn't explain why you didn't tell me *before*. Did you think I was going to get jealous or something? I'm happy for yo—"

Danny rose from the stool and stuck his index finger in my face. "Listen, I don't need anyone riding my coattails," he said. "I have to start getting serious, figure out what I'm going to do with my life. You think I want to live with my god damn father until I'm sixty? I'm tired of supporting his ass. I'm tired of playing these seedy little dives for pocket change. I need to make some real money, and I don't need you and your idiotic platitudes getting in my way." He lowered his finger, then glared at me with burning eyes. At last he broke eye contact and stormed past me, heading backstage.

I stared off into space, not knowing what to do. I'd never seen him like that. It was as if he'd been possessed by an alien being. I was aware of Marion not far away, piddling around with something, trying to act like she hadn't heard the outburst. I just drank my beer, acting as if she weren't acting.

I stuck around to see Danny perform. Something seemed different the moment he walked out on stage. He stuttered and mumbled his way through a twenty-minute set that was usually the most streamlined act in town. Strangely, no one in the audience seemed to dislike it; or rather, they reacted to it in the same lukewarm manner with which they had greeted my own performance. It was as if both the entertainer and entertained were following a conditioned script by rote, without enthusiasm, like an amputee trying to exercise a phantom arm.

I left in the middle of the applause, confused and depressed.

Back home I went to bed early, a terrible headache having bloomed beneath my skull right between the eyes. After taking a couple of aspirins I collapsed onto my mattress and stared at the blank TV screen across the room. I turned it on, just for the hell of it, and saw a news report about Israel and Palestine being on the brink of a nuclear war. I switched the channel and saw a newscaster standing in the middle of the street in South-Central, where a group of children had been shot to death while trying to walk to school. Little chalk outlines stained the crimson sidewalk. I switched the channel again, this time seeing a sermon by Pat Robertson warning the people of Florida that their state would soon be plagued by massive earthquakes if Disney World continued to endorse rampant hedonism and sodomy. Studying Robertson's stone-face puss made me wonder how different the world would be if only people like him could have a good laugh just once in their life, just once. The TV made my headache even worse, so I shut it off and stared at the ceiling instead, welcoming the silence.

The phone rang a few seconds later. Danny was on the other end. "Sorry for what happened earlier," he said. "I've been dealing with a lot of stress lately, what with these crazy contract negotiations and all. I don't know what happened. I just went a little nuts."

"That's quite all right," I said. "I know how it is." I felt uncomfortable even talking about it. He still didn't seem like the old Danny.

After a long, awkward moment of silence Danny said, "How would you like to work with me at Paste-Pot Pete's tomorrow night? We'll riff on whatever comes to mind, just like we used to at the Cyclops."

"I'd love that."

"We'll go at 8:30, okay?"

"Sure . . . see you then." I hung up, feeling a bit dizzy. Somehow I knew then that nothing was ever going to be the same again.

CHAPTER 3

Jimi Hendrix Meets Superman

(September 23, 2014)

I arrived an hour early at Paste-Pot Pete's, a club on Santa Monica Boulevard in Hollywood, in order to work out what Danny and I were going to do on stage that night. We'd teamed up dozens upon dozens of times before when the Cyclops (a comedy club/bookstore/wedding chapel) would host their "All Things Great and Stoopid" night every Sunday on the Third Street Promenade in Santa Monica.

Any other night I would've been comfortable hopping up on stage with Danny totally unprepared, certain that one of us would stumble onto something funny within seconds. Tonight I wasn't so confident. I wanted to make sure that Danny wasn't going to weird out on me again. Perhaps that would've made an interesting spectacle for the audience, but not for me. Unfortunately, Danny didn't arrive backstage until a few minutes before we were supposed to go on. He was out of breath and his forehead was beaded with sweat.

"Where were you?" I said.

"Karen had to drop me off. We got held up in traffic."

I glanced at my watch. "But we're supposed to go on in—"

"I know, I know. Everything will be fine, trust me. It'll be like The Muppets on 9/11 all over again."

A reference to one of our oldest (and stoopidest) routines. I was surprised he even remembered it. "Well, do you have any ideas?"

"It hit me while we were in traffic. What if Jimi Hendrix met Superman?"

A smile broke out across my face. "That's brilliant." Endless possibilities began to bubble to the forefront of my skull.

At that moment the MC introduced us. While walking out on stage we decided I'd be Jimi and he'd be Superman. "Hey, Superman," I said, "are you like . . . *experienced*, man?" "Boy, Jimi, am I ever! Play that groovy National Anthem again while I drop some of this Orange Sunshine." "Hey, Supes baby, Lex Luthor and Braniac are, like, takin' over the world." "So what, man? Let 'em! We have to allow them to create their own karma. I mean, what *is* good? What *is* evil? It's yin and yang, man, it's all yin and yang." "Supes, you are one crazy mothafucka . . . for a white dude, that is." "Groovy, Jimi. I can grok that shit, man. I mean, you're the first darky I've ever seen in this part of Metropolis. In fact, you're the first darky I've ever seen in my entire life." "I bet there weren't many of our kind allowed in Smallville, were there?" "Nope. Ma and Pa Kent would pretty much lynch 'em if they happened to sneak into town." "That's cool, man." "In fact, now that I think about it, none of your kind were allowed on Krypton either. I remember Jor-El warning everybody, 'Hey, we've gotta send all these darkies into the Phantom Zone or else Krypton's gonna explode!'" "And, like, did it explode, man?" "Shit, yeah! And it's all your fault, you dirty stinkin' nappy headed—!" "Like, *no*, Superman, let me down! It's that Orange Sunshine. It's messing up your mind. Don't throw me into the *sunnnnnnnn!*" We had Jimi fall back to Earth and land on Superman's head, knocking him unconscious with the help of some kryptonite-laced cocaine. Jimi went through Superman's tights looking for some cash, finding a piece of lint and a condom made of lead, then set Supes's body on fire like a guitar and scampered off for Woodstock.

This skit ate up a good ten minutes. The audience reacted well to it. You could always expect the people at Paste-Pot Pete's to have a sick twist of mind, which was right up my alley (a proclivity that seemed destined to keep me off *The Tonight Show* forever). We were doing really well until about ten minutes in, when Danny began to stutter and mumble just as he had the night before. He seemed confused, self-conscious, tongue-tied: everything Danny Oswald was *not*. His jokes fell flat, his impressions grew more and more incomprehensible. It was such a dramatic change that the audience seemed convinced he was doing it on purpose. I tried to save the day by coming up with a good punchline for each of his bad ones. It soon degenerated into some kind of mutated Martin & Lewis routine. The audience seemed to like it well enough, though. I was beginning to think they might laugh at anything we said. Were they all high or something? I didn't know, I didn't care. By the end of the set I just wanted to get the hell out of there.

I ended the show with some of my pat jokes (trying to avoid Danny's lame attempts to step on my lines), then grabbed him by the back of the collar and dragged him off-stage where I ripped into him good.

"What the hell's wrong with you?" I said. "Did Griffin slip you some fuckin' ketamine or something? Did you hit your unfunny bone when you got out of bed this morning or did you just wake up and think, Boy, I wonder what it would feel like to completely humiliate Elliot today?"

Danny's brow wrinkled in confusion. "What're you talking about? We did great out there."

"Yeah, at first we did, then you lost it!"

"You're out of your mind."

Danny tried to walk away from me. I grabbed him by the wrist and spun him around. "Listen, there's something wrong. It's like you're lost in a cloud and I can't reach you."

Danny jerked his wrist out of my grasp. "Did you ever stop to think that maybe you're the one who's not funny, huh? Maybe you're the one who's losing it! They laughed at everything I said out there."

"Because I was covering for you!"

"Hey, who has the development deal and who doesn't?"

"Danny, you're letting this thing go to your head. It's just a *development* deal. It's nothing. HBO will probably let it expire in two years without having done a damn thing for you. It's hardly your ticket into Paradise."

Danny waved me away and stormed out of the club through the back exit. The next act, a pianist who did boring political commentary set to music, stared at me strangely as he walked past me on his way onto the stage. I couldn't figure out what had happened. I just stood there for awhile, staring at the wall, only half aware of the jaunty music behind me. I mulled over Danny's words and wondered if he could be right. They *had* laughed at everything he'd said.

Was I the one who was losing it?

CHAPTER 4

The Attack of the Radioactive Mormons

(September 24, 2014)

That night my headaches returned. Once again I took two aspirins and nodded off to the nightly news. I saw footage of lightning-related wildfires in Florida, a Catholic priest attempting to perform an exorcism at the Capitol Building in D.C., the remains of a young black man who had been chained to the back of a truck by a couple of skinheads in God-fearing Texas and dragged across the pavement at high speeds until his head had been sheared off, dancing and cheering in the streets of Pakistan after the detonation of their latest (and vastly improved) hydrogen bomb.

Then I was in my old room at my parents' house, sitting cross-legged on my bed. My dad was in his business suit. I think he'd just gotten home from work. His imposing figure filled the doorway as he pointed at me and yelled and yelled and yelled, ordering me to start getting "serious" about my life. "All you're good at is mouthing off!" he said. "You think anyone's going to pay you to be a smartass when you leave here?" Mom stood in the corner crying, pleading with him to stop. He ignored her, like he always did. I said nothing, hoping he would go away. I had just turned ten.

Then I was back at my elementary school, strolling across the lawn in front of a hallway of open school rooms, lost in boy-thoughts, savoring the precious few moments at "recess" during which I was allowed to finally think what I *wanted* instead of memorizing meaningless numbers and cold sentences written by dead men. The sun was bright and warm in the noon sky, not hot. No, not hot. Just right, in fact. The breeze caressed my skin. The smell of freshly mown grass filled my nostrils. The way the sunbeams bore down upon the red brick wall to my right, brightening it like gloss, remains vivid in my mind for some reason. Yeah, real fuckin' idyllic.

That brief moment of reverie was shattered by the cry "Dog pile on Greeley!" somewhere behind me. I didn't even stop to look over my shoulder. I knew what it meant. This happened to everybody from time to time, at least once during each semester. Some sort of weird group-think would take control of almost everybody on the playground. Somebody would shout out, "Dog pile on _____!" Fill in the blank, whoever the universe chose that day. And this person—could've been a boy, but could just as easily have been a girl—would try to run away. Without even thinking about it, an entire mass of kids would respond to the call by jumping on top of this person; the entire purpose was to crush the chosen individual beneath the largest mass of gyrating flesh possible. These savage outbursts would occur spontaneously, for no reason. It was just something that always happened; you could never know when to expect it. Today was my turn to run. I wasn't fast enough, of course—nobody ever was.

Dozens upon dozens of boys from the playground leaped on top of me, pinning me to the grass, crushing my head against the ground, bending my right pinky back so sharply it snapped. Intense pain seared my brain like a firebrand, imprinting that moment—that overwhelming feeling of helplessness, of suffocation, of being pursued by faceless enemies I could never know because I would never have the time to look behind me—into my nervous system forever. Yes, imprinting all of this and one other thing: As I pulled myself inch by inch out of that pile of gyrating prepubescent male flesh, I kept yelling, "Get off me, get off me!" My finger hung limply from my hand. Tears poured out of my eyes. I glanced to my right and saw two teachers and an aide wander out of their classrooms to see what all the commotion was about. I thought, Thank God, they're going to get me out of this mess. Instead they stood there and watched. I even remember locking eyes with one of them, a lanky red-head with pale freckled skin whose name was Mrs. Love of all things, but she just looked away and did nothing. What was the name of the other teacher? He was well over fifty, balding, thin, wore cowboy boots and loved to talk about fishing. A Math teacher. Ah yes, Mr. Taylor. Like Mrs. Love, Taylor looked away and did . . . nothing. The aide's name has faded into the past, obscured by the pain, but she was forty-something, dumpy, destined only to get dumpier as age dragged her screaming into a well-deserved grave, a dishwater blonde with K-Mart make-up and clothes to match. This nameless woman looked away and did . . . nothing. Did nothing as I cried from the burning pain and dragged myself out of the pile. While inching my way out from under the kids, screaming at them to get the hell off, I felt a hand wrapping around my left wrist in an attempt to pull me free; this lasted just for a second, but it allowed me enough leeway to do the rest of the job on my own. This person was another child, I'm sure of it, but I would never know who. My friends, it seems, were as faceless as my enemies. I scrambled to my feet, trying to run as far as I could before they caught up to me again. After running for only a few seconds, however, I stopped. I stopped because I realized that no one was chasing me. If you've been expecting a punchline, you won't be disappointed. Here it comes: Near the entrance to a nearby hallway I glanced over my shoulder and saw that pile of boy-flesh still humping the earth as enthusiastically as before. They didn't even know I was gone. *They didn't even know I was gone.* I wiped the tears from my face with the back of my forearm, swearing never to cry again, never to show a hint of weakness to anybody. I didn't even go to the nurse to tend to my finger. No, I went right back to class after recess and interrupted Mrs. Love's lecture to ridicule her into less than nothing; I had reserved my hatred not for the kids who had attacked me, but for those in authority who had stood by and done nothing. My impersonation of her reduced the class—most of whom had been crushing me only minutes before—into paroxysms of laughter. I was now a hero, at least for a brief period of time. After an hour of this I was physically dragged to the Principal's office, where someone at last remarked, "Gee, that boy's finger doesn't look quite right, does it?" No one was sued for this oversight. Believe it or not there are fates worse than lawsuits, for I attacked those teachers verbally every hour of every school day until they had to send me to a therapist to cure my most peculiar "attitude problem." I'm not certain of this, but I don't think they succeeded.

Then I was back home in my bedroom watching the TV. Beams of dust-speckled sunlight poured through the half-closed curtains. It was morning. I breathed a sigh of relief, thanking God I had only been reliving the horror in my sleep. I never wanted to be ten again, not if it meant repeating my elementary school years. I'd rather be an eighty-year-old man hooked up to a colostomy bag and a dialysis machine than have to spend even one more second in that nightmare.

I glanced at the digital clock beside my bed. It was 9:08, which was quite early for me. On the television I saw a group of stiffs in neckties and white lab coats standing behind a podium while reporters scribbled notes and photographers flashed bulbs in their faces. It looked like a pretty important event. I searched under the covers for the remote so I could turn up the sound, which I must have lowered at some point during the night. I couldn't find the fucking thing, though, so I said, "Aw, screw it," and walked the six feet to the TV to do it by hand.

I lay back down and listened to one of the reporters say, "What can you tell us about the causes of this disease?"

The various neckties and lab coats looked around at each other, as if all of them were reluctant to respond. At last one of them stepped up to the mike, coughed into his fist, then said, "That's a very complicated question. In brief, our observations suggest the possibility of a cellular-immune dysfunction that manifests itself in a uniquely selective manner, attacking specific centers of the brain almost as if it were designed for that purpose alone—"

At that moment a chorus of questions erupted from the reporters, but the first reporter beat them to the punch: "Uh, doctor, are you suggesting that this disease is a chemical/biological warfare agent? Would you consider Iraq a likely source?"

The lab coat seemed quite panicked now. He opened his mouth to respond but before he could do so one of his colleagues stepped forward and said, "Gentlemen, ladies, please, I urge you not to jump to conclusions. The truth is we don't really have a clear idea what the origin of the disease is. Any answer to that question would be pure speculation on our part." He threw the first doctor a hard glance.

Another reporter chimed in: "Excuse me, when you say 'specific centers of the brain' what do you mean exactly?"

The second doctor said, "I'm glad you asked that question. It's important to underscore the fact that this is not a *fatal* disease. After a full year's worth of study we can firmly state that the virus affects only the humor centers of the brain."

"I don't understand," the reporter said. "Affects it in what way?"

"Well, if untreated the disease seems to, uh, wipe it out entirely."

"How is that possible?"

"We don't know. That's why we're studying it."

Yet another reporter struggled to be heard: "Has anyone developed a vaccine to fight it?"

"No, but within a few years perhaps, if the government provides enough funding. . . ."

Another reporter: "How long has this virus been around?"

"We don't know. We discovered the virus only a year ago, as was already stated. It could've been affecting humans for, oh . . . more than a hundred years."

Coco the Clown leaped up from the back row at that exact second and tossed a coconut cream pie right into the doctor's face. There followed a tense moment of uncomfortable silence, then the reporters turned en masse and helped the security guards beat the clown to death with their fists. Coco screamed, "Get off me, get off me, get off me!" as blood spurted out of his lip. His voice was as high-pitched as a child's. . . .

I vaulted out of bed, my naked body covered in sweat. The sheets were soaked. The sunbeams had shifted since I'd last seen them, covering the bookcase instead of the desk beside it. The clock read 10:22. Some dumb soap opera was on the TV. Though my headache had gone, my mind was very hazy. I couldn't figure out which parts of my dream, if any, had been real.

I switched the TV from station to station, searching for the news. All I found were vapid talk shows like *Wendy Williams*, and a re-run of *The King and I*. I thought, If ignorance is bliss the people who program these stations must dance the rumba to work every morning while singing Zippity Fucking Doo Dah.

I threw on some clothes, an old t-shirt and ripped blue jeans, then ran down two flights of stairs to the newspaper machine outside my apartment building. I peered through the glass and scanned the first page of the *L.A. Times*. Obama urges more "ambitious" action against climate change, three die in shooting spree in Alabama, a second fence goes up outside White House for added security . . . nothing about a strange new virus. But it wouldn't make the papers that quick, would it?

I didn't bother to go back upstairs. I had to talk to some-one more sane than myself. The first person I thought of was Heather. I jogged two blocks to the nearest bus stop and caught a bus just as it was pulling away from the curb. In my haste I dropped one quarter too many into the glass and metal machine near the front of the bus. As usual I sat near the emergency exit, just in case trouble broke out on the bus.

And I was right to be wary. A block later three big burly Mexican dudes climbed aboard. Two of them were dressed the same. Judging from the metal lunch boxes dangling from their hirsute fingers, and their dull gray jumpsuits that reminded me of the attire preferred by such genteel serial killers as Michael Myers in the *Halloween* movies, I concluded they were on their way to work at one of the many picturesque refineries in the area given to periodic explosions, conflagrations, and unexpected malfunctions of various kinds. Two of the men deposited their coins, then sat in the back of the bus. The third man lingered in the front, attempting to force a crumpled dollar bill into the metal and glass machine for which no one in the universe had a proper name. The machine seemed reluctant to accept the man's dollar bill; it kept spitting it back out at him. The man was becoming more and more frustrated. He proceeded to carry on a conversation with the bus driver while also cursing and beating the machine: "God damn. Why won't this god damn thing go in there? God damn! How do you get to Lankershim from here? You can't? What's your problem? Get in there! Wrong bus? Damn it, that last bus driver told me *this* was the bus. What's *wrong* with this machine? I'm gonna have to shoot someone! God damn. . . ."

At last he gave up on the dollar bill and lumbered down the aisle, making direct eye contact with each passenger as he said, "Anyone got change for a dollar?" Each time he repeated the phrase it became shorter and shorter: "Got change for a dollar? Change for a dollar? Dollar? Dollar? Dollar?" One by one the passengers shook their heads and looked away without even bothering to check their wallets or purses. L.A. commuters were a uniquely uncaring lot. You could tell the man's frustration was growing as fast as it had with the machine, perhaps more so. By the time he got to me he didn't even say anything. He just shoved the dollar in my face and stared. I thought, Ah, here's my opportunity to be a Good Samaritan for the day! I dug into my pocket to grab some change, then realized that I had left in such a hurry I hadn't brought any with me.

I said, "Sorry, man, I don't have any change. I thought I did, but. . . ." I spread out my hands.

He stared me down. "Where you goin'?"

"Uh . . . just to a friend's house. Why?"

"How you gettin' home?"

"On the bus. I don't think my friend will mind loaning me some money. If she does mind, hopefully she'll loan it to me anyway."

"Well, that's great," the man said, nodding. "That's great that you've got a friend to *loan* you money. You know I've got to go to work on the bus every morning, every day, back and forth, back and forth, every day, back and forth? Shit, *more* than every day, man! You know how much that costs?"

"To tell you the truth, I was never that good at math. I'd much prefer you ask me a question about English literature. Who wrote *Mill on the Floss*, for example?"

"What the—?"

"No, not What The, though that's pretty close. The proper answer is George Eliot. Or is it Eliot George? Curious George? No, no, Curious George is a monkey, except on off days when he's a Beatle, a dead one. Then he's George Harrison. Or at least he thinks he is. Say, do you ever look at the world and know that it's turning while your guitar gently weeps?"

The man stared at me as if I had just erupted out of a volcano, then walked past me. He must've gotten the change from someone behind me because he returned to the front and plunked some coins into the machine. Then he walked back down the aisle. I stared out the window, watching Hollywood storefronts whiz past me in a bright, gaudy blur. I expected him to sit in the back with the other two Mexican dudes, but instead he plopped down right next to me even though there were plenty of empty seats all around us. He pointed at my t-shirt and said, "What's that say?"

At first I didn't know what he was talking about, then I glanced down and realized I'd thrown on my old Alternative

Tentacles t-shirt that I'd found in a thrift store up in San Francisco during my dim, dark college days (I left before I got a
degree). It had a great illustration on it: a decrepit old man
whose ears are stuffed with bottle corks, whose glasses are covered with brick, and whose mouth is fastened shut with a zip-
per. Stamped on his bald pate are the words "U.S. Government
Inspected." Above the illustration are the words. . . .

"No More Censorship Defense Fund," I said, reading off
the shirt.

"No More Censorship, huh? Yeah, that's good. That's real
good." He shoved a big beefy finger in my face. "You know how
much I make a week?"

Not another math question, I thought. "No, how much?"

"Chickenshit!" The tip of his index finger rammed into my
chest. "Why don't you wear a shirt that says, 'No Chickenshit,'
huh? *Huh?*" He waved his hand in the air. "Phh, forget it, man.
You go to high school?"

"Are you kidding? I'm twenty-nine years old. The only reason for me to go to a high school is to cruise for jailbait."

"I hear you, man." At this point he placed his huge hand
on my knee. I decided to ignore it. "You like the little girls with
the tight asses? I like the tight asses." He smiled broadly, not
looking at me, staring straight ahead.

"Uh, yeah. Whatever you say."

"I've got a thirteen inch dick."

Silence for a moment. "Really?"

"The girls are afraid of it. Sure, they'll make out with me
and stuff, but when I whip it out they get scared and run away."

"Hell, I can understand that."

He began rubbing my knee. "How big is yours? You got a
big one?"

"Not so big. Average, I guess. You know."

"About six inches?"

"Uh, I never really measured it. That sounds about right. So how do you think the Raiders will do this year?" I was a jumble of emotions. I didn't know what the hell I should do. Cry for help? Leap out the emergency exit? Call him a cad and slap him across the cheek?

"I'd trade you any day of the week. I'd love to know what it's like to be inside a woman without making her scream. So don't you feel bad, my friend. Yours is just the right size. Take it from me."

"I'd . . . really rather not."

"It's funny. Sometimes I find that boys are a lot less afraid of it. Young boys, especially. They like to play with it, like taffy."

"Did I mention I wasn't in high school?"

His hand began to travel up my leg. "So what's your name, bro?"

"You know, for some reason I'm drawing a blank at the moment." I wondered what his two friends were doing in the back, holding hands and snuggling? I glanced out the window. My stop wasn't too far away.

"Maybe you've heard of me," he said. "My name's Chino."

"It suits you. Were you named after the prison?"

"It's just a nickname. The real name's Chewey. I run with the Mexican Mafia. The cops know I killed two people, but they can't pin nothin' on me. They're total fuck-ups."

The bus came to a stop. The two guys who I thought were his friends left through the back door opposite my seat, not even glancing in our direction. I suddenly realized that three Mexicans who get on a bus together don't necessarily know each other. Not only was I getting felt up, but I had to deal with the fact that I was prejudiced too.

The bus started up again. Chino, or Chewey (whatever), had lapsed into silence. I stared straight ahead, motionless, my arms folded across my chest. I could feel my heart beating against the back of my forearms. I wondered if he would kill me if I just stood up and moved to another seat.

After a few seconds Chino said, "My dick's wide as a beer can. You could just barely fit those thin lips of yours around the head."

"Driver!" Chino's hand fell off my leg as I shot to my feet. "You missed my stop!" Everyone on the bus turned around to stare at me, no doubt confused by the extreme panic in my voice. "Pardon me, excuse me, pardon me," I said, vaulting over Chino's lap and darting toward the front of the bus.

"Why the hell didn't you ring the bell?" the driver said.

"I was momentarily distracted by the beautiful North Hollywood scenery, sir."

The driver pulled up to the curb. "Smart ass," he said under his breath as I leaped off the stairs and onto the sidewalk. I glanced over my shoulder to see if Chino would burst through the backdoor and pursue me down the street, but thankfully no. He remained on the bus while I continued my rather treacherous journey. Christ, I thought, you can't go anywhere these days without getting your dick grabbed. As I walked down the street my mood darkened. I began to question my own sexuality. Had I brought this on in some way? Was it my provocative clothes? Oh, I felt so used. I wondered, Is that all I am to the world, just a pretty face and a tight ass?

Since I had to abandon the bus well before my stop I was forced to walk about six blocks until I reached Cahuenga Blvd., where Heather's apartment building was located. Normally this would have been a pleasant twenty minute bus ride, but of course there was nothing normal about this day. Heather lived in a three-story building that seemed quite old. Perhaps it was designed to look that way. Because the rent was cheap a lot of old people and college students lived in the building—not to mention one struggling comedian.

Barring entrance into the building was a large black gate that was locked after ten p.m. This annoyed me to no end. I spent most of my childhood in Torrance, a coastal suburb of Los Angeles where almost every gingerbread home had black iron bars over the doors and windows. The areas with the least amount of crime seemed to have the greatest amount of bars and locks and chains. Some people would probably say, "Oh, well that proves the bars and locks and chains prevent crime, doesn't it?" Perhaps, but somehow I doubt it. I think the crime rate would be the same either way. The truth is, people who live in the suburbs are just fuckin' paranoid. Back in high school I remember reading a newspaper article about a fire that had broken out in one of those homes due to faulty wiring in the family's Christmas tree lights. The fire trapped both the parents and the children in their separate bedrooms. In most other homes they could've escaped. Unfortunately, the parents had decided to install bars over the windows only a week before. Imagine them pressed up against those iron teeth, trying to bust their way through a cage they'd made for themselves as the little room filled with smoke. The image horrified me when I first read it. I think I knew then that I had to break out of the suburbs and make a name for myself in the real world. I've hated bars and locks and chains ever since. When I was twenty-two I remember the manager installing a similar gate around the apartment building I was sharing with a couple of friends I was going to college with. At every opportunity I would leave the gate unlocked as my own subtle protest. To this day I did the same exact thing whenever I entered Heather's building.

I buzzed Heather's apartment on the intercom. Like always, I had to wait for a long time. As I did, I noticed a weird bit of graffiti spray painted on a Starbucks across from Heather's building. It was a mural, about twenty feet long and twelve feet high, extremely detailed. It depicted a giant terrier, so finely drawn I could see every single hair on its back, rising up onto its hind legs while sort of dematerializing in a cloud of green vapor. Floating out of the dog's gaping mouth was a wispy word balloon that read: "Good morning!" What that meant, I had no idea. All I knew was that the "graffiti" around here was getting a hell of a lot more sophisticated. This crap would've been worthy of Diego Rivera or Robert Williams.

After leaning on the bell for a full minute, I finally heard Heather's groggy whisper: "Mm, yeah? Who the hell is it?"

"If the Pope had sex with puppies would he give birth to another Pope or more puppies?"

A beat. "Elliot? What the fuck are you doing here so early?"

"It's 11:11. The rest of the world has been up for hours. Now will you please open the door? I'm about to be run down by Cossacks on horses out here. I'm in great danger. I feel as if my enemies are closing in on all sides."

Heather sighed. "Jesus, all right. Hold on a second while I throw on my robe."

"Throw it out the window for all I care, just *hurry*. I've got members of the Mexican Mafia gunning for me."

A few minutes later the door to the building opened and Heather emerged wearing a fluffy white robe and sandals. "This damn well better be important," she said, unlocking the gate with a tiny silver key. There was something fresh and appealing about her mussed-up pillow-hair, her unmade face. From somewhere in the back of my mind came the thought: This is what she would look like if I woke up beside her. Because it reminded me of my drunken attempt to seduce her, I tried to banish the thought as soon as possible.

"Important?" I said. "You know what I had to endure to get here? On the bus I almost got raped by a mad Mexican named after a prison."

"So? You have to expect these kinds of things when you take the bus." She swung the gate open, then spun on her heels and began climbing the stairs two at a time.

"I must've missed that warning in the Commuter's Guide to Los Angeles," I said, making certain the gate was slightly ajar. I then closed the door behind me and followed her up the stairs.

Once we were in her apartment, which was so cluttered I had to kick half-empty luggage and old newspapers out of my way in order to clear a path across the floor, Heather said, "So what was so important that you had to wake me up at this ungodly hour?"

"I saw a weird newscast on television."

"And you couldn't tell me about it over the phone?" She entered her kitchen, which was separated from the living room by a small bar stained with Coca-Cola, bread crumbs, and grease. She began making coffee.

"This is far too important for telephonic communication, believe me. Besides, you always keep your phone off this early in the morning."

"Oh, yeah," she said, trying to sound as if she'd forgotten about that. "So what was so damn ominous about this news broadcast?"

"Well . . . I'm not sure," I said, sliding onto a wicker stool in front of the bar. "It might've just been a dream."

She rolled her eyes up at the ceiling. "Tell me the truth, you just came here for the coffee, didn't you?"

"Now that you mention it I wouldn't mind having a cup."

She glared at me. "You better come up with something good quick or I swear I'll empty this pot right on top of your head."

I threw my hands into the air. "All right, all right, just hold on a second." I tip-toed across the floor, navigating the room as if it were a mine field. Barely avoiding a collision with what looked like either an overturned hairdryer or a postmodern example of abstract sculpture, I switched on the television and surfed the channels until I found the local NBC news. Some tanned male bimbo going by the unlikely name of Johnny Thunder was forecasting the week's weather with a tone of enthused desperation, as if his continued survival depended on convincing the audience that a grown man could reach orgasm by reading inaccurate meteorological predictions off a teleprompter. I wondered if he was a modern day Scheherazade, forced to reel off a thousand and one variations of the phrase "It'll be sunny again tomorrow" in order to prevent the President of NBC from dropping him in front of a firing squad at dawn. If I thought about it long enough I could see the men in ski masks just off-screen, training their submachine guns on the weatherman at all times, thus accounting for the constipated smile affixed to his twisted, herpes-sore-pocked lips. Herpes? What? No matter how hard I tried I couldn't seem to prevent my mind from wandering off on inexplicable thoughts. My teachers, my parents, and my therapist all tried their best to cure this disease, but alas none of them succeeded. I noticed early on that the condition was brought on by boredom but no one seemed to believe me, least of all my teachers. Nowadays they call it "Attention Deficit Disorder" and pump you full of Ritalin until you quiet down to the point of flatlining, thus leaving you in a vegetative state receptive enough for the inducement of such crucial ideas as "I pledge allegiance to the flag," "Be all that you can be," "Support our troops," "Just say no to drugs," and "Congress shall make no law abridging the freedom of speech, except when it violates our right to tell you what to think" at which point Heather said, "Hello? Are you listening to me?" and I realized I'd gone off on another tangent in my mind again.

I turned my attention back to the TV screen and noticed that the weatherman had disappeared to be replaced by the press conference from my "dream." It was real. I hadn't been asleep. "Heather!" I said. "Get over here, they're repeating it!"

She strolled over with a coffee cup in her hand, sipping from it as the doctor behind the podium said, "The truth is we don't really have a clear idea what the origin of the disease is."

Heather glanced over at me, her eyes filled with nervousness. "What disease?"

"Shh," I said, "listen!"

"It's important to underscore the fact that this is not a *fatal* disease," the doctor continued. "After a full year's worth of study we can firmly state that the virus affects only the humor centers of the brain."

"Is this some kind of joke?" Heather said.

"No," I said solemnly. "That's the whole point."

Heather sat down beside me on the floor. We watched the entire press conference in silence. After it was over, and the airheads who read the news had begun reciting pre-scripted ad-libs in response to each other's pre-scripted witticisms concerning the press conference, Heather and I just sat there not knowing what to say. I felt like I was hearing the news for the first time all over again. For some reason I felt a tinge of guilt, as if I had somehow dreamed the disease into existence.

Finally Heather said, "Is this some kind of joke?" Her thought processes must have gotten stuck on one groove. "Could this be true?"

"Yes."

"God damn it, you're probably right. The universe really does work like that, doesn't it?"

"It's an odd-shaped world full of odd-shaped folk."

Heather laughed. "I think God has a hell of a sense of humor."

"Or he doesn't."

"Oh no. You think the virus affects him too?"

"I think it affected him a long time ago. I mean, Jesus fucking Christ on a pogo stick!" I said, slamming my fist into my knee. I rose to my feet and began pacing back and forth in front of Heather. "Doesn't the whole world just make perfect fucking sense to you now? This virus has probably been around for thousands of years. How the hell do you think we got where we are today? Only a society almost totally devoid of humor could elect thirty-eight lawyers as President of the United States, right?"

"But I thought this was a new virus."

"They didn't say that! This is the second time I heard that press conference; I was listening carefully. They said they just *discovered* it, not that it was new. It could've been around forever, longer than the human race. Hell, maybe that's what killed the dinosaurs in the end! The implications of this are enormous. It's putting everything into perspective: my relationship with my father, my experiences in elementary school and high school, my disastrous failure at every honest job I've ever had, my inability to hold onto a girlfriend for more than three months, the reason all my friends keep stabbing me in the back.

I always thought there was something wrong with me, that it was *my* problem, but it wasn't. It was theirs all along. They had the virus, I didn't. I was healthy, they weren't. I had a sense of humor, they didn't."

"Don't you think you might be jumping to conclusions just a little bit?"

"Absolutely not. Everything fits!" I stopped pacing and stood in front of the TV, slapping my fist into my palm at the end of every sentence like a mad orator standing on a bench in Venice Beach. "Think about it. Haven't you ever had a friend, or a relative, or a lover or whatever, who you were intimate with for a long time—you were sure you knew them inside and out, right?—and then suddenly you woke up one morning and realized you couldn't stand to even hear them breathe anymore?"

Heather raised her hand. "Like, try every boyfriend I've ever had."

"There you go. Why do you think that was?"

"Because I got smart all of a sudden."

I waved my hand in the air. "Nah, I doubt that. It wasn't because of you at all. It was because they'd lost their sense of humor *and didn't even know it.* Imagine that. If the virus infected you, how would you know? You'd probably think you were as bright and quick and witty as you ever were. You'd probably even think you were . . . oh my God." Of course, I thought. "Danny. Maybe that's why he's been acting so strange lately." I kneeled down in front of Heather. "Maybe he hasn't sold out after all. Maybe he's just . . . just suffering from a disease." I was so ecstatic I grabbed Heather by the shoulders and shook her. "Do you know what this means?"

"Excuse me, what did you mean by 'Nah, I doubt that'?"

"It means Danny can be cured. Maybe we can get his humor back for him. But we have to convince him that he's sick first."

"Are you saying I'm not smart or something?"

I rose to my feet. "C'mon, get dressed. We're going over to Danny's house."

"If you're saying I'm not smart you can get the fuck out of here right now!" Heather had shot up from the floor and was now sticking her index finger in my face. Her pale skin had darkened to a deep crimson. I was surprised by the outburst.

"When did I ever say you weren't smart?"

"Just now. You said, 'Nah, I doubt that.'" She imitated my voice. "The implication was clear. Listen, maybe you can get away with insulting the stooges who come to see you perform, but don't think you can pull that shit on me."

"I didn't even mean it that way. It was just a—"

"A joke? Well, I didn't think it was very funny. I don't need any more skinny ass comedians making jokes at my expense, okay? And this isn't a fucking virus talking, this is *me*, so I hope you're paying attention."

I raised my hands in the air, surrendering. "Jesus, okay, I'm sorry. I'm not quite sure what I'm apologizing for, but I'm sorry anyway."

"Just as long as you don't do it again you don't need to know what you're apologizing for."

I said to myself, Okay, I'll pretend as if that made sense. "So are you going to help me with Danny or not?"

"I don't understand . . . I didn't even know there was anything wrong with him."

"You haven't seen him in the past couple of days. *I* have. I'm telling you, he's freaking out. He got in my face the other night at Prospero's. I thought he was going to attack me."

"*Danny?*"

I nodded. "It was totally bizarre. I've never seen him act like that before."

"Well, why did he freak out? Did you tell him he wasn't smart or something?"

I decided to ignore that comment. "He said I was jealous because he got a development deal with HBO."

"When the heck did that happen?"

"I guess last week sometime. It seems to have really gone to his head."

Heather smiled. "I hear Griffin's the only one going to his head these days."

"Yeah, well, that's a whole nother issue. But I don't think she's the problem. I don't even think the HBO deal's really to blame. You have to come with me and see for yourself. He's changed into a totally different person."

She sighed. "Well, I guess I have to go. This is too intriguing to pass up, even though it means operating on about three hours sleep. I was up all night working on some new material."

"Cool, but I don't have time to hear it at the moment. We should leave if we're going to—"

Heather planted her hands on her hips and gave me that stern look of hers. "Oh, I see. You don't have time. You're the only one who can tell funny jokes, is that what you're subtly implying?"

"What? Are you serious? Christ, you're way too sensitive. How'd you ever manage to get up on stage with such thin skin?"

"By ignoring jackasses like you." She lumbered toward me with death in her eyes. For a moment I thought she was going to hit me, but then she just stormed past me and entered her bathroom, slamming the door behind her. What could she be doing in there? My mind began weaving horrible scenarios: I saw Heather bursting through the door, screaming Henny-Youngmanesque one-liners as she impaled me through the heart with the sharpened end of a plunger.

I crept over to the bathroom, pressed my ear up against the door, and listened. I could hear nothing. "Uh, are we still going over to Danny's place?" I asked.

Heather's muffled voice came floating through the door: "I said I would, didn't I? Maybe if you knew how to listen better you'd be able to appreciate my jokes! Now leave me alone so I can take a shower, or would you rather I go smelling like you?"

Before I could reply I heard the shower door slide open with a high-pitched shriek like fingernails on a chalkboard, then the sound of the water being turned on. Once I'd heard the shower door slide shut again, I plopped myself down in the sofa. I wondered how long her shower would take. Probably forever. I smelled beneath my armpits. True, I hadn't taken a shower, but it wasn't *that* bad. What was Heather's problem? Why did she always have to be so damn testy?

The doorbell rang at that moment. I opened the door to see a pair of blond, blue-eyed gentlemen in their early twenties wearing neat, no-nonsense black business suits. I thought they might be salesmen until I saw their ties. No salesman wears ties as stylish as the ones these guys had. They consisted of striking, fractal-like geometric patterns that immediately caught one's eye. They were so colorful they almost mesmerized me . . . almost, but not quite.

"Hello," one of the men said, "I'm Brother Lundberg and this is Brother Fleetwood. May we talk to you about the *Book of Mormon*?"

"Uh, sure, I guess," I said, too polite to say no. Heather would've said no immediately. Politeness has always been my Achilles Heel.

"I'm sorry," Brother Lundberg said, "I didn't catch your name."

"Elliot Greeley."

"Hello, Elliot." He shook my hand. "Have you ever heard of the *Book of Mormon?*"

"Sure, I'm very familiar with it."

"What have you heard about it?"

"Uh . . . nothing."

"Have you ever heard of Joseph Smith?"

"Yeah, that's the name I use when I check into motels."

"Oh?" Brother Lundberg was beginning to look a bit uneasy. "Well . . . Joseph Smith is also the name of the prophet to whom God entrusted the golden plates upon which the *Book of Mormon* was originally transcribed by God. Now, you see, Joseph Smith—"

"Where are these plates now?"

"Ah!" Lundberg thrust his index finger above his head, as if trying to poke a hole in the air. "Now, that's a very good question, Elliot. Joseph Smith showed the plates to eleven other men, after which God took the plates back to Heaven."

"Hey, how big is the *Book of Mormon?*"

"Oh, about . . . this big," Brother Fleetwood said, holding up a tome as thick as a Tom Clancy potboiler.

"Jesus Christ, all *that* was printed on gold plates? That must've been a hell of a lot of plates. You know how heavy those suckers must've been? How'd they carry them around?"

"Well, they didn't move around much," Brother Lundberg explained. "It should be noted that this particular edition isn't exactly lightweight either. It's rather special due to the fact that both the front and back covers are lined with a thin sheet of metal to protect the words of God from the vicissitudes of Time itself." He clicked his fingernail against the cover as if to prove his claim. It made a slight clanging sound.

"Hell, at least if you don't like the book you can use the damn thing to clobber muggers over the head."

Lundberg nodded. "Interesting point, Elliot. The word of God is the best weapon we have no matter how difficult the situation. Anyway, as I was saying: Do you know the two biggest problems faced by human beings?"

"I haven't a clue."

"We all die, and we all sin."

"In that order?"

"It doesn't matter. It's bad either way. Tell me, Elliot, have you ever heard of the Holy Ghost?"

"Of course."

"What have you heard?"

"Uh . . . nothing."

"You've heard of a lot of interesting things haven't you?"

"Oh, you don't know the half of it, Brother Lundberg. By the way, let me state that that's a beautiful tie you're wearing." I pointed at Fleetwood's tie. "That one's pretty good. I mean, it's okay, but it's not as good as Lundberg's here. Boy, this one's a keeper all right, you bet. It sure is snappy. Damn near hypnotic."

"Why, thank you," Lundberg said, appearing to be quite flattered.

"Now, let me ask you, did you know that until just recently the Mormons claimed that once a black person accepted Jesus Christ into his heart that black person would then become white?" This is true; I read a whole report on it in the *L.A. Weekly*.

"Of course!" Lundberg said. "I was black myself once!" Actually, he didn't say that. That's just my imagination running away with me again. He said, "No, I wasn't aware of that. But if you read the *Book of Mormon* you'll learn that—"

"Wait a minute, I'm not finished, Brother Lundberg. Did you also know that Joseph Smith found the gold plates buried beneath the earth and *assumed* God gave them to him? How do you know it wasn't space aliens that planted them there?"

At this point Brother Fleetwood decided to step in: "May I ask where you're getting your information from?"

"Why, my source is that well-known expert of Mormonism, John A. Keel."

"I've never heard of him," Fleetwood said.

"He's world famous. He wrote the book *The Mothman Prophecies*. Hollywood made it into a bad Richard Gere flick a few years back." *The Mothman Prophecies* is Keel's magnum opus. In fact, it's possibly the greatest book ever written. It's about a faceless, red-eyed winged beast known as Mothman, phantom photographers, men in fright wigs, strange flying machines, mysterious lights in the skies, ethereal gypsies, Men In Black, disappearing dogs, toxic sludge, Indian prophecies, the phone company, a collapsing bridge, a plot to assassinate the Pope, and as if all that weren't enough you learn new ways of eating Jell-O.

Lundberg and Fleetwood stroked their smooth chins. "Hm . . . Elder Keel," Fleetwood said. "That has a familiar ring to it, I must admit."

"There you go, I told you. By the way, where do you fellas come from?"

"I came from Utah," Lundberg said.

"Boy, that's a surprise." I suddenly remembered one of Jack Varner's routines and said: "Hey, they do a lot of nuclear testing in Utah. You know if there are any radioactive Mormons wandering around out there?"

The Mormons turned to each other with stone-hard faces . . . then abruptly burst out laughing! It was the first time they'd cracked a smile during the entire conversation. I wondered if they were laughing with me or *at* me.

"Elliot," Lundberg said, "we really like you. This has been the first of six lectures. May we come back in two weeks to deliver the second lecture?"

"Sure, come the Sunday after next. Early in the morning."

"Sunday would be rather unusual for us," Fleetwood said, jotting down the appointment in a tiny black book, "but perhaps in this case we can make an exception. How early should we come?"

"As early as you want. If I'm not home feel free to deliver the lecture to my wife Heather. She loves talking about God at seven or eight-thirty in the morning."

"Wonderful!" Lundberg said, shaking my hand. "I hope to see you then."

From the bathroom I heard the sound of the shower shutting off. "Fine, fine," I said quickly. "Nice chatting with you!" Lundberg and Fleetwood gave me a little wave, then began walking down the hall. At the last second I stuck my head into the hall and called out, "Oh, and by the way, if I don't answer the door at first just keep knocking until I do. I'm a deep sleeper." They nodded and waved again, then disappeared.

I closed the door and sat back down on the sofa, crossing one leg over the other, placing my hands on my knee, trying to look as nonchalant as possible. Only a few moments later Heather emerged from the bathroom, running a towel through her wet hair, her fluffy robe wrapped around her slender figure.

"Did I hear someone at the door?" she asked.

"Just salesmen."

"Really? I wonder how they got into the building. What were they selling?"

"Jokes. I told them you didn't need any because you were the master joke-writer of the universe."

Her face darkened again. She threw the towel in my face and yelled, "I don't need to be patronized!" then stormed off into her bedroom, slamming the door behind her.

I peeled the soaking towel off my head and dropped it on the coffee table. You couldn't win with her. You insult her, she gets mad; you compliment her, she gets mad. You might as well insult her and have fun at least.

I glanced over at the bedroom door. What could she be doing in there? My mind began weaving horrible scenarios: I saw Heather bursting through the door, screaming Henny-Youngmanesque one-liners as she impaled me through the heart with the sharpened end of a bedpost. I crept over to the bedroom, pressed my ear up against the door, and listened. I could hear nothing. "Uh, are we still going over to Danny's place?" I asked.

Heather's muffled voice came floating through the door: "Will you leave me alone for one second? I have to get dressed, don't I? What, you want me to go naked?"

"Not unless you want to frighten Danny into a paralytic state, then we'd never be able to talk to him." Something heavy slammed into the door from the opposite side. The sharpened bedpost, perhaps? I retreated into the kitchen . . . where I soon began to feel guilty about the practical joke I had played on Heather with the Mormons. I considered jotting down on her calendar for the Sunday after next: "Mormons Coming At 7:00 a.m. HIDE!!!" Then I thought better of it.

I sat back down in the sofa and waited for Heather to emerge from the bedroom, wondering how Lundberg and Fleetwood would fare against her in hand-to-hand combat.

CHAPTER 5

Never Mind the Orangutan

(September 24, 2014)

Heather owned a fucked-up green Volkswagen Bug that her mother had given her a hundred years ago. It was held together with safety pins, Crazy Glue, and duct tape and was always breaking down on her, particularly on the freeway. I often told her she should just get rid of it and buy a motorcycle, but she wouldn't hear of that. She said the car was "reliable." I told her it was probably cursed or inhabited by the souls of dead Nazis or both. The car gave me bad vibes, but Heather insisted that this was just another excellent reason to keep it.

At any rate the car got us to Danny's apartment in West Hollywood, an area inhabited by queers and junkies and hookers, as well as movie stars and businessmen with excess money to burn looking for varying combinations of the three. The area Danny lived in was pretty expensive. How he could afford to continue living there I had no idea. I know his dad's pension covered the rent and some of the bills, but by no means all the expenses. I always assumed the two of them were just barely making it, which is no doubt one reason why the development deal was so important to Danny. Heather tried to convince me of exactly that as we parked outside the liquor store across from Danny's apartment building. I told her the problem went far deeper. "Just watch," I said, "you'll see."

We walked across the street toward the building, which was a weird, depressing kind of place above a Chinese restaurant where they had avant-garde poetry readings on Sunday nights. The building had always disturbed me, though for reasons that were mostly indefinable. One of the most peculiar aspects of the building was that it seemed to have been built for people no more than five feet tall. I'm almost six feet, and I constantly had to duck in order to squeeze through the doorways. I think the place was originally intended to be an office building; the hallways were too narrow, the windows too small, the apartments too close together. For some reason the pipes in the ceiling were exposed for all to see. At the top of each flight of stairs was a heavy door that had to be forced open. After you'd managed to slip through, it would swing shut behind you with a deafening *slam* like the entrance to an underground cell in an Alexandre Dumas novel. Perhaps worst of all, some rocket scientist had decided to paint every hallway in the building in a dull, bluish-gray color that was deadening to both the eyes and the human soul itself. As far as I knew Danny had lived in this building all his life. No wonder he was so screwed-up.

Danny lived at the end of a windowless hall on the third floor. Across from his apartment were a flight of stairs that led up to the laundry room on the roof. Late at night sometimes Danny went up there and practiced his act with only the stars and the clouds as an audience. He claimed that some of those shows were among his very best.

Heather and I paused outside Danny's door, or at least what I thought was Danny's door. I could hear loud music blaring from within; this disoriented me. For a second I thought I had somehow overshot his floor. Danny's father had stopped listening to music roundabout 1963, and Danny rarely ever listened to music. He always seemed bored by it somehow. I don't think any composer could ever match the dissonant cacophony going on inside his head. Nevertheless, rap music was now erupting from the apartment at such a deafening volume that it was causing the walls to vibrate.

Heather noticed the confusion in my face. "What's wrong?" she said.

I didn't respond. I checked the number on the door. No doubt about it, it was Danny's apartment. I had to knock about eight or nine times before he finally opened the door.

"Elliot!" he said, an uncharacteristic Cheshire grin spreading across his face. He seemed happy to see me—ebullient, in fact. Only a week ago I couldn't have imagined the word ebullient ever applying to Danny. "Come in Elliot, come in Heather, join the party!" It was as if our argument had never occurred.

He took me by the arm, leading me into the living room where Griffin sat on the sofa bending over a glass coffee table. Lines of white powder lay spread out atop the glass like even regiments of soldiers seen from very high in the air. A dozen of Griffin's friends, the avant-garde posse that followed her around like rock 'n roll groupies, stood around the table waiting their turn. I'd run into them several times before at Prospero's and other clubs. A few of them were black, but most were effete whites. They looked like a pack of genetically-engineered, hipster-Goth hybrids that had somehow managed to crawl, unbidden, out of a Daniel Clowes comic book adaptation of Walter Hill's *The Warriors*. For some reason they seemed to be wearing Gothic dark clothes mixed with hipster accoutrements like bowler hats, suspenders, and adhesive walrus moustaches. Despite their clownish attire, these jokers never appeared to clown around. In fact, as far as I could tell they lacked the ability to discern the difference between a joke and a political slogan. Maybe that's why they loved Griffin's routines so much. Most of her act consisted of little more than angry tirades against right-wing politicians, which is probably why Heather couldn't stand Griffin's shtick. Heather despised soapbox sermons dressed up as standup comedy routines.

At the moment Griffin's personality seemed to fill the entire room. A stereo system with huge speakers had been plugged into the wall socket behind the couch. Griffin's updated rendition of "Fuck the Police" (in which the word "police" was replaced throughout with the names of almost every popular comedian on the L.A. circuit, recorded for a CD she had produced on her own that she often sold—or tried to sell—at her shows) was thundering out of the speakers. I suddenly flashed on a routine that Danny used to do a couple of years ago where he'd recite the words from "Fuck the Police" in a high-falutin' voice as if it were a lyric poem by Shelley or Wordsworth. It was one of the funniest routines I'd ever seen on stage. Now Danny was shaking his hips to the rhythm as if he were actually getting into it; he wasn't joking.

"Say hello to some of my good friends," Danny said. "You already know Karen." Griffin glanced up briefly. "Greetings, people of Earth," she said as she craned her head back, held a finger over her right nostril, then snorted like a rhinoceros with a head cold; it was far from the most attractive sound in the world. A few seconds later she leaned over another white line, switching the two-inch long plastic straw to her right nostril.

By this time Danny had begun introducing some of the other people in the room. "This is VoidIndigo, TweeBoy19, Plumlight, and Po'Belly."

"Jesus Christ," Heather said, "it sounds like a law firm that only hires Bronies or pedophiles or *both*."

They glared at her with bloodshot eyes ringed by baggy, purple shadows. Their porcelain-smooth faces seemed to have been untainted by a single laugh since the moment of their conception—perhaps even before.

"Tough room," Heather muttered under her breath.

Danny continued as if Heather had never opened her mouth: "And over here is Count St. Germain, Exegesis, Memewire—" Before Danny could finish rattling off the rest of the Peanut Gallery (thank God), Griffin said, "Yo, Danny. Your turn."

"Oh, okay, uh, hold on a second," he said to me, then started walking toward the coffee table where Griffin was straightening out a line of coke with a razor blade.

I grabbed Danny by the elbow and whispered, "Can I speak to you for a second?"

An expression of utter distress swept over his face. "Can't it wait?" he said, gesturing toward the coffee table.

"Nope. I'd say it's pretty urgent."

Danny sighed, rolling his eyes, then turned to Griffin and said, "Uh, save my place in line, okay?"

I dragged Danny into the bathroom under the disapproving stares of the Peanut Gallery. Before I shut the door behind us I saw Heather staring at me with wide, panicked eyes. "Don't you dare leave me alone with these nutjobs!" her expression screamed. I felt bad for her, but could do nothing. Sacrifices must sometimes be made during wartime.

"What the fuck are you doing?" I said, backing Danny up against the sink.

"What do you mean?" He seemed genuinely confused.

"Since when the hell do you do coke?"

"Since . . . I don't know, a little while ago. Karen gave me some. It's cool, man."

I didn't know what to say. "Is your father here?"

"Of course not. I threw him some pocket change and told him to go to the track. He won't be back for hours. You know him, he'd die at the horse races if he could."

"What would he think about all of this?"

Danny stared at me for a long time, then laughed. "Since when did you become such a moralist?"

"I'm not being a moralist. I just don't understand. Who goes from doing nothing to . . . to doing *cocaine*. It's unheard of. That's like going from diapers to winning a pissing contest in a week."

"Listen, do you want some? If so, I can ask Karen—"

I almost slapped him upside the head. "No, I don't want some! I can't believe this. You get one development deal and you suddenly fall into every Hollywood cliché in existence—and maybe even managed to make up some new ones of your own. Who're those trick-or-treaters out there? You used to make fun of these people, now you're snorting lines with them. What's next, celebrity orgies in Pacific Palisades?"

Danny just waved me away. "Whatever, man."

"Whatever? Is that the best you can come up with? What happened to the quick-witted Danny Oswald? Jesus, how did you lose it so fast?"

"Lose what?"

"The truth is you never would've thought of doing this shit before you lost your sense of humor."

"Are we back on that again? I think you're just jealous. You don't want to see me making new friends. You want me to be tied to you forever so you can ride my coattails to fame and fortune."

"Is that what you think or is that what Griffin thinks?"

Danny just shrugged. Translation: "What Griffin thinks."

"Have you been paying attention to the news lately?" I said.

"What's to pay attention to? Nothing matters. The world's a cesspool; it's a fucking piece of rotting meat and we're the maggots crawling around on its surface."

"Well, make up your mind. First it's a cesspool, then it's a piece of rotting meat. Aren't you mixing your metaphors just a tiny bit?"

"What're you talking about?"

"There's a plague going on out there." I pointed out the bathroom window.

"I know, *we're* it."

"I'm not talking metaphorically, man. The CDC announced it today. They've discovered a virus that's affecting people all over the world. It attacks the humor centers of the brain. Do you realize what that means?"

"Wait a minute, are you sure *you're* not the one who's been sniffing something funny? There are no 'humor centers' of the brain. Someone's pulling your leg, man."

"I heard it on the news!"

"Yeah, like the news never gets anything wrong."

"The doctors went through the symptoms of the disease. They said that anyone who has it will feel just like they always do. They won't realize they're sick, that their sense of humor has been *totally* stripped away."

"Well, that's a pretty convenient disease, particularly for the CDC. 'Hey, everybody, whip out your wallets to buy a vaccine for a disease you don't even know you have!' Can't you recognize a scam when you see one?"

"They're not offering a vaccine."

"Of course not, it's too early. First they'll want funds to 'develop' it. Yeah, they'll probably be able to welch off the government for a good ten years or so before people begin to get wise, just like with the whole AIDS thing. Damn, these CDC guys are clever, aren't they? Right around the time people begin questioning the idea that AIDS even exists, the CDC makes up a whole new disease that you can't prove is real. I mean, a sense of humor is a pretty subjective thing don't you think? Who's to say who has a sense of humor and who doesn't? The CDC is filled with a bunch of fucking charlatans. Oh, man, I'm so glad I hooked up with Karen. She's been giving me a crash course education during the past few days. Did you know that AIDS is really a chemical-biological warfare weapon created by the American government to wipe out blacks and gays? There's this book called *AIDS and the Doctors of Death* that lays out all the hardcore evidence and—"

"Danny?"

"Yeah?"

"Just answer one question. How do you make a hormone?"

A blank stare. "What do you mean? You can't 'make' a hormone. A hormone's a chemical substance formed in the body."

"Nope. You kick her in the stomach."

"What the fuck are you talking about?"

"Good-bye, Danny." I turned my back on him and reached for the doorknob. I didn't even want to look at him. It was far too sad a sight.

I emerged from the bathroom to see Griffin offering a straw to Heather. "Sure you don't want to do some?" Griffin said. "There's plenty to go around."

"You know, that reminds me," Heather said, wagging her finger in the air. "The other day I was walking down the street and this scummy lookin' dude comes up to me and says, 'Hey, honey, you want to buy some crystal?' Well, I hadn't done amphetamines in a long time so I said, 'Sure, let's see it.' The guy reaches into his coat and whips out a stack of clear crystal plates. I go, 'What the hell's that?' And he goes, 'This is the crystal. You want to buy some silverware with it?' and pulls out a couple of shiny forks and knives. So I just told him I was on the wagon and walked away. I wasn't in the mood for jokers, you understand."

The Neo-Gothic Hipster Peanut Gallery stared at her with dead, empty expressions.

"So . . . is that a yes or a no?" Griffin said.

"Uh, that's a no, I think," Heather said.

I placed my hand on Heather's shoulder. "We have to go now."

"Aw, so soon?" Griffin said, trying (not so hard) to pretend that she was sad.

"Yes, it's unfortunate I know, but they who play cannot stay." I motioned for Heather to follow me toward the door. She was more than happy to do so. Out of the corner of my eye I saw Danny emerge from the bathroom. One of the Neo-Gothic revelers—Plumlight, I think—said, "Next time you must really stay longer. We hardly got to know each other." His voice dripped with fey sarcasm. Something about the way he said it made me intensely paranoid. All of a sudden I imagined the pinheads attacking us en masse, sinking their teeth into our necks and drawing the humor out of our bodies pint by pint. I sensed I was in great danger, but then again I often feel that way—sometimes (I suppose) with no justification. This time I wasn't taking a chance, however.

"We demand walrus litigation!" I declared, swinging the door open. I thought I might unbalance them momentarily with snatches of surreal political slogans. "Don't tread on my mimetic avalanche! Lobster beard! Cancerous nightgown! Never mind the orangutan!" While they were still bobbing and weaving from this ruthless assault we managed to slip into the hall. We ran for the stairs and didn't stop running until we were far away from that terrible, claustrophobic scene.

On the sidewalk below, once we had enough time to think about what had just happened, we began laughing non-stop for a full five minutes.

"So . . . I guess it's safe to assume that they're infected?" Heather said, which only caused her to giggle some more.

I thought to myself, The sad thing of it is some people don't even need a virus. They're just born like that. "C'mon," I said, "let's get out of here before those incubi decide to pursue us into the streets." I began walking toward the car.

"Wait a second," Heather said, still trying to catch her breath, "I don't understand, whatever happened to me talking to Danny?"

I just waved my hand in the air. Nothing needed to be said. The gesture said it all.

Just let him be.

CHAPTER 6

How to Get Rid of Telemarketers

(September 25, 2014)

The phone woke me up out of a deep sleep. It wasn't yet fully light outside. I glanced at the clock beside my bed: six o'clock on the dot. Who the hell was calling this early?

"Hello?" I said groggily.

"Is this Elliot Greeley?"

"Uh, yeah. I think."

"Hello, my name is Judy and I'm taking a survey for San Francisco State University." Oh, joy. My old alma mater. "Do you mind if I ask you a few questions?"

"Yes, I do."

Despite this answer she just continued onward like a mindless automaton. I began to suspect that she was, in reality, a very clever pre-recorded message with long silences placed strategically in between her questions. What the purpose of this blatant act of psychological warfare would be, I had no idea.

Perhaps it was just a bureaucratic plot to drive non-compliant outsiders like me over the edge of sanity, a quite precarious edge upon which I teeter back and forth almost every day anyway. They knew it would just take a slight push to send me on a one-way trip, with no hope of return, down the slippery slope of total boundary dissolution and reality breakdown. . . .

But the bastards wouldn't get me that easy. I decided to turn the tables on them. I'd keep them on their toes. After all, psychological warfare is a two-way street. It'd be a good idea to copy that last sentence and tack it onto your refrigerator. I've learned the value of that maxim during these past few years.

"What was your favorite experience at SFSU?" she asked.

I didn't even have to think about it. "Leaving."

"Have you used any of SFSU's facilities since completing your studies?"

"Yes."

"What was that?"

"The bathroom."

"I see. Uh, well, Mr. Greeley, have you ever considered donating money to SFSU in order to help students who are poor and unfortunate and have no ability to pay the exorbitant admission fees necessary to gain access to the learning facilities and opportunities open to other members of the population far more fortunate in terms of monetary security?"

I was so tired I think I blacked out for a couple of seconds. I didn't even know what the hell she was saying. I was certain it made sense in an alternate dimension closely aligned with our own, some Bizarro world where it was commonplace for female-sounding simulacra to verbally harass exhausted professional comedic linguistic technicians at six o'clock in the morning for no other reason than the sheer sadistic pleasure of it.

After an extended moment of silence, during which I was simply attempting to prod my synapses into firing in a proper fashion once again, I at least managed to form the following words: "So, when do you get off work?"

Now it was her turn to be quiet for a few moments. "Uh . . . why?"

"You want to go out to dinner? You'll have to pay, of course."

"Excuse me?"

"Forget it, I withdraw the offer. I have better things to do than to go to the horse races. I mean, Santa Anita's a drag this time of year. All those old fuckers with their smelly black cigars, and all that yelling? Who needs it?"

The simulacrum seemed confused. Maybe the computer would explode while trying to unscramble the message it perceived to be hidden deep within my words, tucked away within the syllables themselves. "Uh . . . I was wondering if you wanted to donate a hundred dollars in four installments of twenty-five dollars, or fifty dollars in five installments of ten dollars?"

"How about six installments of zero dollars?"

"What, don't you have any money?"

"Of course not. Why do you think I have to go all the way to the damn campus to take a piss?" Seconds later I was left speaking to a dial tone. Jesus, I thought, maybe she wasn't a computer after all.

Well, I couldn't bring myself to hate her too much. Sometimes I took telemarketing jobs myself in between gigs just so I could pay the rent on time. Eating tends to be difficult when you make . . . oh, about five bucks per show.

Which may or may not be an exaggeration. Trust me, I knew a hell of a lot of comedians who were making *way* less than that.

God, I never wanted to be forced into a mind-deadening job like that ever again. It was so painful reading from those fucking computer scripts. But it was even more painful having to listen to them. . . .

I cradled the receiver and glanced at the clock. It was 6:16. I was too wired to go back to sleep. I switched on the TV and lay there staring at the screen, not really paying attention to it. My mind was on the strangeness of the previous day. After Heather and I had left Danny's apartment, I'd asked if she wanted to go to Ye Rustic Inn for a drink. She told me she had to go home and pack; she had a plane to catch later in the afternoon. Her agent had booked her for six nights at the Holy City Asylum, a nightclub that was a hot spot for alternative standup comedy in San Francisco. Heather's (and Danny's) agent happened to be mine as well, a fifty-something farrago of personality disorders named Marsha Ruskind. I'd heard she'd fallen on some hard times a few years ago, something having to do with a hardcore drug addiction, and she was just now building up a stable of clients again after all her old clients—many of whom had since gone on to fame and fortune, mostly due to Marsha's efforts— had abandoned her at her lowest point. Marsha was eager to reestablish her presence in the business. One advantage of having an agent as desperate as you was that you knew she'd devote every second of the day to improving your career; your success, by extension, would be her success. This wasn't the case at the larger, more prestigious agencies where you could easily get lost within the more obscure corridors of the labyrinth.

Before leaving for the airport Heather had said that Marsha might have a gig for me; she'd mentioned something about it over the phone Tuesday night. Heather said Marsha might call me about it early this morning, but I didn't think she'd meant 6:22 a.m.

The phone rang. Of course, I thought it was that SFSU automaton calling back for another round.

"Look, you bitch," I yelled, ripping the receiver off the cradle, "I already went into debt going to your damn school for four years and now you want to rob me again? Fuck you! Sit on a harpoon and spin on it, you Lovecraftian mass of protoplasmic evil!"

After a moment of silence I heard: "Been smoking that devil weed again, Greeley?"

Marsha. "Oh, it's you."

"That's right, the bringer of good tidings."

"Is that so? Is that what They told you to say?"

"Who's 'they'?"

"I think you know: the guys behind the curtain, the ones pulling the strings, the Controllers, the shadowy cabal who ordered you and their crazy mechanical harlot into calling me back to back at six o'clock in the morning just to disrupt my beauty sleep and make me cranky. Don't act like you don't know what I'm talking about."

"I don't know what you're talking about."

"Well, you would say that, wouldn't you—particularly if you had something to hide."

"It's hard to argue with your logic."

"I'm glad you finally admitted it. Now can I go back to not sleeping, please?"

"No, you have to hear about this now."

Affecting a thick Southern accent, I replied, "Now, don't give me none of your crazy bullshit, Jew girl. I'll kick your big sweet ass from here to Texarkana, where George Aitch Dubya Bush and those evil retarded sons of his bury young boys in the sand just for the fun of it, where Aryans are real men who behead defenseless colored hitchhikers with machetes and chainsaws to impress the Lodge Brothers on initiation night at A&M University, where steers are queers and queers are steers and the skies are not cloudy all day." I sang that last part. "Ain't that right, Bubba?"

"I hate to interrupt your impromptu monologue, but I've got a chance for you to make some real money for a change. You want to hear about it or not?"

I dropped the accent. "Money, did you say? Why didn't you mention that in the first place? Proceed."

"I got a call today from Gerald Bloom, an old agent friend of mine. We go way back. Turns out he's representing this weird . . . I don't know, *punk band*, crabcore band, whatever they're calling it these days. Doesn't matter. That's not the point. The point is they're big fans of yours and they want you to open for them. And I know how you love weird stuff."

I shook my head back and forth. I couldn't believe it. "Aw, c'mon, how many times have I told you? No more fucking bands."

"Now, wait a second—"

"It's death, total death. You don't know what it's like."

"So you had one bad experience, so what?"

"So *what*? That's easy for you to say. You're not the one who has to go out there and face an auditorium packed full of screaming teenagers expecting tits 'n ass covered with tattoos— not to mention laser beams, gel lights and propane explosions. Instead they get some skinny bastard telling peripatetic stories about suicide? What do you *think's* going to happen? It's a volatile situation, Marsha. I almost got my head blown off by some kid with a stolen .44 and a serious lack of appreciation for the art of the spoken word."

"Okay, so maybe you and heavy metal don't mix—"

"No, no, scratch that. How about me and a singer and two guitars and a bass and a drum don't mix. The problem's much more general, you see."

"I'm telling you, these guys are fans of yours."

"So what? That doesn't mean *their* fans are going to be fans of mine."

"Gerald tells me your attitudes mesh. Anyone interested in them will be interested in *you*."

I sighed. She was a single-minded, stubborn, lying pimp. That's partly why I liked her, of course. "Who are these guys?" I said, just to give Marsha some false hope that I would actually agree to this madness.

"Doktor Delgado's All-American Genocidal Warfare Against The Sick And The Stupid."

"Excuse me? That's their name? How the hell do they fit that on the marquee?"

"Most of the times they don't. They're still enjoying *cult status*, you see, but they've got a loyal following that's growing day by day."

"So Gerald Bloom tells you."

"I *know* the man, Gerald doesn't lie. The band's got a unique sensibility he says. Real existential, like you. They're the only band in history made up of musicians who are all dying of terminal illnesses."

"Ah, real cheerful. That won't be a tough room to crack."

"Twisted, huh? Right up your alley."

"Great. So do you wake up in the morning intent on finding new ways to challenge my patience?"

"Elliot, listen, this is a way for you to get some big money, some exposure outside of those art museums you insist on playing at. Are you going to be a dilettante for the rest of your life or do you want to break out and earn enough money to buy more than Saltine crackers for dinner?"

I stared at the TV screen. Bugs Bunny was chasing Yosemite Sam around a tree, or perhaps it was the other way around; it was hard to tell. At that moment, for some reason, I realized I was licked. Why fight Marsha and San Francisco State University and Danny and Yosemite Sam and the Neo-Gothic Hipster Peanut Gallery and the CDC and the Mormons and Elijah Mohammad and Doktor Delgado's All-American Genocidal Warfare Against The Sick And The Stupid all at the same time? It was useless. They would win in the end, they always did. The whole of human history was on their side. "So when's this gig?" I asked.

I could sense Marsha beaming through the phone. "Next Friday night at ten at The Brink in Hermosa Beach. You go on for twenty minutes, then you leave. What's so difficult about that?"

"Think they might throw a bullet-proof vest into the package?"

"Hey, they just might. That could be funny. You want me to ask?"

"Forget it. I prefer to live dangerously."

"I hear you, my brother. So you want me to call and confirm?"

I sighed again. "Might as well." Just as Marsha was about to hang up I said, "Hold on a second, I wanted to ask you something."

"Yeah?" She sounded worried. She'd had bad experiences in the past with people wanting to ask her questions, people like IRS agents and stiffed drug dealers.

"Did you help Danny sign a development deal with HBO?"

"Didn't he mention it to you?"

"No, not until a couple of days ago."

"Oh. I thought he would've mentioned it to you sooner."

"Well, he didn't." Silence, for a moment. "You think Danny's changed a bit since the deal?"

"Changed? What do you mean?"

"Don't you think he's been acting more erratic?"

"I don't think so. Of course, I haven't talked to him much in the past week. Why?"

"Have you, uh, heard about this plague on TV?"

Marsha laughed. "Plague? There's no plague. That's just some hoax cooked up in the White House to get our minds off the collapsing economy. It's like that David Mamet movie. What was it? *Wag the Dog.*"

"That's kind of like what Danny said."

"There, you see?"

"But haven't you noticed people acting stranger lately?"

"Excuse me, I make a living by sucking parasitically off the earnings of people who do things like blow up condoms with their nose and impersonate Bela Lugosi on speed. How the hell would I notice if people were acting stranger or not?"

"You've got me there."

"Say . . . did something happen between you and Danny?"

"I guess you could say that. He almost ripped my throat out at Prospero's."

"Danny? I can't believe it. What did you say to him?"

"Why does everybody say that? I didn't say anything to him. He just started yelling at me for no god damn reason. Twice now he's accused me of trying to ride his coattails, whatever the hell that means. Meanwhile, he's flubbing his lines on stage at Paste-Pot Pete's! I had to cover for him, but for some reason he doesn't *see* it. He thinks it was the other way around! It's hard to gauge why he's acting this way. It could be because of the HBO deal, it could be because Griffin's pumping up his ego, it could be this plague thing, it could be—" I stopped myself before I said "the drugs." There was no reason Marsha had to know that, at least not yet. I didn't want to rat the guy out. I just lapsed into silence.

"Hell, this isn't right," Marsha said. "You're two of the funniest guys I know. Man, when you did that Muppets on 9/11 routine at the Cyclops I almost fell on the floor. That was the first day I met you two, remember?"

"Yeah, I remember."

"Well, it's not right that you two are fighting. Did Abbott and Costello ever fight?"

"All the time. They hated each other."

"Okay, so that's a bad example. Forget that. What about Lucy and Ethel?"

"They hated each other too."

"They were sluts anyway. Screw 'em. I don't want to hear about these dead comedians anymore, I'm talkin' about you and Danny here. That's what's important."

"You're the one who brought them up."

"Listen to me, you've got to focus for a second. You and Danny have an incredible chemistry on stage, a real kismet—"

"Doesn't kismet mean fate?"

"Let's not get bogged down in semantics. I don't want to see what you and Danny have together just die on the vine."

"Assuming that's true, how come you struck a deal with HBO for Danny but not me?"

"Ah, I was wondering when we were getting around to that. I think now we're getting to the heart of the problem between you and Danny, aren't we?"

"*Absolutely* not. I'm telling you, that has nothing at all to do with it. I'm just curious."

"The answer's simple: They didn't ask for you. Listen, there's no reason to be jealous—"

"I'm not jealous, I don't *care*."

"These deals happen all the time. Usually they expire without a sitcom or anything else coming out of it except some quick, easy money. I'm hoping to at least secure a half-hour HBO special for Danny, but even that's up in the air. Don't be frustrated, Elliot, you're talented too. Your time will come."

"I'm *not* frustrated. Who says I'm fucking frustrated?"

"All right, all right, you're not frustrated. Nevertheless, I'd advise you to calm down and take a deep breath. While you're doing that I'll call Gerald and confirm the gig with Doktor Delgado's etc. etc., then right after that I'm going to call Danny and—"

"No, no, please don't—"

"Elliot, wait a second, I'm your agent, correct?"

"Correct."

"And what does that mean?"

"It means you get ten percent of my already meager salary by chatting away on the phone with your friends."

"Yes, but besides that?"

"I give up, you've got me."

"Elliot, I'm like a drill sergeant, a big brother, and a father/confessor all rolled into one—"

"Jesus, it must get crowded over there in that broom closet you call an office."

"—and right now it's time for the drill sergeant to step into the fray. I'm *telling* you what's best for you. I'm going to call Danny and straighten this mess out and you damn well better appreciate it. Now stay by the phone and wait for Danny's call. Bye."

"Wait—!" The dial tone mocked me with its incessant drone. I sighed and cradled the receiver. Defeated again. On the TV Bugs Bunny was digging a hole in the ground at super speed. I thought I might join him soon.

I continued to watch Bugs Bunny for the next twenty minutes. I suddenly realized that this was how long my act would have to be next Friday night. In my mind's eye all I could see were a bunch of long-haired freaks holding up lighters and screaming at me to get my skinny ass off stage. Time, of course, is relative. While watching Bugs Bunny twenty minutes can seem like nothing. While attempting to entertain an auditorium filled with glueheads twenty minutes can seem like twenty fucking years. I hoped this upcoming experience would be mellower. The Brink was a much smaller venue than an auditorium, of course, but I didn't know if that was more or less dangerous. It just meant your enemies had less of a space to cross if they wanted to kill you.

The phone rang as Porky Pig stuttered out, "Th-th-th-that's all, folks!" I considered this an ominous portent, a Jungian synchronicity of the most dire proportions. I picked up the receiver anyway. It isn't possible to outrun fate, or "kismet" as Marsha might say (though no doubt in the wrong context).

"Hello?" I said.

A beat. "This is Danny." His tone was very somber. "Marsha told me to call."

"Yeah?"

Another beat. "Well . . . so I'm calling."

"Am I supposed to get down on my knees and praise the Lord or something?"

A sigh. "Look, I'm sorry I accused you of trying to ride my coattails. I know that's not true."

"Then why would you say it?"

"I don't know. Maybe the deal did go to my head a bit. Marsha straightened me out."

"Did she straighten out Griffin too, or is she just going to keep filling your head with this bullshit?"

"Look, man, don't blame Karen. It was entirely my fault. I'm taking full responsibility."

I'm taking full responsibility. Is that something the old Danny would've said even a week ago? I didn't ask this question out loud, of course. Why ruin the moment? All I could do was hope that the old Danny figured out a way to come back somehow, somehow.

"All right," I said. What else was there to say?

"Listen, there's a Godzilla marathon playing at the New Beverly all month. You want to go catch *Destroy All Monsters* next week? It's playing with *King Kong vs. Godzilla.*"

Besides the awkward shift in the conversation, this was something the old Danny would've suggested. Perhaps things were looking up. "Uh, sure," I said.

"It'll just be me and you. I'll leave Karen at home."

"All right."

"I'll call you before then."

"All right."

Danny hung up. So did I. A few feet away Elmer Fudd was threatening to shoot Bugs Bunny with a shotgun.

Didn't these cartoons ever end? I thought as I shut off the TV with the remote and went back to sleep.

CHAPTER 7

The Dinah Shore Tea Party

(October 1, 2014)

About a week later, on Wednesday night, Heather called to tell me she'd finished her gig at the Holy City Asylum and was now off to play a couple of nights at some obscure lesbian club called The Dinah Shore Tea Party.

"Don't you have to be a dyke to play there?" I said.

"No, you just have to harbor a deeply imbedded hostility toward all carbon-based lifeforms with male reproductive organs. I figure I've got that down pat, so I should fit right in."

For the past six nights I had been wondering (at occasional points during the day the thought would invade my brain, I just couldn't help it) if Heather had met anyone while in San Francisco, and more importantly if she was having sex with him. I was surprised that it concerned me so, but nonetheless it did.

In as humorous a manner as possible I said, "You mean you haven't gotten lucky yet? Aren't there plenty of comedy groupies wandering around up there?"

"Sure there are, but every single one's as queer as a three-headed Pope."

I was relieved, but tried not to show it. "Maybe you'll get lucky at The Dinah Shore Tea Party."

"Yeah, right, with who? Hell, I'd have sex with *you* before I fucked some motorcycle bulldyke with a hook for a hand."

"Oh. Why, thank you. I guess."

"No problem. Look, I've gotta go. Marsha set up a phone interview with one of these free newspaper rags, and they're supposed to be calling any second. Now I've gotta recite all my routines to some stranger over the phone."

"The littlest publicity helps."

"So they tell me. Listen, I'll talk to you later, okay? Good night."

"'Night." I cradled the receiver, imagining the journalist from the free newspaper rag being a huge Aryan with a leather fetish who seduces Heather with the mere sound of his voice, hypnotizing her into taking a cab to his dungeon lair in the Haight where he straps her down on a gynecological table, then approaches her steadily with a cat-o-nine-tails in one hand and a glowing hot branding iron in the other. . . .

What? Where the hell did that come from? I shook myself out of the daydream. I decided to force Heather from my mind, so I retired to my desk to write some new material for the show coming up Friday night. The humor needed to be perfect, just the right balance of sadomasochism and silliness, otherwise the testosterone-filled teenagers would drag me into the mosh pit and beat me to a pulp with deadly blunt objects, most notably their heads. Striking such a balance was not going to be easy.

After about twenty minutes of intense work, during which I drew indecipherable doodles in the margins of my notebook paper, I released a frustrated sigh and threw my pen against the wall. Creating comedy in a vacuum wasn't the easiest thing in the world. I needed real people to bounce ideas off of, people who understood my humor . . . people like Heather.

I leaned back in my chair and stared at the wall for what must have been a very long time.

CHAPTER 8

Destroy All Monsters

(October 2, 2014)

Except for my near death at the hands of a mad man, the next day was rather uneventful.

Danny called me around ten in the morning, the first I'd heard from him since our awkward conversation a week before.

"A bit early for you, isn't it?" I said. He'd just roused me out of a deep sleep.

"Early? I haven't gone to sleep yet."

"Late night with Griffin?"

"Oh, you could say that. Listen, the movie starts tonight at six. So you doing anything or what?"

It took me a couple of seconds to remember what the hell he was talking about. "You mean *Godzilla*?"

"No, no, *Destroy All Monsters*. It's the best one—you know, the one where Godzilla, Rodan, Mothra and the whole crew are confined on Monster Island, then they have to band together to fight Ghidrah who's being controlled by those weird aliens on the moon? Is this ringing any bells?"

"Okay, wait a minute," I said. "Is that the one where aliens take control of Godzilla and Mothra to destroy the Earth, but then the military or whoever uses high-frequency sound waves to fuck up the alien mind control devices?"

"No, no," Danny said. He sounded somewhat frustrated, as if he were attempting to teach advanced calculus to a four-year-old. "That's *Monster Zero*, the sixth one."

"It's got Ghidrah and Planet X in it."

"Right!" From the tone of his voice I could detect that Danny was pleased with the rapid ascent of my learning curve. "*Destroy All Monsters* takes place much later, in 1999. It's directed by Ishiro Honda, who directed the very first Godzilla movie back in 1954."

"Is that the one with that old fat guy who died of AIDS?" I said.

"Yeah, Perry Mason. But they just added that guy into the American version; he wasn't in the original Japanese version."

"So Perry Mason and Godzilla never actually shared a scene together?"

"Exactly."

"Maybe that's good, otherwise Godzilla might've caught the AIDS."

Danny paused, no doubt contemplating this possibility, before replying, "Nah, I doubt it. If anyone's protected against various errant sexual diseases, it's Godzilla."

"Jesus, I hope so. Can you imagine the size of the condom he'd have to use?"

"It'd be half the size of a football field, perhaps longer. Hell, Christo could make an art object out of it."

I laughed aloud at that one. I thought, Maybe the old Danny isn't dead after all.

For the next twenty minutes we chatted some more about equally nutty topics, then Danny told me he'd pick me up at around four-thirty.

"Pick me up? With what, a shopping cart?"

"Karen said I could use her car for the night."

"Since when the hell do you drive?"

"Karen's been teaching me."

"How can you learn to drive in a week?"

"You'd be amazed at what Neuro-Linguistic Programming enables you to do."

I rolled my eyes. Whatever, I thought. "I'll be here with bells on," I said. "And a crash helmet."

Danny, infamous for his habitual tardiness, surprised me by arriving at 4:28 in Griffin's Saab 900. It was strange seeing Danny behind a steering wheel, but I got used to it. It wasn't as easy getting used to Danny's appearance. He looked haggard. Always lanky, today he seemed even skinnier than usual. There was a slight yellowish tinge to his flesh, purplish rings under his eyes. It appeared as if he'd been up for five days straight.

"Before we head on over to the movie I have to stop some-where first, okay?"

"Sure," I said, shrugging.

Danny removed a Stooges CD from the glove compartment and slipped it into the player, then pulled away from the curb with jerky, stop-start motions. Somehow I knew it wasn't going to be the most pleasant of rides.

We sped onto the 405 freeway toward the suburbs while listening to Iggy Pop sing "We Will Fall." Halfway through the CD we had penetrated deep into the heart of Torrance, which in terms of its venal fascist ideology is worse even than Orange County, home of the John Birch Society. (Those poor souls unfortunate enough to dwell within Orange County referred to it as living "behind the Orange Curtain"—a term of endearment.)

We wound our way through the quiet, tree-lined streets. I stared at the linear square lawns and the empty birdbaths and the wizened garden gnomes and the precisely clipped hedges as if observing my past through a misty eyeglass, remembering all over again why I had tried my best to leave it far behind. Why was Danny dragging me back here? Though I didn't recognize the neighborhood,—this was the north side of Torrance, rather far from the area where I had spent my oh-so-idyllic formative years—the resemblance was near enough to disturb me. I felt like a Vietnam vet who freaks out and falls into convulsions whenever he hears a helicopter flying too low.

"Why the hell are we here?" I asked.

"Don't worry, this'll just take a second. We won't miss the movie, I promise." Danny pulled up to a curb outside a little white house that looked like all the other little white houses surrounding it. The scene was perfect enough for the setting of a '50s sitcom, where all was as right as toxic rain and no one ever seemed to hear the sound of the laugh-track behind them. "You want to wait out here?"

"Well, how long are you going to be?"

Danny chewed the inside of his cheek, something he always did when he was deep in thought. "I don't know, this might take awhile." He began climbing out of the car. "You might as well come in, I guess," he said over his shoulder.

Before I could ask him what on earth we were doing, he slammed the door behind him. Grumbling to myself, I followed him up the driveway and onto the porch. A wooden bench, suspended from the roof of the porch by a pair of thin chains, swung back and forth as if ghostly young lovers were sitting there just a few feet away from me, holding hands, whispering sweet nothings into each other's unseen ears.

Danny pounded on the door nine times in a row.

I said, "Jesus, what're you trying to do, bring down the walls?"

"He won't hear it otherwise."

I sat down on the swing. "You mind telling me who we're visiting?"

"Just a friend of Griffin's. His name's Mike, met him last week."

The door creaked open slowly. The man who stood in the doorway appeared sluggish and sleepy-eyed. He wore nothing but a ripped black t-shirt and black shorts, which accentuated his pale skin and emaciated body. The faintest blue veins stood out against his flesh like a neon billboard in the L.A. night. A thick carpet of dark hair was sprouting up from his scalp, as if he'd been too lazy to shave it during the past few days. His icy blue eyes seemed to be filled with an all-encompassing sadness that stemmed from everything and nothing.

"Hey," Danny said, giving him an awkward little wave. "Remember me from Saturday night? You know, at the party? Karen told me I should drop by."

It seemed to take a few seconds for the man to focus on Danny; at last the light of recognition flared up in his eyes. "Oh yeah, hey, how you doing. C'mon in." He wasn't excited, nor was he sad. Just another diversion to fill up the hours, perhaps?

The interior of the house was the exact opposite of the picture-perfect surface outside. It was dark and depressing, totally devoid of furniture. The light was dim, the walls bare. The place smelled musty, like a pack of wet dogs. The only objects sitting upon the dull brown carpet were cardboard boxes filled with books. I ran my finger along the surface of a Time/Life book about cells, and it came away coated with dust.

Danny gestured toward me as if he were about to introduce me to the man. "Dr. Steinberg," he said, "I'd like you to meet Dr. Steinberg." Then he turned to me. "Dr. Steinberg, I'd like you to meet another Dr. Steinberg. And it just so happens by a very strange coincidence that I'm *also* Dr. Steinberg." At that moment a wet Labrador retriever came padding into the room, sniffing the carpet for food. "And, uh, there's Steinberg Jr."

"*A Day at the Races*, MGM, 1937," I said, identifying the source of Danny's impromptu routine.

The man snapped his fingers and said, "Speaking of Groucho Marx, did you know that Groucho took LSD with—"

"Paul Krassner!" I said, beating him to the punch. He smiled (I think, though perhaps it was just a twitch) and nodded. I was impressed that he knew this rather obscure fact.

As the man led us into the hallway Danny said, "Mike, this is Elliot. Elliot, this is Mike."

Mike turned and said, "Hey."

In the cramped hallway, standing only a few feet away from Mike, I noticed that his skin was as smooth as porcelain. It was very hard to discern his age; he could've been anywhere from twenty to forty.

Mike led us into his bedroom. The walls were gray—not due to paint, but to dirt. From the ceiling hung a bright yellow buglight around which a halo of flies buzzed, the room's only source of illumination. Posters of ten year old punk bands lined the walls. Billowing cobwebs had consumed the corners of the room as well as the piles of trash and paperback books that lay in shadowy niches. The carpet, or what remained of it, was cluttered with books about serial killers and obscure rock 'n roll magazines.

Mike plopped down on his bed, a thin mattress lying on the carpet. Above the bed hung a series of silk-screened photographs of various famous people. Most prominent were those of Nixon, Hitler and Henry Kissinger; each of the photos had rifle sights superimposed over them. Mike pressed his back against the wall and shut his eyes for a moment. "I just woke up, man."

Danny sat down on the bed beside him. There was a wicker chair near the bed, but it was occupied at the moment by yet more books and magazines as well as an electric guitar with red rectangular "WARNING: FLAMMABLE" stickers plastered on almost every inch of it. I decided to stand rather than disrupt the pile. Who knew what was lurking beneath, ready to bite my hand off at the slightest disturbance?

I scanned the posters on the walls, tripping out on the names of some of the bands: Johnny Fistfucker & the Strap-ons, Flesh Eating Virus, Candy Jones & the Presidential Models, Lavender Brain Tumor, Frogfall, Psychic Dictatorship in the USA, The Bilderburgers, The Flaming Quakers, Mary Ferrie and the Monkey Virus, The Bigfoot Jazz Trio, The Trouble with Chinks, and (my favorite) Nazi Fuck Boys! Now *that's* class.

When I glanced back at Danny to comment on the band names, I saw him slipping a needle out of his inside jacket pocket, followed by a plastic baggie filled with a dark, tar-like substance. Mike handed him a spoon, the bottom of which was blackened as if it had repeatedly been held over a flame. Danny placed some of the tar-like shit into the spoon, held a lighter under it until it liquefied. He soaked the liquid into a cotton ball, then drew the liquid into the needle. I watched all this, transfixed. I felt as if I had taken a turn into The Twilight

Zone. I expected to see Rod Serling emerge from beneath the pile of books on the wicker chair and say, "Consider, if you will, Elliot Greeley: a small-time standup comedian, none too bright, lacking direction, adrift in the waters of life, suddenly plunged into the dark underbelly of the twisted narcotics underground, a grotesque wonderland of petty thieves, murderers and syphilitic junkie whores, a wonderland known in some quarters of the world as . . . The Twilight Zone." Then I started hearing that freaky music in my head and knew I'd really gone over the deep-end.

Danny handed the needle to Mike, who then held it out to me and said, "You want to do this first? I'm kind of like, HIV-positive, you know."

Before I could respond Danny said, "He doesn't do drugs."

Mike looked at me for a moment as if I were a Fabergé Egg under glass, some rare artifact he'd never seen before (certainly not in this bedroom). Then his attention drifted away from me as he ran his fingertip along his forearm, searching for the proper vein. All of a sudden I grew self-conscious when I realized I was staring at him with far too much fascination. As the needle punctured a bulging blue vein near the crook of his elbow I glanced away, embarrassed, as if I were peeping through a keyhole trying to catch a glimpse of a couple making love.

Danny, at last realizing that I was standing in the middle of the room, gestured toward the wicker chair. "Have a seat," he said.

I didn't know what to do. Should I move the pile of books and risk Rod Serling biting my hand off?

"Oh, I'm sorry, man," Mike said. His embarrassment seemed genuine. "Let me clear that off for you." With the needle still dangling out of his arm Mike got up and began pushing shit off the chair. This was the strangest image of the whole evening: that needle bobbing up and down like a jack-in-the-box as he waded through strata of dinosaur fossils, uranium deposits, dead television stars, and who knows what else.

Staring at the needle with some uneasiness, Danny said, "Uh, let me do that for you," and finished shoveling the shit onto the carpet. Mike sat back down on the bed and tended to his business.

I settled into the wicker chair. At random I plucked a paperback book out of the pile that was now on the floor. It was called *Hunting Humans Vol. I*. On the inside front cover was an advertisement that read, "Wait for *Hunting Humans Vol. II*!" How many volumes could there be?

After the brown liquid had descended into Mike's vein, he handed the needle back to Danny. I said nothing as Danny drew more of the brackish substance into the syringe. I didn't understand why Danny was using the same needle, particularly if Mike was HIV-positive. I'm not sure why I didn't say anything. Shock, perhaps? Or maybe I just figured, hell, he must know what he's doing, right? Besides, I couldn't think of a polite way of saying, "Hey, uh, you really think you should be sharing a needle with this AIDS-ridden freakazoid?"

Within seconds he had already slipped the needle into his arm, had already injected the substance into his vein as if he were a past master at this, a life-long user. The sight brought back memories of one of Danny's earliest routines, a story about being forced to go to the doctor as a kid. He used to do five minutes on needles, on how much he hated them. What the fuck had happened to change his mind?

I glanced back at Mike again. I was surprised to see that he was staring at me; that bemused, Fabergé-Egg-look had returned to his eyes.

"So . . . you don't do drugs?" he said. He looked like he couldn't believe it.

Falling back on one of my old routines, I laughed and said, "The other day I stopped at a Wienerschnitzel to buy a hot dog and I saw a big banner outside that said, 'Do Dogs, Not Drugs.' I thought, What the hell is this? Does Wienerschnitzel advocate bestiality?"

Mike continued to stare at me with a stoic expression. Don't feel bad, I thought, perhaps he's laughing inside. He said, "What do you do for a living?"

"I'm a comedian."

He nodded. "You make good money doing that?"

I wiggled my hand in the air. "It fluctuates."

"You know, you could pick up a lot of extra cash with your urine."

"Excuse me?"

"Yeah, some people even make a living off it, especially in D.C. In D.C. the whole drug testing thing is out of control. If you're arrested you can't even see a judge unless you piss in a bottle first. There's a huge demand for clean urine out there. I know a guy who makes about $20,000 a year."

"That's pretty good—for urine, I mean."

"Fuck yeah, I'd take it! Hell, you can make fifty bucks a pop from scumbags in the street. You could probably rake in even more from the white collar areas like Orange County. Those guys are desperate 'cause they're all on speed. Speed will stay in your system anywhere from twenty-four to forty-eight hours. A surprise drug test on Monday morning is their worst nightmare."

"Maybe I'll head on over to Orange County tonight and set up a little lemonade stand on the sidewalk."

"Or Silicon Valley. That place *runs* on cocaine, and coke can stay in your system for up to twelve hours. Those guys have lines of cocaine waiting for them in their office. It's a perk of the job. It wouldn't surprise me if they had a coke break clause in their contract. I think they do lines at their board meetings."

I instantly had an image of yuppies in neckties standing around a long table, all of them bent over one of those large graphs, snorting cocaine sprinkled along the jagged red line that measures the economic growth of the company. The image made me laugh. "I think I'd rather peddle my urine in D.C. It seems more appropriate somehow."

"Yeah, D.C.'s a cool place if you've got a stomach for high strangeness. I was thinking of maybe moving back there soon. Hell, any place that had a crackhead for a mayor for as long as that can't be all bad, eh?"

The scariest part of this conversation was that I was only half-listening; the other half of my mind was seriously considering how to begin selling my urine. "So . . . where would I advertise my urine, the Yellow Pages?"

"Word of mouth would work better."

"Is, uh, selling urine illegal?"

"You wouldn't think so, but they'd probably find some way to classify it as a drug-related crime. Everything else is."

All of a sudden we heard a noise out in the living room. Mike said in a panic, "Shut the door! That's my dad. He'll get mad if he sees me shooting up heroin again."

Well, you don't hear that sentence every day of your life. I started to get up, but Danny (with the needle bobbing out of his arm) leaped off the mattress and made a mad dash for the door, slamming it shut and slipping a chain over it. Two seconds later someone knocked on the door so hard I thought it was going to fall off its hinges.

"*Michael, who've you got in there?*" a gruff voice boomed through the door. "*Are you shooting up heroin again?*"

"No, Dad!" Mike said. "I've got a couple of friends over! We just want a little privacy, is that a crime?"

"If I find out you're doing heroin in there I'll rip your fucking head off!"

Mike rolled his bloodshot eyes. "So do it already! Put me out of my misery!"

"Don't tempt me!"

Mike picked up a black combat boot and threw it against the door. "Get the fuck out of here! Leave me alone, that's all I want! That's all I've *ever* wanted from you, you stupid son of a bitch!"

I heard heavy, Frankenstein-like footsteps lumbering away from the door. My hands were clutching the arm rests of the chair as if I were hanging on for dear life. Mike leaned his head against the wall and covered his eyes with his hands. In the pocket of silence that followed Danny sat back down in the bed and slipped the empty needle out of his vein.

Finally the silence became far too nerve-wracking. I said, "It looks like *you* may need my urine in a few minutes."

Mike removed his hands from his face and said, "I think you're right. How much would you charge me?"

I shrugged. "Fifty bucks."

"Aw c'mon, man, no discount? You wouldn't even have thought of it if I hadn't suggested it first!"

"Okay, forty."

"Thirty."

"Thirty-five."

"Uh . . . all right."

"Bitchin'." He slipped his hand beneath the mattress and pulled out a blue velcro wallet that was falling apart. He withdrew three tens and a five, crumpled them up into a ball and threw them at me. They pulled apart and drifted through the air like feathers, falling onto the carpet between us. I leaned over and snatched them up with great eagerness. You know how many cans of chicken noodle soup you can buy with that?

Mike rose to his feet and began rifling through the top drawer of his dresser. He pulled out a tangled ball of torn socks, a narrow glass jar containing a katydid on a slab, and a plastic toy that looked like Lumpy Space Princess from *Adventure Time* before he found the object of his search: an empty mason jar. He tossed the jar to me and said, "Fill it."

"What, here?"

"Hey, I coughed up the cash, now you cough up the product!"

"Excuse me, but if you want me to *cough* it up we're going to be here for awhile." Mike waved his hand in the air, then plopped back down on the mattress. I glanced over at Danny, but he just shrugged. How had I gotten into this? "Can't I do it in the bathroom?" I said.

Mike pointed at the door. "With *him* out there?"

I could still hear the echoes of those elephantine footsteps reverberating through my skull. "I guess you have a point." I released a huge sigh, rose to my feet, wandered over to the corner of the room. Turning my back to Mike and Danny, I unbuttoned my Levis and held the jar up to my penis. "Can't you run some water or something?"

The best he could do was play a New Age CD of whale sounds. That didn't quite hit the mark, I'm afraid. While I thought of rain storms and garden hoses, desperately trying to make something happen, I said to Mike, "So your dad makes you take urine tests, huh?"

"Ever since I was fifteen." He sighed. "Man, I told myself I'd never do this shit again." He turned to Danny. "I was doing fine until you came over."

Danny said, "Dude, don't worry about it. We'll stop doing it—tomorrow."

"Yeah, right. Tomorrow. I just realized it's been six years to the day since I was diagnosed HIV positive. I know people who were diagnosed at the same time and they're all dead now. They took AZT, I didn't. Did you know that AZT is nothing but fucking salmon sperm? Oh God, oh God, I'm so depressed. I look in the mirror these days and say, 'Jesus, you're thirty-four. Where did all the time go? It went by so fast.' Not only that, my girlfriend's being a fucking bitch."

"I hear you," Danny said. "Hell, my girlfriend's a fucking dyke. She cheats on me almost every day. She's probably cheating on me now."

"Sometimes I start crying for no reason," Mike said. "At night. Around three a.m. When I'm all alone."

"I cry too," Danny said. "All night sometimes."

"One day I cried for twenty-four hours," Mike said. "At least, it seemed like twenty-four hours. I cried today. I'm *so* depressed. Sometimes I feel like killing myself. I know exactly how I'd do it too. My dad keeps his .22 in the drawer next to his bed, says he keeps it there in case of 'intruders.'" He released a hollow laugh. "Man, it'd be so simple to sneak in there, slip the gun out of the drawer, press it against my right temple, and then just—" He placed his index finger against his temple and lowered his thumb as if it were the trigger of a gun. Then he dropped his hand to his side, his eyes glassy and without emotion. "Actually that's what I was thinking about right before you came over."

There followed a long, uncomfortable moment of silence. I said, "Uh . . . I had a hangnail yesterday."

At that moment someone pounded at the door. A long, arcing stream of golden liquid shot out of my penis. I didn't anticipate it having such a long reach; I had to compensate as quick as possible and just barely managed to catch the piss in the jar.

"*Do I hear someone pissing in there?*" said the voice.

I immediately cut off the stream, stuffed my penis back into my Levis, and buttoned up.

Mike said, "No, Dad, you're just being paranoid!"

I screwed the lid on the jar as tight as possible, then hid it behind a pile of porno magazines on the floor as Mike's dad said, "If I find out anyone's been pissing in there, I'll rip their fucking head off!"

Of course, I wondered which head he was referring to. The sudden and unsurgical displacement of either one was an experience I preferred to avoid as long as possible.

"I'd like to see you try it," Mike yelled.

"Don't tempt me!"

I waved at Mike to please be quiet, but he wasn't paying attention to me. "Get out of here," he screamed, throwing another boot at the door. "Leave me the fuck alone!"

Once again those golem-like footsteps thundered away from the door. I realized I'd been holding my breath during the entire exchange. "How're we gonna get out of here?" I said.

"Oh, don't be scared of him," Mike said. "He talks loud and carries a small stick."

"How small? Small sticks can cause as much damage as big sticks if used properly."

"Speaking of getting out of here," Danny said, glancing at his watch (since when the hell did he start wearing a watch?), "we better get scootin' if you don't want to miss the beginning of the movie."

"What're you seeing?" Mike said.

"The New Beverly's showing *Destroy All Monsters*."

"Is that the one where Godzilla and Mothra and Rodan and baby Godzilla are all on Monster Island and they have to fight those weird alien dudes on the moon?"

"That's the one."

"Damn, that's my favorite."

"You want to come with us?"

Mike thought about it for a second, then waved his hand in the air. "Nah, I'm way too depressed. I'll just bring you down."

I couldn't disagree with that. Danny glanced at his watch again and said, "Okay. Well, I guess I'll see you later."

"Yeah, later." He just stared at his mattress, as if thinking about smothering himself with it.

"Uh . . . you think you can walk us out?" Danny said.

"Can't we just crawl through the window?" I suggested.

"Don't worry about my dad. I'll *cut* him if he tries anything." Mike reached under his pillow, whipped out a switchblade, and dropped it into one of the pockets on his shorts. A determined, implacable expression washed over his face as he rose from the bed and opened the door. Danny and I fell in behind him, peering over his shoulders fearfully as if expecting ninja warriors to erupt from the shadows of the hallway and begin attacking us with Samurai swords. Somewhere in the house I could hear a television blaring some kind of game show. I was relieved; perhaps we could reach the front door without laying eyes on the fearsome apparition I imagined Mike's dad to be.

Just as we were about to leave the hallway one of the side doors swung open and out shambled a huge bear of a man with broad shoulders and a thick neck, two hundred and seventy pounds of angry flab that may have been firm and muscular twenty years ago but had since softened into a mass of walking dough. We froze. The man's eyes, as bloodshot as his son's (though no doubt for different reasons), bulged out of his head as they scanned all three of us as if considering which one to attack first. At last a pair of meaty hands reached out and grabbed my head; toughened, leathery skin pressed against my skull and began squeezing like a vice. "Have you been giving heroin to my boy again?" he yelled.

I grabbed his wrists, which were so thick my fingers couldn't even wrap around them, and tried to scream, "It wasn't me, it was the other guy!" but he was pressing my cheeks so hard the words came out garbled and incomprehensible.

Somewhere to my left I heard Mike say, "Leave him the fuck alone!" and the next thing I knew I was watching a long silver blade plunge into my attacker's right forearm. Blood squirted out of his flesh as he howled, released my head, then swivelled around to face his son. I staggered backwards into the doorway of Mike's bedroom. Danny ducked under the mad man's outstretched hands and followed me into the room. We slammed the door shut and slipped a chain over it once again.

"Maybe the window wouldn't be a bad idea after all," Danny said.

I couldn't disagree with that either. We trampled Mike's mattress, unclasped the window above it, and spent the next two minutes struggling to raise the damn thing—which apparently hadn't been opened in years—while behind us we heard shouting, the crash of large heavy objects, and the dull thumping sound of flesh beating flesh. In the end Danny and I prevailed, thank God. We slid the window open just high enough to squeeze through, landed head first into a tangle of bushes full of those annoying little brown prickly things which clung to our hair like fleas, then rounded the house and ran toward Danny's car as fast as possible. We scrambled inside with as much finesse as a pack of drunken clowns piling into a midget car in a three-ring circus, while behind us we heard the front door slamming open. I peered through the window to see Mike's dad stumble out onto the porch, blood pouring down his XXL Beefy-T Hanes t-shirt, and wave his hairy fist at us.

He yelled, *"You come back here again I'll rip your head off and stuff it up your ass sideways, you hear?"* This alone would've been disturbing enough, but the fact that he said it while dashing across the lawn toward us made it even more distressing.

I rolled up the window and said, "Get us out of here, get us out of here!"

I glanced over at Danny to see him picking through the three dozen keys on Griffin's key ring. "I'm just trying to find which one's the key to the car," he mumbled.

"Hotwire the damn thing then! That guy's gonna kill us!"

Mike's dad slammed his full weight against the side of the car. At that moment I noticed I hadn't locked my door. Just as he made a grab for the door handle I slammed my fist down on the lock, then did the same to the door behind me.

"Lock your door!" I said to Danny.

He didn't bother. "I'm pretty sure this is the one," he said, slipping a key into the ignition. The sound of that engine starting up was probably the most beautiful, angelic sound to ever bounce off my ear drums. We peeled out into the street with Mike's dad running along beside us, cursing our mothers and calling us bastards and faggots and even more horrible things. His kind words sparked a wave of nostalgia. For a moment I thought I was back in high school.

Mike's dad tried his best to keep up, but within a few seconds we had left him in the dust. I peered over my shoulder and watched him shrink into the distance.

A blanket of uneasy silence fell over the car, but only for a brief time. A weak smile appeared on Danny's face as he said, "Now wasn't that pleasant. We'll have to do it again sometime."

Any witty rejoinder that might have followed had been knocked out of my skull long ago. "How long have you been doing it?" I said.

He maintained that weak smile. "Doing what?"

"The heroin."

He shrugged. "Not long. This is only my third time."

"Only? Don't you know what heroin does? Haven't you seen the ads? 'This is your brain. This is your brain on drugs.' It fries eggs, Danny, it fries *eggs!*"

"Yeah, yeah, that's what they said about marijuana. You smoked that a couple of three or four times, right?"

"It's hardly the same thing."

"We'll see."

I sighed and slumped down in my seat. It felt as if the world were going mad and I was the only one who was even aware of it.

"Are you pissed at me?" Danny said.

"Yes."

"Does this mean you don't want to see *Destroy All Monsters?*"

"No."

"No you want to see it, or no you don't want to see it?"

"No I want to see it."

"Good. I think we'll just make it. We might miss the opening credits, but that's okay."

I didn't say anything for the rest of the ride. I strapped on my seat belt and hoped Danny wouldn't nod out on the 405.

CHAPTER 9

Squid Sitting

(October 2-3, 2014)

I had been looking forward to goofing on the movie with Danny, like we used to do while staying up late at night watching stupid sci-fi movies like *Angry Red Planet* and *Samson vs. the Vampire Women* on cable, but fifteen minutes into the film Danny nodded out. Throughout the evening he continued to fade in and out of consciousness, his head bouncing back and forth as if his neck were made of rubber, his eyelids fluttering like dying insects. Once in awhile he would become very alert and sit straight up; over the course of the next few minutes he would then slump down ever so slowly and nod out all over again. At times he would be as lucid and communicative as anybody else; nevertheless I knew it was useless to talk to him. I had known plenty of heroin addicts back in high school and sooner or later you realized that anything you said to them while they were high was lost in the ether twelve hours later. You might as well talk to the air. I was so pissed off I said nothing to him the rest of the evening.

After the movie I took the keys from Danny and drove him to his apartment building. Upon arriving he apologized over and over again for what happened at Mike's place (as if that's what I was angry about!), then staggered up those claustrophobia-inducing stairs and disappeared into the shadows within the building. To be honest I was glad to be away from him. From a shit-stained phone booth down the street I called for a cab, though I could ill-afford such a luxury. I paid the driver with part of the $35 I'd gotten for my piss.

Within an hour I was back home in bed, wide awake, staring at the ceiling. I was a nervous wreck—not because of Danny, but because of the gig tomorrow night. I still didn't know what I was going to do. I knew my standard act wouldn't go over too well, not in such a crazy setting. I needed a gritty, realistic story to start off the show—some darkly humorous vignette that a bunch of teenage misfits could relate to.

Then it struck me. Why not tell them what had happened to us tonight at Mike's house? It was perfect: fucked-up and weird enough to be funny, if told in the right way, and just realistic enough to be believed. Hell, why shouldn't they believe it? It was true! (Then again, throughout my career I'd noticed that the truest stories were the ones nobody ever believed. This was a universal law, the reason for which no comedian could ever hope to understand.)

I leaped out of bed, dashed over to my desk, whipped out a notebook and began jotting down the story as I might tell it on stage. Often I would get up and relate parts of the story to the mirror first,—wishing Heather was in town so I could try it out on her instead—then transcribe the monologue onto paper. This sudden burst of creativity sparked a string of other ideas, all of which I worked on well past the witching hour and into the wee hours of the morning.

I think I fell asleep at the desk; the next thing I knew daylight was pouring in through the windows, my cheek was pressed up against the desktop, a stream of saliva was trickling out of my mouth, and some bastard was knocking on my door with ten jackhammers and refused to let up for even a second. I shot up out of my straight-back chair and glanced at the clock. It was 4:30 p.m. Jesus Christ, I'd have to be at the club soon. Of course, the heathens at the door didn't care about that. They just kept pounding away.

"All right, all right," I said, "I'm coming!" I swung the door open and yelled, "Now what the hell do you—?" I cut myself off in mid-sentence when I saw none other than Brothers Lundberg and Fleetwood standing in the doorway holding out copies of the *Book of Mormon*. Their ties were different, though just as snappy as before.

Brother Lundberg did a little double take before his eyes widened in recognition. "Ah, Elliot!" He seemed very happy to see me again. His brow wrinkled. "You don't live in two apartments, do you?"

"No. This, uh . . . this is just a friend's place. I'm watching their pet squid for them while they're away."

"Their pet what?"

"It's a squid. Named Cuddles. It's a real bitch taking the thing for a walk but it's fun watching it play with the neighbor's poodles."

Lundberg and Fleetwood glanced at each other sideways. Fleetwood cleared his voice and said, "Do you know when your friends will be back?"

"They won't be coming back. They went on a euthanasia cruise."

"A what?"

"Nothing, forget it, it's very difficult to talk about. My friends are dying of various terminal illnesses at once. I-I'm sorry—"

"Oh no, *we're* sorry," Lundberg said. He grabbed Fleetwood by the elbow and began leading him away. "We'll leave you with your grief."

"Thank you for understanding," I said.

Fleetwood pulled away from Lundberg and handed me his copy of the *Book of Mormon*. "Maybe this will help you in your sadness."

"Thank you," I said, reaching out to grab the book. Before I could do so, however, Lundberg pushed Fleetwood's hand downwards, then turned to me and smiled. "Excuse me," he said. He grabbed Fleetwood's sleeve and guided him toward the opposite side of the hall where he began whispering into his ear. By craning my neck I could just barely make out the words: "What do you think you're doing? You're aware of The Elders' directive. A free book is not to be given out until *after* the second lecture."

Fleetwood stared at the ground and shrugged. "I'm sorry. I just thought—"

"Your job isn't to think, it's to follow the Word of God. Now c'mon." Lundberg marched back over to the door, shook my hand, and said he was looking forward to delivering his second lecture to me on Sunday morning.

"Oh, so am I," I said. "You can't possibly know how much I'm looking forward to it."

I waved and closed the door, listening for a moment while they visited my neighbor's apartment. Lundberg managed to get out two words before my neighbor told them to fuck off and slammed the door in their faces. My neighbor's approach wasn't subtle, but effective nonetheless. Sometimes I wished I could deal with the world that way. I just didn't have the heart to be that upfront with people; instead I stood around insulting them without them knowing it, which was far more time-consuming. Heather was the exact opposite; she was sort of like my neighbor, but worse. She would insult you into the dirt, insult you again just in case you hadn't noticed, *then* slam the door in your face. If that didn't work she'd kill you. She was as tough as titanium, and I envied that strength. Brothers Lundberg and Fleetwood would no doubt have a far different reaction. I hoped Heather would be back from San Francisco in time to meet them. The effect of my little prank would be even more gratifying if the Mormons decided to drop in only a few seconds after Heather had returned from a jet-lag-inducing red-eye flight through the turbulent winds of El Niño, a crowded airport packed full of annoying tourists, and four lanes of weekend traffic on the 405. The result might very well be the ruptured remains of a couple of Mormon medulla oblongatas splattered all over the walls of a certain junk-cluttered North Hollywood apartment.

At the moment, however, I had far more important things to worry about than a pair of (soon to be) dead Mormons. I had a gig to get to with only a half-remembered routine in my head. I took a quick shower, grabbed some relatively clean clothes off the floor, pulled them on while somehow consuming a bowl of banana nut cereal with two pieces of buttered toast, stuffed my wallet into my back pocket, then sped out the door, keeping my eye out for wandering bands of radioactive Mormons armed with sling shots and tire irons and even more awful things.

CHAPTER 10

Doktor Delgado's All-American Genocidal Warfare Against The Sick And The Stupid

(October 3, 2014)

It was a long ride from Hollywood to Hermosa Beach. I used the time to practice my act in my head over and over again. This was difficult, what with drunken old men ranting in the back seats, pregnant teenage girls yakking to each other while their children ran wild, black gangstas blaring ghetto blasters the size of Volvos, and a bus driver with a penchant for running red lights. Not only that, I could feel that familiar horde of butterflies beginning to flutter their little wings within my stomach. My nervousness would continue to grow over the next few hours, then peak right before I went on stage. I'd learned long ago how to deal with it. I would imagine that I wasn't actually Elliot Greeley; in reality I was a convicted murderer strapped into an electric chair, waiting for the throw of a switch that would end my life forever, wishing that I was actually a struggling standup comedian sitting on a smelly, noisy bus on his way to a gig—a standup comedian whose biggest worry in life was dealing with stage fright. I would imagine the scenario so vividly that I would soon feel the coldness of the steel arm rests beneath my hands, the wires attached to my head, the rubber underwear wrapped around my crotch. My heart would start beating faster and faster as I imagined a calloused hand gripping the switch and. . . . Compared to this grim scenario, telling a few jokes to a club full of punk kids didn't seem all that distressing.

I arrived at The Brink just before 8:00. Since I didn't have to go on until 10:00, this might appear a bit premature. I know Heather would think so; she could jump into a spotlight blindfolded and deliver a good show. I needed somewhat more security than that. When I was faced with a new stage—this was my first gig at The Brink—I wanted to make sure I had more than enough time to scope out the place and get used to the idea of being up there in front of all those people.

Eddie Milstein, the owner of the club, greeted me backstage. While shaking his hand it was difficult to ignore the distinct odor of beer on his breath. He was a dumpy, middle-aged man with a dark black moustache and mismatched smoke-gray hair ringing a bald pate. To me he looked more like an undercover cop than the owner of a club. In my paranoia I actually found myself considering this possibility. After all, it would be a good cover, wouldn't it? Once I got an idea like that into my head it was hard to shake. I remained wary of the man throughout the evening.

Eddie informed me that the band hadn't shown up yet, and probably wouldn't until the last possible second, just soon enough to complain about not having enough time to tune up. The first ten minutes of the show would consist of them tuning up on stage while their fans screamed and danced just as much as if the real songs were being played. Eddie said most of the fans couldn't tell the difference, nor did they care.

Eddie said, "They just want a good excuse to jump around and beat each other up, and who can blame them? Sometimes I like to leap into that mosh pit and crack a couple of heads together myself. You need to go a little crazy once in awhile, know what I mean?"

I said that I did, though it was hard for me to imagine this weird fat dude holding his own with hundreds of teenage speed freaks.

Eddie glanced at his watch and said, "I hope they remember to show up. I went out of my way to promote this gig, paid a shitload in advertising, more than I usually do, all because Gerry Bloom's a personal friend of mine and he says these kids are the next big thing. He's never steered me wrong once, so what can I do, eh? He's the one who turned me onto you, you know."

"Wait a second, I thought the band requested me. I'd heard they were fans of mine."

Eddie waved his hand. "Aw, that's just Bloom greasing you up. He was desperate and needed an opening act quick. Originally he wanted The Sno-Cones, but they were finishing a tour in Canada and couldn't make it down here in time. I tried to tell him comedians don't mix well with rock bands, but he never listens to me. When he makes up his mind he sticks like gum to the bottom of your shoe until you give in. So what could I do?" He threw his hands in the air. "I gave in."

I could feel the color draining out of my face. "Does *anyone* in the band know who I am?"

"Oh, sure, Ogo does. He's the one who told Bloom to go see you down at that club there in West Hollywood, what is it, Sneaky Pete's or something—?" He snapped his fingers.

"Paste-Pot Pete's."

"That's it! Ogo's caught your act there a few times. He says you're funny sorta, but he's got a pretty damn weird sense of humor anyway. I think he's a pedophile."

"Am I supposed to know who Ogo is?"

"He's the bass player. He's a real clown. You'd probably like him."

"Yeah, it's funny, just the other day I was talking to my agent and I said, 'You know what? We really need to add some more pedophiles to my fan base. That should help my standing at the networks. Maybe if you throw in a couple of transvestites and serial murderers too, my star will really begin to take off.'"

Eddie stared at me with blank, unreadable eyes, then nodded and said, "Yep, you and Ogo should get along well together."

This comment propelled me toward the exit. "I'm going for a walk," I said, "I need to get some fresh air."

"Don't stray too far!" Eddie called after me. "I'd rather you didn't fall into the ocean before your performance. Afterwards you can do whatever the hell you want, of course."

The Brink was located near the Hermosa Beach pier. This being summer, the sun was just now setting. Portions of the twilight sky were as red as blood. I strolled down the sidewalk, breathing in the salt-laced air blown in on a strong gust of wind from the Pacific, which I could see rolling away from me, flat, fiery orange and infinite, only one block away. Beachside condos were woven into the panorama, preventing a totally unobstructed view, but I didn't mind. This was good enough. I could just make out a scattered group of tiny white dots, which I took to be sailboats, slicing through the waves like giant knives. For a moment I fantasized swimming out to one of those boats— even though I couldn't swim—and climbing aboard, sailing the hell away, leaving Doktor Delgado's All-American Genocidal

Warfare Against The Sick And The Stupid far, far behind me. But this, of course, was impossible. I was locked in, and all I could hope for was that the audience would have more of a sense of humor than Eddie Milstein.

After strolling around for about a half-hour, I paused by a newspaper machine outside a bong shop and did a double take when I saw the headline on the front page of the *L.A. Times*: "Newly Discovered 'Humor Virus' Feared To Be Incurable." The paper had even included a sidebar to the story, the headline of which read, "Ironically, Most Americans Think 'Humor Virus' Is A Joke." I dug a handful of quarters out of my pocket, bought the paper, and read it on the way back to the club. The scientists claimed the virus was growing more and more destructive, and as it did so its victims grew less and less aware of the problem; the stronger the virus, the more complacent its victims. The colored pie graph to the right of the article indicated that most Americans believed the CDC had made up the disease just to have something to occupy their time.

On my way back to the club I saw something that made me stop in my tracks: another piece of "graffiti," one so sophisticated it just had to have been created by the same artist who'd painted that giant talking dog on the front of the Starbucks across from Heather's apartment. This particular image, a breathtakingly detailed mural, had been sprayed on the side of *The Easy Reader* building. (*The Easy Reader* was a local newspaper given away for free, really nothing more than a bunch of puff pieces wrapped in ads.) The mural depicted a giant mouse with its butt and tail facing the viewer. You could just barely see its head turning toward the right, its whiskers overlapping a closed window. The mouse was surrounded by a trail of purple sparkles. Rising out of its black lips was a wispy word balloon that contained the following message: "I was along this way, and thought I'd drop in!" There was a definite hint of intelligence in the rodent's beady black eyes.

Whoever was responsible for this stuff should've been receiving a whole lotta remuneration for his efforts. Instead, two little Hispanic dudes were sloppily painting over the mural with white paint. I walked away, shaking my head in disgust.

I entered the club through the back door. The backstage area where I had been talking to Eddie was now empty except for a clown. The clown was crouched on the ground, flinging various objects into a black Gladstone bag. The objects were scattered across the floor, as if they had fallen out of the bag only a few moments before I'd entered. Among the objects were a pile of rubber snakes, a bottle of seltzer water, a hand buzzer, a whoopi cushion, two banana peels, a severed mannequin hand, a half-eaten cream pie, and about three dozen marbles. My first thought upon seeing the clown was something along the lines of: A fuckin' clown? What the hell's next, ten midgets in mime outfits?

I walked over to the clown and said, "Would you like some help with that?"

The clown glanced up at me. "No, I'd rather you stood around watching me with your thumb up your ass!" He seemed eager to throw out some more caustic cracks until he squinted at me, tilted his head and said, "Hey, you're Elliot Greeley!"

From the raspy tone of his voice I couldn't quite tell whether this made him happy or mad. "I suppose that's possible," I said, reluctant to commit further than that.

The clown rose to his feet and held out his gloved hand. His gloves might've been white at one time, but had turned gray-ish-yellow after years of accumulated dirt. "Nice to meet you," he said, "the name's Ogo. I'm the guy who got you the job here."

"Are you the bass player?" With some reluctance I shook his hand.

"That's right. Have you heard of us before?"

I recalled what Eddie had told me about Ogo: "He's a real clown. You'd probably like him." It hadn't occurred to me to take him literally.

"Not until I got the call to play this gig," I said. "I'm sorry, I don't really keep up with the new bands."

"That's okay, neither do I. Most of 'em suck. Here, I'll give you a free CD." Ogo lifted the bag off the ground and began rooting through the junk he'd just thrown inside it. The clown stood a little over five foot eight and was a bit chubby. Because of the make-up it was difficult to tell how old he was. Perhaps he was in his early twenties. His outfit was no run-of-the-mill clown costume. It was rather disturbing to look at. Except for his blood-red lips, the color scheme was entirely black and white. The outfit consisted of a mixture of chaotic black and white swirls that could make you dizzy if you stared at them long enough. The same chaotic swirls adorned his face, the only differences being the subtle inclusion of the twenty-two sigils of the Kabalah amongst the otherworldly streaks. If I hadn't taken a Comparative Religion course in college I wouldn't have recognized them as anything more than meaningless squiggles. I was about to ask him about them when I heard the back door opening behind me.

I turned and saw a muscle-bound, middle-aged punk rocker backing through the door with an amp in each hand and a guitar case slung over his shoulder. He was short, standing a little over five foot five, but was well-built; his head was shaved, and he wore nothing more complicated than a black t-shirt, black Levis and combat boots. His arms were covered with tattoos, stunningly detailed renderings of surreal, nightmarish beings that looked like they'd been plucked out of a Max Ernst collage.

"It'd be nice if you could carry your own god damn guitar," the man said, lowering the equipment to the floor beside Ogo's oversized shoes.

"This is the opening act I was telling you about," Ogo said, gesturing toward me.

The man encased my hand in a grip that could've damaged me permanently if he'd wanted it to. Somehow, though, it was clear he wasn't trying to impress me with his strength; he just didn't realize how strong he really was. "Elliot something, isn't it?"

"Elliot Greeley," I said.

"This is Jesse Lazar, our drummer," Ogo said.

"So I hear you're some sort of a comedian," Jesse said.

I shrugged. "I guess so."

"So tell me something funny."

I hate it when people say that. It's like cornering a doctor in the men's room and asking him to give you a free rectal exam. "Oh, I don't know, I haven't had much time to think up funny shit lately. Howzabout this one? What do you call a forty-year-old man who's still playing drums in a garage band?"

The brute glared at me with eyes of fire. "What?"

"Stupid."

Jesse said nothing. His hands suddenly transformed into fists and he came at me. Ogo slipped in between us, just in time.

Ogo patted Jesse on the chest, like an animal trainer at a circus calming down an enraged lion. "No worries, m'man. The guy's a silly comedian, you know that. Just relax. Chill."

The fire in Jesse's eyes began to die down. "Well, I dunno . . . if you say so, Ogo. I'll relax, but that guy better watch himself, that's all I'm sayin'."

"Now don't you worry your pretty little head none," I said, "I'll just go in the dressing room and stand in front of a mirror and do my best Narcissus impersonation—I promise."

Jesse glared at me again, as if trying to puzzle through my words.

Ogo leaned toward my ear and whispered, "Don't worry about him. He's a little slow. Believe it or not he's a Gulf War vet. He's lost a couple of brain cells to that (quote) non-existent (unquote) Gulf War Disease, if you know what I mean." He twirled his index finger around his ear.

"Hey, what're you saying?" Jesse said, stepping forward and expanding his chest outward like a gorilla ready to attack. His t-shirt drew tightly against his body, revealing what seemed to be a shallow dip in his chest. It was as if someone had bounced a bowling ball off his sternum a few times too many. "You makin' fun of me again?" he said, pushing Ogo against the shoulders.

"Why, you—!" Ogo said. "I'd horsewhip you if I had a horse!" Ogo threw me a knowing glance.

"Professor Quincy Adams Wagstaff," I said. "*Horse Feathers*, Paramount, 1932." I was amazed. What were the chances of meeting two separate people—within only a few days—with esoteric, intimate knowledge of Groucho Marx?

Jesse seemed confused by our exchange and demanded to know what Ogo had been saying about him. Ogo responded by sticking out his long, grayish tongue. The squabble might have come to blows if not for the interruption that came from the back entrance.

"Will you two stop fighting for a second and help me with this shit?" This sentence came out rather garbled due to the drumstick lodged in the mouth of the speaker. All three of us turned toward the exit.

Leaning against the doorway was a puckish sprite of a girl with a ballerina's figure. Even with a complete drum set in her arms and a guitar case strapped over each shoulder, she managed to maintain the svelte movements of a natural-born dancer. This gracefulness was rather discordant compared to the saltiness of her language.

"Both of you cocksuckers are hopeless," she said, allowing the drumstick to fall from her mouth. "What does it take to get you retards off your lazy asses, anti-fucking-gravity?"

"Hey, that's a good idea," Ogo said. "Maybe I should begin researching that in my spare time. I could develop an anti-grav-ity zeppelin, perhaps."

"The only thing you're going to develop is a black eye if you don't get the rest of your shit out of the van," the girl said. "You couldn't even alphabetize a bag of M&Ms. How're you gonna research anti-gravity?"

I laughed pretty hard at the M&M line. No doubt about it, she was a beautiful girl. She had long auburn hair, green eyes, and a childish face with chubby cheeks that made her look like a twelve-year-old with a stripper's body. She wore a long trench coat, a belly-shirt that showed off a disturbing fetus tattoo on her midriff, a mini-skirt, knee-high stockings and combat boots: an all-black ensemble that caused her to blend in with the walls of the club.

Since both Ogo and Jesse made no attempt to help the girl, I stepped forward and took the drum set from her arms, placing it down beside Ogo's bass. The girl breathed a sigh of relief and lowered her two guitar cases to the floor. "Jesus Christ, at least there's one gentleman around here," she said, shooting a nasty glance at Ogo and Jesse.

"This is Esthra," Ogo mumbled, waving his hand toward the girl with complete disinterest. "She fiddles around with the guitar a bit."

"Fiddles around!" Esthra said. "Phh! I'm the main draw of the show, you dick! You think people come to see your ugly ass dancing around on stage?"

"As a matter of fact, yes I do," he said.

Esthra laughed. "In your dreams."

I held my hand out to Esthra. "I'm Elliot Greeley," I said, "your opening act."

She shook my hand. "You're the comedian?"

"So everyone keeps telling me."

"Don't you know that rock bands and comedians don't mix?"

"Sure do."

"Then why are you here?"

"Because I'm sick or stupid or both."

Esthra laughed. "Then you're in fine company." She pulled her hand away slowly. Did she brush her fingers against my palm a bit longer than necessary? Perhaps this was just my imagination. Even so, I was growing quite thankful to Marsha for having talked me into this gig.

Ogo cleared his throat. "Aren't we forgetting someone? Where's our fearless leader?"

"Where do you think?" Esthra said. "In the back of the van doing his Stephen Hawking impersonation."

"Before or after the onset of amyotrophic lateral sclerosis?" I asked.

"Definitely after." She turned to Jesse and Ogo. "Well, are one of you going to help me haul in the rest of the shit or are you going to leave it to the fucking comedian?"

Ogo pointed at the junk on the ground and said, "I have to finish cleaning up my bag o' tricks."

Esthra rolled her eyes and appeared just about ready to rip into the clown when Jesse said, "Don't get all out of sorts, I'll do it."

Esthra glared at Ogo, turned on her heels, then stormed out the door with Jesse following close behind. I realized that she reminded me of Heather.

"She must be easy to work with," I said.

Ogo waved his hand and continued rooting through the bag. "And she's not even on the rag yet," he said. "Just wait until she's on the rag."

"Pretty strong-headed, huh?"

"That's the diplomatic way of putting it. The only one who can tell her what to do is Mr. Aster."

"Who's Aster?"

"The singer and songwriter, the brains behind this here operation. Esthra's his girlfriend. Well, kind of. They break up every other day. Ah! I knew you were hiding around here somewhere." From his bag Ogo pulled out a huge magnifying glass and a CD, both of which he tossed up to me.

A magnifying glass was necessary to make out all the details hidden within the cover's illustration. It was a silkscreen of the infamous autopsy photo depicting the back of JFK's head. In the circular space that should have been the gunshot wound, the artist had inserted a colorful collage made up of the most memorable images from the latter half of the twentieth century and the beginning of the twenty-first: the burning monk in Vietnam, Nixon flashing the victory sign, a peace activist in a gas mask tossing a smoke bomb, a regiment of Black Panthers armed with rifles, LBJ picking his dog up by the ears, Marlon Brando in *The Godfather*, Bugs Bunny chomping on a carrot, the Pepsi logo, the Spruce Goose in flight, J. Edgar Hoover lying in his coffin, Charles Manson grinning, Hunter S. Thompson's peyote-button-in-fist symbol, Roger Patterson's Bigfoot footage, the space shuttle *Challenger* exploding, Oliver North testifying before Congress, Ronald Reagan kneeling before a Nazi grave in Bitburg, the flying saucer from *Close Encounters*, Nancy Reagan sitting on Mr. T's lap while he was dressed up as Santa Claus, George Bush vomiting into the crotch of the Japanese prime minister, a C-140 Cessna crashing into the White House, Bullwinkle pulling Rocky the Flying Squirrel out of a top hat, an array of blue cellular phone towers made up to look like palm trees, the whirling tea cups at Disneyland, the smoking remains of the Twin Towers in New York, and dozens of other images that were far too small to make out. Running across the top of the cover in messy, dripping letters was the title of the album: *Adventures in the Head Wound*. At the very bottom, if you looked hard enough, could be found the name of the band in microscopic letters.

"Interesting cover," I said. What else could you say?

"Aster did that. He's pretty good when he puts his mind to it."

This Aster was multi-talented, a real renaissance man. I hated him already.

Ogo continued to toss his junk back into his bag. "Please listen to that as soon as you can," he said. "Don't just toss it out or anything. Aster's got a hell of a talent for quirky, funny lines. I think you'll really like them."

I flipped over the CD and scanned the song titles on the back: "Dr. Seuss Was a Junkie," "Queen of Conspiracies," "How Assholes Came to Bleed," "Suicide Boy," "O, Petra Beter, Won't You Marry Me?," "The Olive Garden Fellatio Incident," "Momma's Got a Death Ray," "Suicide on Sunday, Poolside on Monday," "Don't Fuck with the Phone Company," and "Damned If You Do, Dead If You Don't."

"Quirky is a word that applies," I said.

Ogo finally packed away the last of his shit and zipped up the bag. As he stood up he said, "I realize it's nerve-wracking for a comedian to do his routines at a rock concert, but don't worry about it. I saw Jack Varner open for Matachine and he killed. The audience loved him. You're not going to regret taking this gig."

"Well, I sure hope not." At that moment I remembered something Marsha had told me. "Do you mind if I ask you a question? I hope it's not too personal."

"Nothing's too personal." He reached into his ear and pulled out a pair of polka-dotted underwear.

I tried not to seem too surprised. "I hear everyone in your band is dying of a different terminal illness. Is that just a gimmick or . . . ?"

"No, it's true. I'm suffering from a rare skin disease, a cancer that's slowly eating me alive."

"Jesus, that's horrible."

Ogo shrugged. "It could be worse."

"How could it be worse?"

"I could be dead already." (I experienced a sudden sense of déjà vu. Hadn't Heather told me something similar only a couple of weeks before?) The clown added, "I contracted the disease from the face paint I'm wearing."

"Then why don't you take it off?"

"Oh, I couldn't do that. I've been wearing it nonstop since I was thirteen."

"Doesn't that get uncomfortable?"

"Not as uncomfortable as it would be if I took it off. I couldn't even talk to people without it. It's my father's make-up and his father's father's make-up. It's as much a part of me as my DNA. I have to stand or fall with it, just like my father did."

"Did your father die of the same disease?"

"No." For the first time I detected a defensive, hardened edge to his voice. He didn't want to talk about how his father had died. "He passed away when I was thirteen. Afterwards I took his name and his make-up, everything that made him who he was, then ran away from the circus I'd been with all my life."

I couldn't help but laugh. "Most kids want to run away from home to join the circus, not the other way around."

"I've always done everything ass-backwards. Anyway, I hopped a freight train just outside San Francisco. You meet a lot of strange characters on freight trains. That's where I met Jesse."

"What was he doing hopping freight trains?"

Ogo shook his head. "Oh, it's a long story. When he came down with the Gulf War illness he lost everything. The VA wouldn't help him, the Pentagon told him he was crazy, his wife abandoned him. He was suffering from a whole laundry list of horrible symptoms: stiff joints, chronic fatigue, diarrhea, vomiting, partial loss of eyesight. He even developed a large circular hole in the middle of his chest."

I wrinkled my nose in disgust. "A hole? What do you mean?"

"He can pass his hand right through it. It doesn't bleed, and the insides are as smooth as glass. In fact, they are glass. You can even see his organs through the inner walls of the hole; the glass is perfect and neat, as if a laser bored a hole right through him."

"Oh, c'mon. You're pulling my leg."

"No, really! He might even show it to you if you're nice to him. He only shows it to people he's really comfortable with."

"So what happened to all his other symptoms? He seems as healthy as a horse—however healthy that is."

"Once his wife left him he decided to leave everything behind him and began riding the rails up north. He was surprised to meet a lot of other Gulf vets doing the same exact thing. Some of these guys had experimented with a whole panoply of drugs, trying to cure themselves since the government refused to help them. Without the freight train riders Jesse would be dead by now. They turned him onto an obscure drug called doxycycline that dampens the pain of the disease and at least renders life bearable from time to time. He's still in a lot of pain, but he refuses to show it. He has too much pride for that. I've known him for six years and I've never heard him complain once."

"What about Aster?"

"What does he have to complain about? He's just dying of AIDS. Lucky bastard! I'd trade with him any day of the week. He gets a steady stream of government subsidy checks every month. Without those checks we wouldn't have been able to buy any of this equipment or practice as much as we have. Hell, thank God for AIDS, that's what I say."

"You know, it's funny. Just the other day I met another guy who was HIV positive." I think that's when it hit me. "Say, what's this guy's first name?"

Jesse appeared in the doorway carrying a keyboard and an electric six-string bass. Staggering behind him came Esthra with her arm around an emaciated, pale fellow who was wearing nothing but a black t-shirt and black shorts, the same clothes he'd been wearing when I'd seen him in his bedroom the day before. Esthra was doing everything she could to help Mike into the room. He had a purplish-black eye and fresh cuts all over his face; he appeared to be half-asleep.

I turned to Ogo and said, "This is your lead singer?"

"Yeah, but don't worry. We'll just give him some speed and he'll be in fine shape for his performance."

"Isn't that dangerous?"

"Of course, but what else can we do? We've got to go on."

"I thought he promised to stop doing this shit," Jesse said as he leaned the equipment against the wall.

"He did," Esthra said, easing Mike down on an upturned crate. "Last time when he was kicking he promised me he was never going to touch the shit again. I don't even know how he got ahold of it. Some fucking idiot must've given it to him."

Jesse shook his head in frustration. "If I could find the guy who gave it to him I'd—!" He slammed his fist into his palm.

"Uh, maybe I should leave you guys alone with him," I said, backing away toward the exit.

Ogo said, "Aw, don't go. I've been wanting the two of you to meet each other for awhile now. Believe it or not you think very much alike."

Mike slumped down on the crate, his legs spread out wide, his head tilted back against the wall, his mouth hanging open as if he were mentally retarded. It was difficult to interpret Ogo's words as a compliment.

Noticing the disfavor in my face Ogo added, "I mean when he's lucid, of course."

Esthra leaned down and stared into Mike's drooping eyes. "I think he's coming out of it now."

"How can you tell?" I asked.

Mike's whole body snapped forward suddenly, as I've often done during a dream of falling. He glanced around as if trying to figure out where he was.

"Are you all right?" Esthra said, caressing his swollen cheek.

Mike slapped her hand away. "Don't touch me! Are you trying to hurt me or something?"

"I'm sorry," she whispered. She crossed her arms over her chest and stared at the floor, shrinking into herself like an abused child. She was the exact opposite of the self-assured woman I'd seen only a few minutes before.

"Think you can perform?" Jesse asked.

"Perform?" Mike uttered the word as if wondering what it meant. "I don't know. . . ." The sentence just trailed off. Mike seemed to be nodding out again.

"Maybe we should get you to the little boys' room," Ogo said. "It's definitely time for some medication." He held up his bag o' tricks, indicating that the "medicine" was inside.

"It looks like he's had too much medication already," I said.

At the sound of my voice Mike's head swivelled toward me in a jerky, rubbery motion. He peered at me through half-closed, Mr. Magoo eyes. "Wh-who are you?"

"He's our opening act," Ogo said. "I'm sure I've mentioned him to you. His name's Elliot Greeley. He's a brilliant comedian."

"H-have I seen you before?"

"I don't know," I said. "I've been on a couple of cable talk shows. Maybe you saw me there."

"He doesn't have cable," Jesse said.

"So maybe he was at a friend's house. How should I know?" I felt sweat breaking out on my forehead.

"I'm sure it doesn't matter," Ogo said, reaching his hand out to Mike. "C'mon, let's go find that bathroom."

Esthra moved between Mike and Ogo. "I think Elliot's right," she said. "Maybe he's got too much shit in his body already. If you give him speed too, who knows what could happen? He might die."

Ogo said, "Excuse me, do I have to remind you that he's dying already?"

"But why speed up the process? I don't like it. We should be trying to cure him, not make him worse."

Mike laughed and rose from the crate on quaking legs. It seemed as if he almost toppled forward a couple of times. His blank, stoic expression transformed into a disgusted sneer. "Why do you even bother to act like you care about me? When you're around other people you do such a good job of pretending like you're *so* in love with me. If you're so in love with me why do you fuck every man, woman or child you can get your hands on when I'm not looking? Hell, you don't even care if I'm looking. You'd fuck a dog in front of me if you thought you'd get off on it." He cast a hateful gaze at Jesse. Jesse wavered and glanced away.

Over the course of Mike's diatribe Esthra's lower lip began to tremble. She wrapped her arms tightly around herself, her fingernails digging into her shoulders. At one point she whispered, "That's not true," as tears began to trickle down her cheeks.

Mike lunged forward and grabbed her wrist, ripping her hand away from her shoulder. "Stop crying! You have no fucking right to cry, no right to criticize what god damn drugs I take! You think I'd have to do this shit if it weren't for you?"

Jesse took a step toward them. "Mike, let her go."

Mike just looked at Jesse and laughed with what seemed like utter disgust. Then his eyelids began to droop. He released Esthra's wrist, weaved back and forth slightly. His eyes became blank and glassy again. He began to topple forward. Esthra and Jesse moved to catch him, but he caught himself at the last second. At least he almost did. He fell backwards onto the crate, slamming his head against the wall with a painful-sounding *crack*, then resumed his comatose position.

Eddie strolled in from the stage area, saw Mike propped up on the crate like a corpse, and said, "What the hell is this?" He walked over to Mike.

"Oh, he's just resting a bit," Ogo said.

"Resting?" Eddie picked up Mike's hand, then released it. The hand dropped like a stone. "You call this resting? I call it unconscious. Oh, shit." He lowered his face into his hands, shook his head back and forth. "This is the last time I do a favor for Gerald Bloom, the very last time."

Ogo said, "Look, all he needs is his medicine, then everything will be fine."

Eddie shoved his index finger into Ogo's face, his fingertip almost touching the clown's bulbous nose. "You give him whatever you have to, I don't care. Just make sure he's lucid enough by 10:20 to walk out there on that stage and deliver the fucking goods, you got that?"

Ogo nodded quickly, wide-eyed, then turned to Jesse. "C'mon, help me get him into the bathroom." Ogo grabbed one arm while Jesse grabbed the other, then they lifted Mike from the crate. "Uh, where *is* the bathroom?" Ogo asked.

Eddie gestured toward the hall to his left by jabbing his thumb over his shoulder. As the mismatched pair dragged Mike away Eddie turned to me and said, "If that freak's not fully conscious by 10:20 your act may have to go on a bit longer than we'd planned. Don't worry, I'll make it worth your while. Is that all right with you?"

"Well, I don't know. My act is sort of timed to last exactly twenty minutes."

"But you must have more material than that, right?"

"Well, of course—"

"Fantastic! I'll be standing at the side of the stage right here. If you see me give the wrap-up sign at twenty, you can finish up and haul ass off stage. If not, keep on going. It doesn't even matter if you're funny, just fill up time." I didn't find this statement very heartening, but I nodded anyway. "Fantastic,

fantastic! You're a life saver, m'man." Eddie gave me a little tap against the shoulder, then followed Ogo and Jesse down the hall.

Now I didn't know what the hell to do. My whole act was based on an encounter I'd had with some strange heroin addict named Mike who happened to be the lead singer of the fucking band! Could I disguise the names so the rest of the band wouldn't know who I was talking about? No, that was impossible. The truth of the situation was a hell of a lot funnier. Unfortunately, the truth might get me rent in two by a Gulf War vet. Maybe I would be lucky and Jesse would think it was funny. After all, I wasn't the one who gave him the heroin, it was Danny. Of course, I sat around and did nothing to stop it, but so what? What am I, the Thought Police? I'm going to tell people what they can and can't do with their own bodies? Oh, dear. Now I was getting a headache. What was I going to do? Would I have to make up a whole new act within forty minutes? The butterflies in my stomach were fluttering up a tsunami.

I snapped out of my worry-filled reverie and glanced about the room, realizing that everyone had left except for Esthra. She was standing very still, her arms crossed over her chest as if she were trying to hold herself in, her eyes crimson and glassy. We locked eyes for a second, then she glanced down at the floor, too embarrassed to look at me. She lowered herself onto the crate that Mike had been sitting on, folded her hands between her knees, and stared off into space.

"I hope band practice is somewhat less exciting," I said. She didn't respond. Perhaps she wanted me to go away, I couldn't be sure. "Does he always treat you like that?"

She remained quiet for a long time. I was just about to walk away, the silence having become far too unbearable, when she said, "No, not always. Hardly ever. It's just the drugs."

"Does heroin make him act that way?"

She laughed a little. "I think he did more than heroin. A speedball, probably." I didn't know what that was, but acted like I did. She continued, "I'm not what he said, you know. I'm not a whore. Do I look like a whore to you?"

I was a bit taken aback by the question. I just shook my head no.

"Why did he call me that then?"

"Well, I don't remember him using that word in particular."

"Everything but. I've *never* cheated on him, *never*." She slammed her fist on her bare knee each time she said the word "never."

She looked like she was about to start crying again. "I believe you," I said, hoping to prevent this.

"Do you really?" She looked up at me and smiled. Her smile was wide and bright, so wide it seemed to fill her entire face, so bright it was hard to imagine anyone wanting to harm her. The perfection of her face was offset only by the crimson streaks staining her eyes.

I nodded yes.

"Thank you," she said. "You're about the only one who does." She laughed sadly. "Then again, you don't even know me. If you knew me you'd hate me as much as Mike does."

"How do you know he hates you? You said yourself it was the drugs making him act like that. Maybe he didn't know what he was saying."

She shook her head. "Mike doesn't need drugs to hate me."

I didn't know what to say. When I don't know what to say the first words that pop into my mind are often the most inappropriate ones you could possibly imagine. For example, what I wanted to say was, "Would you like to go out to dinner tomorrow night?" but somehow I knew that wouldn't go over too well at that particular moment.

Eventually she said, "What time is it?"

I glanced at my watch. "Just about 9:30."

"Jesus, we have to get set up." She looked around as if expecting roadies to emerge from the walls. She threw her arms in the air. "Am I supposed to do this all by myself?"

"I'll go find Eddie," I said, hoping to calm her down before she started freaking out again. "I'm sure he has people to help you." Part of me just wanted to get out of there before I said something stupid.

"Wait a second," she said. I stopped and turned. "Please don't listen to Eddie. It *does* matter if you're funny. Don't just fill up time. I think I really need to laugh now more than ever."

I shrugged. "I'll do the best I can. I don't guarantee anything."

She waved her hand. "Oh, I know you won't let me down. Ogo says you're one of the funniest comedians he's ever seen."

I wanted to say, "Well, that means a lot coming from a cancer-ridden clown who plays bass in an obscure punk band," but bit my tongue. I think I mumbled something like "Thank you" and shuffled away in search of Eddie. Now I felt really bad. My damsel in distress requests a simple little laugh, and instead I'm planning on insulting her boyfriend. "Hey, honey, here's a real belly laugh for you: Your boyfriend's a junkie fag who regularly gets the shit kicked out of him by his father, ho ho!" Yeah, that was sure to win her over.

Whoever said comedy was easy? I'd like to find the fucker and pop him in the nose.

CHAPTER 11

Keep the Ravioli in Orbit

(October 3, 2014)

Eddie strolled out on stage at ten o'clock on the dot and introduced me to a giant room filled with wild teenagers. I was so nervous I thought I might stumble and fall on my face before I even reached center stage. Part of my nervousness stemmed from the fact that I had decided to follow through with my original game plan. What else could I do?

Hanging on the wall behind me were a series of American flags of various colors—magenta, orange, black and blue, pink paisley, etc.—with dripping, messy stripes that merged into one another like wet paint. Set up in front of the flags were the drums, the keyboards, and the upright bass. The last time I had checked, which was only a couple of minutes before, Mike was still comatose in the bathroom. I was beginning to think that I would not only have to go over the standard twenty-minute mark, I'd have to do the whole god damn show. However,

Esthra had assured me she could sing the songs if Mike wasn't able to go on, though she preferred not to. She didn't know if her voice was strong enough to carry a whole show, but if worse came to worse she said it would have to do.

The lights above the stage were the brightest fuckin' lights I'd ever seen. Apparently Eddie had decided to shoot a video of the band's performance which required the most intense illumination this side of the sun itself. I couldn't imagine how the band could play under them for more than a few minutes. I could already feel myself beginning to sweat. The lights were shining directly into my eyes. I couldn't see a damn thing. I found myself squinting as if I was at the beach. All I could hear was the incessant shouting. Of course, I couldn't start my act until these stupid bastards decided to calm down. I raised my hands, then lowered them slowly, trying to clue them in on the fact that it was time to begin the show. For a long time I couldn't figure out what the hell it was they were screaming. At first it sounded like "Extra! Extra!" but that made no sense. Then I realized they were shouting Esthra's name.

I said, "Excuse me, I'm only going to say this once, *shut the fuck up* or I'm going to have to kick all your asses at once."

Suddenly a beer bottle erupted out of the brightness and whizzed past my ear, slamming into one of the cymbals behind me, creating an interesting musical sound for a single moment. I said, "Hey, the next beer bottle better be a Heineken or I'm leaving!"

A Heineken arced over my head and smashed into something behind me, I don't know what, sending little glass shards skittering across the stage. I was just about to abandon ship, narrowly avoiding two more bottles and a full Coca-Cola can, when Esthra came striding out onto stage. She had taken off her trench coat, showing more skin than not. The beer bottles stopped flying, but the shouting grew louder. She grabbed my mike from me and said, "Greetings, you wasted little shit-heads!" Just when I thought the screams couldn't get any more ear-shattering they would rise another decibel. "Listen up," she continued, "I want you to give my friend here the utmost respect. If you conduct yourselves like the cultured, urbane gentlemen I know you truly are, perhaps I'll give you a special little treat later on." She wrapped one leg around the mike stand, drew the microphone toward her, and ran her tongue slowly around the head of the mike. The crowd erupted into cheers. She wrapped her bright red lips around the mike, then shoved it deep into her mouth. Moist, intimate sounds echoed through the club. She tipped her head back and eased the mike all the way down her throat. It was the most amazing spectacle I'd ever witnessed. My gag reflex kicked in just by watching it. I actually had to glance away for a second for fear that I might whoop my cookies all over the stage. Meanwhile, the crowd's animalistic grunts had reached an orgasmic high.

At last Esthra pulled the microphone out of her mouth and said, "Okay, you sloth-browed troglodytes, now just kick back and get ready to laugh your ass off for the next twenty minutes and if you don't I ain't comin' back and neither is the rest of the band so as the man says, '*Shut the fuck up!*'"

She tossed the mike back to me, flashed me one of her Esthra-bright smiles, then turned widdershins and marched away to the hoots and hollers of the crowd, who continued to chant her name until she disappeared backstage. To my surprise, they then calmed down like kids in a little country school house and waited politely for me to speak. The silence almost knocked me back on my feet.

"Now how the hell do I follow that up?" I said. "Uh, let me tell you a little story about how I first met Mr. Michael Aster."

Someone cheered at the mention of his name, then I proceeded to lay out the whole scenario, beginning with the simple intent to see the Godzilla flick and going straight through watching Danny shoot up for the first time, the selling of my urine, the assault of Mike's berserk father, my and Danny's panicked retreat out the window, all the way up to meeting the band backstage and my indecisive turmoil over whether or not to tell the story at all. The pitiful absurdity of the story had the crowd in stitches. I think hearing about their aloof, unapproachable, badass icon being involved in a domestic dispute as violent and silly as the situations they themselves were probably involved in on a day-to-day basis made the story even funnier.

The story took a little over twenty minutes to tell. I filled up the rest of the time with a lot of my standard jokes, though I mixed in some brand new ones too. Near the end of the set I realized I was actually enjoying myself. In front of these twisted punks I could get away with some of my favorite, sickest, least appreciated jokes, jokes I could never hope to get away with even at the most underground of alternative comedy clubs. For example, I told them about my idea for a game show I planned to pitch to Fox Television. It was called *Celebrity Date Rape*. You could pick a normal, everyday shlub out of the studio audience to go out on a date with Bono or Sean Penn or Kylie Jenner or some other quasi-star like that. At some point during the date the contestant could rape the celebrity, in full view of the television audience, and as a reward the celebrity could have money sent to his or her favorite charity. The sick fuckers ate that one up like candy. Hell, I tried pulling that crap at The Land of Laughs in Oakland one night and almost got tossed off the stage.

All in all my act was a rousing success, if I may say so myself. After telling a joke about a male hooker with twelve assholes,

I glanced to my right and saw Eddie giving me the wrap-up sign at last. I reeled off a short routine about being married to a severed head, then said, "Goodnight, ladies and gentlemen and everyone in between! Keep the Ravioli in orbit, for God's sakes!" Then I got the hell off stage.

Backstage I saw Eddie and the band standing there waiting for me. Eddie was jubilant, but that was to be expected. As long as the crowd was happy so was he. Esthra and Ogo were both laughing uproariously. Even Jesse was grinning. In distinct counterpoint to these reactions was Mike himself, who loomed over Jesse's shoulder like a demonic wraith waiting to bite him and everyone else on the neck. The guitar I'd seen in his bedroom, the one with red rectangular "WARNING: FLAMMABLE" stickers plastered on almost every inch of it, hung from his shoulder by a black strap. Plastered on his face was a scowl far more flammable than the guitar; it seemed to me as if the scowl might at any moment ignite into berserk rage worthy of his father. Worst of all, his bloodshot eyes were fixed onto me and me alone.

Between guffaws Ogo said, "Man, that was great, the best I've ever seen you! That was unbelievable! I had no idea you knew Mike already."

"Neither did I," I said.

As Eddie walked out on stage to introduce the band, Esthra slipped her hand into mine and said, "Thank you. That was perfect. You were hilarious."

"Well, it's good I took your advice instead of Eddie's."

She laughed and squeezed my hand gently, then followed Ogo and Jesse out onto stage. Mike brushed past me, glaring at me as if he might kill me right then and there. The coldness emerging from him was tangible enough to chill my very insides. I couldn't even maintain eye contact. I had to stare down at my shoes after a couple of seconds. When I knew he had passed I glanced over my shoulder and watched the band file out onto stage to the roars of the crowd. I had a strong urge to stick around and watch them perform, if only to see Esthra jumping up and down with her guitar, but I had an equally strong urge to get the hell out of there before Mike decided to do an impersonation of his father on my skull.

Before I could make a decision either way Eddie returned from his on-stage introduction, slapped me on the back and told me to stick around for awhile. He wanted to buy me a drink at the bar and discuss booking further engagements.

"Marsha knows my schedule better than I do," I said, "but I'll take you up on that drink."

"Perfect," Eddie said. "Do you mind hanging out here for a moment while I visit the bathroom? I have to clean up after Aster. We were in such a rush to get him out on stage I think we might've left some incriminating evidence behind if you know what I mean. I don't want anyone getting to it before I do. Shit as pure as that is hard to come by these days unless you live in New York. And who would want to move all the way there just for some china white?"

I told him I understood perfectly, though I didn't. "I'll be right here," I said as the opening feedback of the band's first song screeched out of the amps.

"That's 'Suicide Boy,'" Eddie said, backing away down the hall. "I hear it's in the top five of the college radio charts. If they manage to break out into the mainstream we'll have a hot little item on our hands with that video we're shooting tonight, yes sir." He held up his stubby fingers and crossed them, then sprinted away down the hall.

"We"? I thought. Who the hell's "we"? I probably wouldn't see a dime from the damn video, even though I sweated like a pig in a fucking steam room just so it could be produced. While in the flow of my act I had been able to put the heat out of my mind, but now that the adrenalin rush was tapering off I suddenly realized that my face was soaked with sweat. Streams of perspiration were trickling out of my armpits and down past my ribs. I felt like a bug who'd almost burned to death beneath a child's magnifying glass.

I pulled my t-shirt up to my face and wiped the sweat away as the instrumental opening to "Suicide Boy" came to an abrupt end. Without warning Mike launched into the heart of the song, thrashing away on his guitar while screaming into the mike with the rhythm of an AK-47. Whatever Ogo had given him had certainly taken effect big time. The clown knew his medicine, you had to give him that.

Remembering what Ogo had said about Mike's lyrics, I tried to pay extra special attention to the words.

Suicide Boy

Suicide Boy
Thinks he's a greater artist than Goya
But plays little jingles on his Casio toy
Suicide Boy
Suicide Boy
Wraps a broken rope 'round his throat
Puts an empty gun to his head and writes a blank note
He thinks he's clever but he'll never die
He's a damn coward and his suicide's a lie
Suicide Boy
Suicide Boy
His mommy gives him a Christmas present almost every day
He makes his grandparents pay and pay

He's great at acting oh-so-depressed
The boy who cried wolf was in greater distress
Suicide Boy
Suicide Boy
Pushes the envelope right off the table
Likes to suck cock whenever he's able
Like his dead father he's a closet faggot
His brain's as soft as a pale white maggot
Suicide Boy
Suicide Boy
His girlfriend Shannon's a psycho-whore
His videos and music are a big fat bore
He sits in his room and records TV shows
His brain's a sieve and his poetry blows
Suicide Boy
Suicide Boy
Checks into AA like a hotel stay
His mommy's payin' but ask and he'll say
"I'm on my own tomorrow and today"
He's independent and he wants to get laid
With the stripper whose face was hit by a truck
Or Fred the heroin addict who he loves to fuck
For a swift needle prick or a tummy tuck
Either way he's stupid and shit outta luck
Cause he's a Suicide Boy
He's a Suicide Boy
He's a Suicide Boy
He used to work at Citicable 22
Now he's got a website and he's surfin' for you
Lookin' for a date with a girl or a boy
He'll take either cause he's a Suicide Boy
Suicide Boy

Suicide Boy
He thinks he's good at saying goodbye
Over and over he tries and tries
He thinks he's good at his little lies
I wish he'd just fuckin' up and die
Suicide Boy
Suicide Boy
Why don't you die die die die die
Why won't you die die die die die
Why don't you die die die die die
Why won't you die die die die *die*!

The kids were going nuts, and I could understand why. It was one of the most intense songs I'd ever heard. Mike delivered the lyrics with such anger I almost expected him to excrete pure hatred through the pores of his skin as a big finale. It was obvious to me that the song had been written about a specific person, someone who Mike despised more than his father, Nixon, Hitler, and Henry Kissinger all combined. Was it about himself? At the same time, however, I got the funny feeling that some of that anger was directed toward me.

Before the echoes of the last chord had faded away, the band dived right into another hardcore jingle called "Queen of Conspiracies," which Mike dedicated to someone named Mae Brussell. I wondered if that was a friend of his. If so, he must have cared for her a great deal. For this song Ogo had set aside his bass guitar and now stood behind the upright bass, sawing a bow across its six strings to create a weird flapping sound like the beating of vast, leathery bat wings. Esthra, meanwhile, had thrown down her guitar and was now pounding away on the keyboard. During the chorus Jesse peeled off his t-shirt, revealing the impossibility that Ogo had told me about before:

a glass-lined hole the size of a bowling ball right in the middle of his chest. Through the hole I could see the stripes of the American flag behind him. Whatever the anomaly was, it was no hallucination on my part. Everyone else in the audience saw it too. The mere act of revealing the hole elicited a wave of swoons from the females in the audience as if Jesse were a Chippendales dancer stripping away a skimpy loincloth.

I felt Eddie's hand on my shoulder. "Hey," he said, "Earth to Greeley! They haven't blown out your eardrums yet, have they?"

I guess he'd been babbling about something, but I hadn't heard him; I'd been too engrossed by the band's performance. "Have you ever seen anything like that?" I asked, pointing at Jesse's hole.

Eddie shrugged. "Aw, I've seen all kinds come through here. What's a glass-lined hole compared to a naked eighteen-year-old albino chick who belts out old Tom Jones tunes while letting a Doberman lick her cunt?"

"You've had acts like that *here?*"

"Well, no, not exactly, but you do get some weird auditions in the back office from time to time."

"They couldn't possibly think you'd book such a thing. You'd get shut down in two seconds."

"Hey, it's hard to know what *anyone's* thinking, particularly when they've got a dog's schnoz stuffed up their fuckin' muff. I was forced to turn the act down, of course, just out of general principle. Boy, it was sure fun while it lasted, though." He had a joyous gleam in his eyes, as if he were remembering the high point of a distant, perfect day.

I snapped my fingers in his face. "Hey, Earth to Eddie!" Lucidity returned to his eyes. "Didn't you say something about a drink?"

"Oh, of course," he said, just now remembering the offer, obviously still dazed from the Doberman memory. "We have business to discuss, don't we?"

I said nothing (which, of course, people always take as a yes) and let him lead the way to the bar.

CHAPTER 12

I Was a Psychic Spy for the FBI Part I

(October 3-4, 2014)

The bar was at the very back of the club. I allowed Eddie to babble on about future bookings while I watched Esthra swaying back and forth to the slow chords of a demented love song entitled "Melanoma Heartbreak." In the back of my mind I wondered if the brief physical contact I'd had with her was a foreshadowing of things to come. You idiot, I told myself, just because a girl touches you for a second doesn't mean she wants to go to bed with you. You're an egotistical jerk to think you can steal her away from a fuckin' rock star, no matter how screwed up he is. You basically live a boring life. *He* lives on the edge every day. Girls love that kind of lifestyle, even if they have to submit to being a punching bag a few days out of the week to maintain it.

After a few beers I had changed my position. While watching her swing her hips to the free form, jazz-like rhythm of

"Suicide on Sunday, Poolside on Monday" I was convinced she was transmitting secret signals to me through subtle thrusts of her groin, giving me (and me alone) The Eye from over two hundred feet away. Though the idea that she could even see me through those lights was rather improbable, I believed it nonetheless. Or at least I wanted to. Hell, so did every other guy in that room over six years of age. Imagine a woman like that casting her wayward gaze on my sorry ass. It was silly to even think about it, but that didn't stop me. Probably didn't stop anyone else either. That's why most of these kids had come to the show, after all. Esthra hadn't been lying when she'd told Ogo that she was the main draw.

I wondered what it felt like to be on that stage in front of all those hungry eyes, knowing that each one of them was undressing you, touching you, perhaps even fucking you in the darkest alcoves of their minds. I was a bit disgusted by the idea that I was one of them, only one of hundreds upon hundreds of psychic rapists.

To my right I heard Eddie saying, "Fuckin' A, I don't even know why I try to have a conversation with you."

"Huh?" I said, not taking my eyes off the stage.

"*Huh, huh?*" He imitated my voice. "Your fucking tongue's hanging out of your head, man. Could you be any more obvious?"

"About what?" I tried to look confused and annoyed as I downed another swig of beer.

"About what." He laughed. "She's one hot tottie, isn't she?"

"Who?"

"You know damn well who."

I shrugged. "She's okay."

"Okay, hell! She's perfect. What more could you ask for?"

"How about the sudden disappearance of a certain boy-friend with a hair-trigger temper?"

Eddie waved his hand. "Don't worry about him. Just wait until he nods out, then you can make your move. She looks like she'd be up for anything. I think you know what I mean by anything."

I looked up at the ceiling. "Uh . . . *Super Mario Galaxy 2?*"

"What?" He drew the word out to three syllables. "No, no. I'm sayin' she's up for some backdoor action, man."

"Backdoor action, hm . . . she wants to play *Super Mario Galaxy 2* near the backdoor?"

"Quit with the jokes already, I know you're interested in her. Let me tell you a secret, the feeling's mutual."

"Who are you trying to kid?"

"I'm *tellin'* you. I could see it in her eyes when she was watching you from backstage. Man, you were the only person in the world to her while you were doing your act."

"Sure, while I was doing my act. That's natural."

"Nah, it was more than just you being funny. Her poontang was dripping, I could smell it."

I wrinkled my nose in disgust. "Jesus Christ, Eddie!"

"It's *true!* I've got a hyper-sensitive sense of smell, I always have. It's a blessing and a curse. It's nice to know when a girl's hot for you, but when it's time to do the unspeakable act and you've got your nose hovering over a real musty one sometimes you almost gag the god damn scent is so overwhelming."

"And to think I actually had an appetite a couple of seconds ago."

"Don't play innocent with me, I can tell you've been around the block a few times. There's *a lot* of girls out there who like funny guys."

"Yeah, harelips and lepers are the first two examples that leap immediately to mind."

"Okay, okay, keep downplaying it. I know it's all part of your routine. It's easier to get girls if they think they're doing you a favor."

"You think so? Hell, maybe I should cut off my arms and legs and act like a retard, then I'll have a whole chorus line of charitable broads camped out on my doorstep day and night."

"You're quick with a comeback, I have to admit, but that doesn't change the facts. Esthra was giving you the verifiable, guaranteed, one and only Look of Love backstage and it was pissin' off Punk Boy something awful."

For the first time I began to take Eddie's meanderings seriously. "Mike noticed it?"

"He sure as hell did. He looked like he was gonna haul off and deck her right then and there. Perhaps that was just the cocaine kickin' in, but I don't think so. I've seen a lot of jealous rages break out at this club from time to time, and he looked like about twelve of them waiting to happen all at once."

"That's reassuring."

He waved his hand again. "Like I say, don't worry about it. After this performance he'll taper off again pretty fast. Jumping around up there takes a hell of a lot out of you. You want my advice?" I gestured for him to continue; I knew he was going to give it to me no matter what I said. "When I was in the bathroom trying to wake Punk Boy out of Slumberland, Ogo told me they were planning on going to a party after this. I suggest you tag along. Why not? You heard them, they all loved you (except for Punk Boy, of course). How could they say no? At the party Punk Boy will be more interested in scoring some more junk than anything else. While he's having pleasant dreams you can move right in."

"Seems kind of underhanded."

Eddie spread out his hands. "All's fair. . . ."

"Yeah, but I'm not in love and nobody's at war."

"Aw, everybody's always in love with somebody. They may not know it, but they are. Same with the other thing. There's always a war on, though not everyone is always aware of it."

"Are you getting philosophical on me? That's when you know you've had too much to drink, particularly when you're not making any sense."

"I've only had three beers."

"Yeah, in the last half-hour. I don't know how much you had before I arrived."

Eddie swivelled his rheumy eyes back toward the stage, where the band was starting up a new song. He watched Esthra dancing to the repetitious, hypnotic beat of "I Was a Psychic Spy for the FBI Part I."

"Yeah, I'd fuck that bitch," he mumbled, "I'd fuck that bitch in a second."

"Hey, you're talking about the woman I love," I said in a listless voice. I settled back against the bar, closed my eyes, and allowed the music to wash over me. I was impressed by how distinct each of the songs were from each other. The band's repertoire appeared to span a number of different musical forms. I listened to Mike belt out a droning chant in a flat, sleep-inducing tone that was rather unique compared to the voice he had used on all the songs preceding it. . . .

I'm undercover with a psychic coven
I eat young trim like chocolate chip muffins
I commune with spirits like Marilyn Monroe
I play poker with the Egyptian Tarot
I'm undercover with a psychic coven

I stuff young boys into microwave ovens
I follow the order of the FBI
I'm down with nirvana and the occultic third eye
I'm undercover with a psychic coven
I lure in hippies for a Leary-style love-in
I dope 'em all up with Ecstasy and smack
I strip off their clothes and tie 'em to a rack
I'm undercover with a psychic coven
I staple open vaginas and shove a white dove in
I perform this ritual as a sign of peace
I could've used eagles or vultures or geese
I'm undercover with a psychic coven
I castrate penises as small as a nubbin
I don't waste time with organs like that
I require members as large as Iraq
I'm undercover with a psychic coven
I cook baby flesh until it browns and toughens
I need the skin to stitch a vast fleshy robe
I can give it to Christo who will blanket the globe
I'm undercover with a psychic coven
I mate with serpents smokin' and puffin'
I hypnotize hippies in a cave near Reno
I conspire with colonels like Michael Aquino
I'm undercover with a psychic coven
I hope to find a nun with whom to have a run-in
I hope to strip her of her virgin pure habit
I plan to introduce her to a destructive drug habit
I'm undercover with a psychic coven
I grow so tired of choppin' and stuffin'
I think I'll bloat up, become fat 'n rolly polly
And soon I'll be as flabby as Aleister Crowley

Ogo was right, Mike did have a strange sense of humor. The man was clearly gifted, I had to give him that much. But what was a guy like that doing living with his abusive father in Torrance? Was it just the heroin? Could very well be. Any money he made from the CDs or the live shows probably went right into his arm.

I sat in that stool listening to each and every song for almost two hours. The ultimate strangeness came when they ended the show with a hardcore punk version of the Groucho Marx song "Whatever It Is, I'm Against It" from *Horse Feathers*. I wondered if that was Ogo's or Mike's idea.

When they began the song Eddie stood up and said, "Well, I've got to go up there and do the outro. I'll tell them you're still here so they can invite you along to the party."

"No, no, you don't have to do that," I said, rising from the stool. "Maybe I should just head on out of here—"

Eddie pressed his meaty hands on my shoulders and pushed me back onto the stool. "Sit. I'm tellin' you, this is going to be as easy as key lime pie." He snapped his fingers, then headed backstage. For a moment I considered bailing through the front entrance. Only the half-full glass of beer sitting in front of me prevented that. I can't stand to waste things, particularly not beer. I told myself I'd wait until I drained the glass. If Esthra and the others hadn't approached me by then I'd take off.

I drank slowly.

I still had quite a lot left by the time I felt Ogo's gloved hand on my shoulder. "Hey, Bunky," I heard him say, "we're headed on over to a friend's house on Pier Avenue. They're havin' a little party or somethin'. You want to tag along?"

"Will there be wild music and nubile young native girls?"

"Sure. We'll even be having animal sacrifices at midnight. That's always a treat."

"It's difficult for me to pass up a good animal sacrifice, I have to admit." I slid off the stool, ready to follow him out of the club.

"Wait a second." Ogo pointed at my beer. "You haven't finished your drink."

I waved my hand. "Eh, it doesn't matter, I didn't pay for it."

"Hey, whoa, hold on there." Ogo lifted the glass to his blood-red lips, tilted his head back, and consumed the contents in one gulp. He brushed his forearm across his mouth, then smacked his rubbery lips together. "I'm sorry, I just can't stand to see perfectly good beer go to waste. By the way, do you have a car?"

"No."

"How did you get here then?"

"I had to take the bus."

"The bus? Jesus, how do you stand it? All you meet on the bus are freakin' weirdos." This as I left The Brink side by side with a clown.

The beach air hit me like a cold glass of water on a hot day. It was such a relief compared to the stifling confinement of the smoke-filled club.

"I used to take the bus to kids' birthday parties," Ogo said. "Those were the only gigs I could get when I first moved to Los Angeles. It was a real bitch, let me tell you. One time I had to work all day in the pouring rain—some friggin' outdoor birthday party. Rain or shine, the kid had to have his god damn party. Shit, I never had a birthday party when I was a kid. The best I got was a broken beer bottle in the back, but that's a whole nother story."

"How're we getting to the party?" I said.

"Don't worry, we'll take my van." He jerked his thumb toward the right and motioned for me to follow him. We rounded the club and began strolling toward the back parking lot. The narrow area to the side of the club was quite dark. None of the street lamps were on for some reason, causing me to imagine sinister muggers lurking behind every trash bin waiting for the best opportunity to relieve me of my cash. I had a fantasy of Ogo saving me at the last second by whipping out a submachine gun from his bag o' tricks and blowing the vagabonds away, yet another example of my tendency to digress from the point. . . .

"Yep, takin' the bus was a real bitch," Ogo continued. "I had to take the bus home in the friggin' rain. Even the winos were laughing at me. At one point I took off one of my shoes and held it upside down and a bunch of rainwater fell out. The driver got pissed and wanted to throw me off, so I took a gun out and kicked *his* fat olive-skinned ass off instead. I took the bus on a joy ride around town doing about fifty miles per hour down one-way streets. Those winos weren't laughin' any more—no, they were scared shitless! Ho, it was a laugh riot, let me tell you." He raised his knee high enough to slap it, cracking himself up. "I got arrested, of course, but that was okay. I'd spent time in the slammer before, so I knew how to handle myself. It was worth it just to see the look on that asshole driver's face as I left him choking on his own exhaust fumes."

I was still stuck one sentence back on the slammer comment. "When you were in jail didn't they make you take off your face paint?"

Ogo's entire demeanor changed. He suddenly became quite somber. He paused awhile before answering, "Yes. But I'd rather not talk about that."

I backed off from the question immediately; I didn't want him turning a gun on *me*. Nonetheless I couldn't help but think that if he'd stayed in jail sans face paint he might never have come down with cancer. I thought it might be dangerous to voice this opinion out loud, though.

Ogo led me behind the club into a parking lot reserved only for employees. A few yards away I could see Jesse, who had slipped his shirt back on, piling the instruments into the back of a brightly colored van decorated with images of happy happy clowns and hula-hoops and monkeys in bellboy outfits juggling torches.

"Yorkshire pudding wile T-man gesticulate imputable bac-illary," Ogo said.

"Excuse me?" I thought I was going nuts.

"I'm sorry," he said, "I lapsed into harlequinese for a moment."

"What?"

"Harlequinese. It's a language I made up in jail. What you do is, you replace every word in the English language with the third word up in the dictionary."

"Why?"

"What do you mean, why? Isn't it obvious? To open your mind. Break it free of the constraints imposed upon it by the unnecessary and false impediments of language. I mean, think about it. Why do we use the word 'chair' to describe a chair? We could easily pick the word 'chainsaw' and use that to describe the concept represented by chair. It's the same thing."

"No . . . no it's not at all. 'Hi, welcome to my abode. Pull up a chainsaw and relax.' That's absurd."

"To you. But only because you've grown up thinking chairs are 'chairs' and not 'chainsaws.' See what I mean?"

"You're mad."

"Or 'maculate.'"

"You should be a philosopher."

"Yeah, maybe. Or President."

"Is 'President' the third word up from 'philosopher'?"

"No, 'Philomena' is. I'm speaking English now. I'm serious, chum. I want to run for President someday."

"Whatever. I wish you a lotta luck, man."

"Wharfmaster. Hysteron proteron wisenheimer yorkshire pudding zymosthenic loss leader oestrogen luciferous, mammon."

"What's that . . . a *translation?*" He nodded. "Hey, wait a minute, what the hell were you gonna say before?"

"Before what?"

"Before you lapsed into . . . whatever the fuck you call it. . . ."

"Oh . . . yeah. I was just going to say that you'll have to get in back," Ogo said. "Jesse's riding up front with me."

Jesse tossed the last amp inside, then gestured for me to enter. I climbed into the darkness, looking forward to a few moments of peace and quiet after such a brain-warping, raucous event. I was to be disappointed. Inside the van, sitting side by side on a little red love sofa, were Mike and Esthra. Esthra's hand was draped over Mike's, as if his hand had just been lying there on the seat and she had been attempting to hold it. He was staring off into space, not looking at anything.

"Hi," Esthra said. She seemed a bit drained. "I'm glad you decided to tag along."

"Wouldn't miss it for the Seventh Coming," I said. In contrast to the bright colors of the van's exterior, the interior was entirely black and had a pentagram painted in blood on the ceiling. The horns of Baphomet's goat-like head filled the two upward points of the pentagram, but the ominous nature of the sigil was off-set somewhat by the googly eyes someone had painted beneath the goat's bushy brow. "Mighty nice place you have here," I said, stepping over the musical equipment and plopping down in a gold-colored love sofa opposite Mike and Esthra. I pointed up at the pentagram. "Is that, uh . . . ?"

"Don't worry," Esthra said with a smile. "It's just goat's blood."

"Oh, is that all." I settled back into the sofa, slipping my hands behind my head. "Now I can rest easy." I flashed back to Ogo's comment about animal sacrifices at midnight. Of course, I'd assumed he was being sarcastic, but now I was beginning to wonder.

Mike continued to stare at a space on the wall somewhere just to the left of me as I said, "That was a great show. Better than I expected."

"Were you expecting us to suck or something?" Esthra asked.

"Oh, no no no . . . well, yeah."

Esthra shrugged. "S'okay. Most bands do suck. I'd probably expect the same thing."

I turned to Mike and said, "Your lyrics are, like, really great. Even Leonard Cohen and Tom Lehrer would be proud."

Mike said nothing. I figured I might as well do the same.

Staring downwards, I couldn't help but notice a pile of old flyers covering the floor like a carpet. Most of them advertised Doktor Delgado performances long out of date. One of them stood out from the mess. It was a sophisticated drawing of two immense crows perched upon a full moon. The moon was so detailed, deep craters could be seen pitting its ivory surface like scars. Both of the crows seemed to be staring directly at the viewer, as if daring you not to believe in their existence. There was something powerful and mysterious about the look in those deep set, onyx eyes. Woven into the craters were these words: DON'T FIGHT DESTINY—HAVE *SEX* WITH IT! The artwork reminded me of those weird murals I had seen around town, the one with the talking dog and the other one with the sparkling purple mouse. Was this illustration created by the same artist? I wondered if Mike knew who the hell had painted those murals. But I could tell he was definitely not in a mood to answer such trivial questions. He remained silent during the entire ride.

The party was at a house near The Lighthouse Café on Pier Avenue, only a few blocks away from the ocean. Sounds of music and laughter grew louder and louder as we approached the house. I would've hated to be the people living on either side of that place. Ogo parked at a crazy angle, one of the front wheels resting on the curb; anyone who's ever been to a circus knows that clowns aren't the best drivers. We piled out of the van and followed Mike up the pathway. Mike walked on ahead of us, not talking to Esthra, not even looking at her. Esthra and I walked side by side behind Ogo and Jesse.

"Is there a problem?" I whispered to Esthra.

"He just gets jealous easily, that's all. Now he's going to punish me by not talking to me for awhile. It has nothing to do with you. He gets jealous of everyone, even Ogo sometimes, which is flat-out bizarre. We don't know what the hell Ogo's into. We've never seen him with a girl, or anything else for that matter."

Mike opened the front door of the house without even knocking. He was immediately greeted with a series of cheers and Heys and How's it goin' and Great show, Mike and You blow everyone else away, man and other variations of these same salutations. Ogo whipped out his bag o' tricks and began performing magic for the crowd. Someone handed Jesse an acoustic guitar, on which he started improvising strange new riffs. Someone tried to hand Esthra a guitar, but she just waved them away. She grabbed a beer instead, pulled away from the crowd, motioning for me to follow her. We stood in the corner of the room, watching the commotion swirl around us.

"I hate crowds," she said. "I like playing in front of people, but I'm a lot more uncomfortable with them when I have to be face to face."

"I know exactly what you mean. It's difficult for me to talk to people." I laughed. "For some reason I push people away, even when they're going out of their way to be kind to me. I don't know why that is. I guess I don't trust them."

Esthra shrugged. "Everyone mistrusts each other. Everyone hates each other for things they haven't even done yet."

"The problem is other people. I once toyed with the idea of declaring myself my own separate nation, that way if someone attacked me it would be an international event and the UN would have to get involved."

"Well, that's the ultimate way to cut yourself off from the world, isn't it?"

"There are better ways. More permanent ways."

"What does that mean?"

I shrugged. "Doesn't matter."

"Have you ever tried to . . . you know . . . ?"

I furrowed my brow. "What?"

"You know . . . damage yourself? Permanently?"

I took a deep breath. I nodded. "When I was eighteen."

"Really? May I ask why?"

I sighed. "Same reasons anyone else does. I was feeling lonely and confused. God, I don't think I've ever felt more alone than at that time in my life. I had isolated myself from everyone in the world. I was too ashamed to talk to anyone. Ashamed of my looks, ashamed of my clothes, ashamed of my personality, ashamed of everything. I almost went through my entire four years in high school without talking to a single person. I don't think anyone even knew I was there. I was Peripheral Boy. You could only see me out of the corner of your eye as I zipped past in the hall. But it's not like people didn't come up and talk to me. Sometimes they would, but I would just find some excuse to push them away. I think that's why I do what I do today. I can interact with people through my humor, and at the same time keep a safe distance from the rest of the world." While saying all this I had been staring at the crowds of people wandering past, all of them laughing and talking. I was reeling off this monologue more to myself than to Esthra. Then I suddenly glanced to my left and saw Esthra staring at me with a blank expression. I wondered if I'd become too morose. "Sorry," I said. "I must sound like a wingnut."

"Nah, I don't think so. I act the same exact way. I think everyone in the band does to some extent or another. The only difference is *we're* hiding behind music instead of humor." She chugged back a gulp of beer then belched.

"But you get to release a whole bunch of different emotions on stage. I wish I had your job. I mean, sometimes I feel like screaming for hours at a time, but I'm sure the neighbors would probably arrest me if I did that. Now if I was on a stage with a guitar in my hand. . . ."

"What frustrations do you have?"

"Plenty. More than you can know."

"Really? Are you dying of a terminal illness too? If so maybe you can join the band. You can be our go-go girl."

I remembered what Ogo had told me about the various illnesses of which the band members were dying. He hadn't mentioned Esthra's condition. For some reason this didn't occur to me until that moment. Perhaps I hadn't wanted to think about it. What if she was dying of AIDS?

"I know what you're thinking," Esthra said.

"Is that so?"

"You're wondering what I'm dying of."

"No, of course . . . well, yeah, I guess I am."

Esthra opened her mouth as if she were about to speak, but then she glanced around the room and said, "I can't stand all this smoke, can you?"

Cigarette smoke mixed with acrid clouds of marijuana fumes wafted throughout the room. There was more smoke in here than in your average night club, pre-Orwell. My eyes were already beginning to water, but I had been reluctant to say anything. I just pointed to my eyes as an answer.

"Let's get out of here," she said, leading me through the crowd and back toward the front door. In my peripheral vision I could see Mike playing acoustic versions of his songs for the crowd. He spotted us walking through the door, but continued playing his song anyway.

It was nice to get outside. We strolled down the path until we reached the sidewalk, then headed west. It'd been so long since I'd taken a walk at night. It's not wise to take such walks alone in Hollywood after, oh . . . sundown, I'd say. In Hermosa Beach it's a bit different.

"It's hard to have a private conversation with a hundred people listening," Esthra said. "So what were we talking about? Terminal illnesses, right?" I nodded. "The doctors say I'm suffering from a completely unique degenerative disease, a variation of a C type RNA tumor virus. You know what that is?" I shook my head. "It causes life to remain in stasis, actually freezes the human body in whatever state of development it was in when it became susceptible to the virus. Some people would think of that as a godsend, but there's a major drawback. I'll remain twenty-two for five, ten, even fifteen years—but then all those accumulated minutes, hours and months will converge on me all at one time, in a single second, and then cause my life to reel backwards at an incredibly fast pace until there'll be nothing left of me but a human cell undetectable to the eye."

A long silence followed as we passed a diner on Pier Avenue that looked as if it had been picked up by a UFO in the 1950s and set down here in the middle of 2014. Next door was a funky used bookstore. During the day one could usually pass by the windows and see a black cat lounging in a sunbeam atop a stack of books, the color of the dust jackets being leached away by the sun. At the moment all the lights were out and there was a sign that read CLOSED hanging in the door. We stopped anyway to look at the books in the window. I was perusing the cover of an oversized collection of M.C. Escher drawings when I said, "You know, I think I've finally discovered someone who has more of an overactive imagination than I do."

"Say what you want. All I know is that the doctors wanted to study me, to show me off to their colleagues like a freak, but there was no way in hell I was going to let myself be turned into a living trophy for a group of fucking men all over again, not after I—" She stopped herself before she could say more. She turned away from the window and continued walking westward, toward the pier. I followed her.

She said, "I left that hospital as fast as possible. I swore I'd never enter such a sterile place again. I mean, think about it, if hospitals are so fucking great how come people are always dying in them?"

I have to admit I never looked at it that way before. Esthra seemed so distraught, so serious, that I began to believe her unbelievable tale. If she was lying she was one of the best actresses I'd ever seen. But what reason would she have to lie?

We crossed the street, passed the elegant 1920s Art Deco building that once housed the eclectic Bijou Theater where I remember seeing *City of Lost Children* when I was eleven years old (it's now a branch of the Chase National Bank, alas), a coffee shop where I could hear a woman playing acoustic versions of Janis Joplin tunes, and a series of quaint oceanside cafes. We strolled down the pier and paused only when we could go no farther without drowning. We leaned over the railing and stared down into the night-black waters. The moon wasn't visible. The night was so black you couldn't tell where the ocean ended and the sky began; it was as if an infinite dark void lay out beyond the beach.

I said, "When did you first find out that you had the disease?"

Esthra sighed. "Oh, about six months after I met Mike and joined his band. That was the best six months of my life. Then everything turned to crap."

"How'd you hook up with him?"

"Now there's a story. I met Mike in San Francisco. He'd been singing in another band called Lavender Brain Tumor. He has a knack for horrible band names. Anyway, I came to the show to avoid going home to another beating. I was living with a guy named Daniel at the time. No one called him Daniel, though—not if you wanted to stay alive. He liked to be called D. He was pimping me out to raise money for our heroin habit. I went along with it because I thought I loved him." Though I was slightly shocked she was telling me all this, I found her total lack of self-consciousness refreshing. "Go ahead, feel free to call me stupid, everybody else does."

"I don't think you're stupid."

"Well, you're in a minority. But maybe you're right. Maybe I was just temporarily insane. So, like I was saying, I went to the show just to have a place to hang out. I saw Mike up there on stage, lookin' so fine with all his tattoos. He was in much better shape back then. He was well-cut and had these huge arms that looked like they could just scoop you up, wrap around you, protect you from the rest of the world. I went backstage specifically to talk to him, though I hate doing such stupid little groupie things. I hate feeding the egos of attention-starved rock gods. But somehow I thought Mike was different. I think it was his lyrics, and the way he carried himself on stage. He didn't dance around like a monkey on speed, he was very reserved, almost shy. It was so refreshing, so different from what you usually see in places like that."

She sighed again, grabbed a pile of pebbles off the planks of wood, then began tossing them into the sea one by one. Her red lips arced into a wistful smile. "We were only talking to each other for a little while when I happened to mention that I'd played guitar a little bit as a kid. Right then and there he asked me to play in the very next set to replace the original guitarist who'd fallen face down on stage in a drunken stupor only a few minutes before. I told him I hadn't played in years, but he said, 'Don't worry about it. Just make as much noise as possible and no one will notice.' It was good advice. I still follow it to this day. After the show he asked me to play at their next gig up north after they decided to abandon the original guitarist in Golden Gate Park. I didn't even pick up my things from D.'s apartment, I just took off.

"Six months later I came down with the disease. In a weird bit of synchronicity we met Ogo and Jesse that same week. When we realized what we all had in common we decided to dissolve Lavender Brain Tumor (by that point we were ready to kill the drummer and the bass player anyway) and formed Doktor Delgado's All-American Genocidal Warfare Against The Sick And The Stupid. That name was Mike's idea too."

"What the hell does it mean?"

"The name Delgado comes from José Delgado. He was a mad scientist who moved from Spain to research electrical stimulation of the brain at Yale University. Most of his research went to the military, or so Mike says. Delgado wrote a book called *Physical Control of the Mind*. You might want to check it out, just for the hell of it."

"Mike's really into conspiracies, isn't he?"

She tossed the last pebble into the ocean, then shrugged. "Yeah. Some of the conspiracies are imaginary, some of them aren't. Just like everything else."

"He's really paranoid about you."

The smile left her face. She stared up at the stars and said, "I'm a man-killer. I don't know why, I just am. I don't think I'm the most attractive woman in the world. I can be in the worst shape and men are still falling all over me. When I was in the hospital kicking heroin the doctors had me on all this weird-ass medication that made me gain forty pounds. Yeah, hard to believe, isn't it? My belly was hanging over my belt as if it were trying to run away. Not only that, acne broke out all along my forehead right here. Looked like someone had tattooed the Milky Way on my skin. Not to mention the track marks on my ass, but we needn't go into that. Anyway, even in this sorry condition guys still seemed to be attracted to me. Hell, more than attracted—obsessed. This one guy I know named Zack (short for Prozac), who I met when I was locked up in this mental ward, wouldn't leave me alone after I kicked my drug habit and realized he was a fuckin' shithead. He even burned all my clothes when I told him I didn't love him anymore, as if I *ever* did. He asked me to marry him every fuckin' day and wouldn't stop calling."

"Guys get attached very easily. They're screwy that way."

"I think it's more than that. Even if I'm dressed like a slob and walking down the street without any make-up on guys still come onto me. I've developed a theory." She held up her index finger like a college professor, then coughed into her fist. "My theory is this: My body gives off some weird-ass pheromones that attract men to me no matter what. I could be wearing a potato sack or a barrel, I could be three feet tall with a harelip and a hole in the middle of my fuckin' forehead and it wouldn't make a difference. Penises would still be slithering down the sidewalk after me like snakes. What the hell is it with penises? They're such funny looking things too. I always thought they looked like roosters, roosters without legs."

I know it may sound cockeyed, but I wanted to say I loved her right then and there. Guys get attached very easily. They're screwy that way.

We talked for a long time out on that pier. There were more than a few times when I felt like leaning over and kissing her, but I didn't think she wanted that, despite what that schmuck Eddie had said. Besides, it felt nice just listening to her, talking to her. I had never talked to anyone as openly as I had with Esthra, except perhaps for Heather. Even with Heather it had taken me months to get past the joking phase with her, while with Esthra it had taken me only a few hours. I thought it might be kind of nice to have a girl who was just a friend. I was usually too busy trying to con girls out of their pants to ever allow such a relationship to develop. In the back of my mind I wondered how many potential friendships I'd passed up on because of my single-mindedness; of course, I was also wondering what Esthra would look like naked. I'm sorry, I can't be reformed in a couple of hours.

Once our little talk began to wind down Esthra suggested we return to the party. "Before Mike comes out looking for me," she added. Since I knew such a scenario could only end with me being dumped in the drink, I followed her advice. On the way there I suggested we enter through the back so as not to draw attention to ourselves.

"That'll look like we're trying to hide something," she said, horrified. "I'm not slinking around like some filthy whore. I'm walking right through the front door."

What could I do except go along with her and pray she knew what she was doing? We walked through the front door to find Mike still at the center of attention. In fact, he had about a dozen pretty young groupies circled around him on their knees. They gazed up at him with lovey-dovey moon-eyes as he said, "Here's a new little ditty I've been playing around with. It's not quite finished, but . . . well, tell me how you like it. It's called 'Masonic Stew.'" With a hip-hop delivery he belted out the following lyrics:

Freemasons here
Freemasons there
Freemasons everywhere
Freemasons from all parts of the world
Comin' to Washington just to unfurl
An esoteric flag and rape a young girl
Punch her big belly and cause her to hurl
Up comes a fetus for a weird Masonic stew
A bubbling witches liquid, a black mystic brew
Filled with yeti armpits plus an undiscovered flu
Two copper Tesla coils and nigger lips too
Bubble and bubble, toil and trouble
Masons in orbit and lurking inside the Hubble
They're floatin' out there just waitin' to perform

A ritual most rare to make us conform
They'll heat up the ionosphere and conjure up a storm
That'll wipe out Jupiter and its alien lifeforms
Freemasons here
Freemasons there
Freemasons hiding in your girlfriend's hair
Freemasons at the post office, Freemasons at work
Freemasons at the Pentagon love to circle jerk
Bubble and bubble, toil and trouble
Masons kill Washington, replace him with a double
Hop to your feet for the Masonic sockhop
Bop to the beat of Adam Weishaupt
Freemasons here
Freemasons there
Freemasons lurking in their underground lairs
Hip to hip, cheek to cheek
Masonic feet dancin' to a weird wild beat
Bubble and bubble, toil and trouble
Masons dancing in the nuclear rubble
Jitter-bugging fast to an ancient tune
Amid the lost remains of Solomon's tomb
Fuck, we're dying while they're flying to the moon
The world's ending, couldn't happen too soon

All the groupies laughed and clapped as if they were in on a
private joke I didn't fully understand.

Esthra pushed her way to the very front of the crowd. I
stood beside her. Mike couldn't miss us. Upon seeing Esthra he
said, "This is a song I just made up on the spot. It's called 'Kiss
Me, Kill Me.'"

Esthra grabbed my hand and pulled me away from the
crowd, while behind us Mike improvised a clever little song

about a girl who "gives head to get ahead"; she clings onto a talented rock star just to get famous, then abandons him when he needs her most. The entire song was a not-too-subtle insult against Esthra and it seemed as if everybody in the room knew it. The entire mood of the party had become quite uncomfortable.

Esthra cleared a path through the crowd and dragged me into the hallway. I didn't know where she was taking me. She swung open various doors in the hall. The first was a closet, the second a bedroom filled with strange people smoking pot, the third a bathroom. There was a teenage boy and girl sitting cross-legged and smoking pot on the fluffy white rug. Esthra yelled, "Get the fuck out!" and kicked the guy in the ass with her boot. They both scrambled to their feet and dashed out of the room. Esthra slammed the door shut, then locked it.

"What are you doing?" I said.

"If he wants me to be a whore so bad, then maybe I should become one." She pressed her face up against the door and moaned loud enough for everyone in the neighborhood to hear, "Oh yeah, Elliot, *yeah,* that feels so good, touch me right there, right there, oh yeah, yeah, fuck me like a monkey in heat, unh, unh. . . ."

My right hand shot to my mouth as my other hand gestured wildly for her to stop. Who knew what they could hear outside? "Esthra, please, what're you doing?"

She whispered, "Giving him what he wants," then yelled, "Oh yeah, baby, that's it, give it to me good, give it to me hard, *harder . . . !"*

I grabbed her by the shoulders and forced her to turn around. Despite the tears streaming down her cheeks, she persisted in her act.

"Oh yes, slap me, Elliot, hit me!"

As softly as possible I said, "Please. Stop."

In mid-sentence Esthra broke off and looked at me with such sad eyes. Such sad, wounded eyes. She fell into my embrace, wrapped her arms around my shoulders, held on tightly, as if she might fall if she let go. She buried her head into my chest and cried for a very long time. I stroked her long auburn hair, whispered in her ear: "Shh, shh . . . it's okay, Esthra . . . it's okay."

After awhile she calmed down, stepped away from me a bit, keeping her palms pressed against my chest. I lifted my fingers to her cheeks and brushed the tears away as best I could.

"God, I don't know," she said, "I don't know what else I can do. I've stuck by him every step of the way, I've taken care of him when he was junk sink, I've never cheated on him, but it's not enough, nothing's ever enough. Do you know how hard it was for me to kick heroin? I was locked up in a psych ward for ten fucking months. I almost hung myself with an electrical wire I dug out of the plaster wall in my room 'cause I thought the nurses were going to rape me and cut off my toes. A couple of them *did* rape me." She released a weak laugh. "At least they didn't cut off my toes; I guess I was only halfway paranoid. They had me pumped full of so many drugs I didn't know what the fuck was going on. I lived in a weird-ass cartoon world for almost a year. I endured all of that just to kick heroin. But with heroin you don't give a shit about the past, or how much pain you went through the first time . . . or the second time, or the third time. . . . I still crave that damn spike, you know? Every day is a struggle, and it's a lot more difficult if your idiot boyfriend is waving a needle in your face every two seconds. God damn it, he's made me sit there and *watch* him shoot up. 'C'mon, baby, it's no fun without you there.' Did he ever stop to consider what that was doing to me, *ever?*"

I stroked her hair for a few minutes more, then she pulled away entirely, giving me one last pat on the chest. "Thank you for listening to me babble," she said.

"It didn't sound like babbling to me," I said. "I think you needed to get a lot off your chest. I think you're stuck in a fucked-up relationship and you need to get out."

She nodded while looking at the floor. "Maybe you're right. I don't know."

"What more does he have to do to you until you're sure?"

"I don't know." I had a feeling she said those words a lot. I felt like kissing her: first a gentle peck on the cheek (when was the last time someone kissed her on the cheek?), then her forehead, her other cheek, her neck, her chin, and at last her lips. I pictured all of this as I stared at the contours of her beautiful face, but I didn't act on the impulse. I didn't think it was the right time. I figured she needed a friend at that moment, not another fucked-up lover.

I brushed the hair out of her eyes and said, "You don't have to worry about it now. You'll know when it's time to dump him."

"You *must* think I'm stupid."

"No, I don't think that at all. I think you've got yourself trapped in a situation you can't find your way out of. That happens to a lot of people every day. Most of them didn't get that way because they were stupid."

"Why, then?"

"Because they trusted somebody too much."

Esthra laughed her usual sad laugh. "That's me, all right. I've trusted a lot of people I shouldn't have."

"But that doesn't mean you give up on everyone, does it?"

"No, of course not. I think—"

Esthra's next words were cut off by a pounding at the door followed by an angry voice: "Hey, why don't you move it somewhere else! I need to take a piss!"

Esthra and I exchanged amused glances, then burst out laughing. "Well, maybe we should rejoin the party," she said.

"Maybe so."

As the pounding continued Esthra took my hand and led me to the door. Just as she was about to open it I gestured toward our hands and said, "Uh, what if Mike thinks . . . ?" I allowed the sentence to trail off.

"Who cares what Mike thinks?" She swung open the door and dragged me into the hall. A hefty biker dude with an incongruous tattoo of Alice in Wonderland on his hairy forearm pushed past us, flashing us an annoyed glance. A whole line of people were waiting outside, sighing and tapping their feet against the carpet. I could see them looking at us sideways. I ignored them as best as possible.

Esthra took me into the bedroom at the end of the hall. I don't think she cared where she was going, just as long as it wasn't the room where Mike was holding court. A half-dozen spacecases were lounging about on a circular waterbed, smoking marijuana and listening to an old Tom Waits album.

In the darkest corner of the room were a clump of empty beanbags near a closed door. Esthra was about to plop down in one of the beanbags when I heard a familiar, hyena-like laugh. Karen Griffin rarely laughed, but when she did she sounded like a pack of hyenas giggling to themselves as they fought over the corpse of a baby tiger.

I opened the door to find myself staring at another bathroom. This one was a lot smaller than the one in the hall, or perhaps it just seemed that way because there were so many people packed inside it. Griffin was sitting on the counter with her legs dangling over the edge, laughing uproariously at Twee-Boy19, he of the now-infamous Neo-Gothic Hipster Peanut Gallery. TweeBoy19 was leaning against the wall across from Griffin, sinking a needle into his pale arm. Danny sat behind Griffin, his hands resting on her stomach, his long legs wrapped around her slender waist. The rest of the Peanut Gallery was sitting on the edge of the bath, watching TweeBoy19 with a strange, dull-eyed fascination. On the lowered toilet seat sat a burly, olive-skinned man who seemed somewhat familiar, though I couldn't quite place his face right off the bat. Black wraparound sunglasses obscured the top half of his face.

Danny's eyes grew wide when he saw me. He smiled and said, "Hey, Elliot, what brings you here?"

"Oh, I was just passing through," I said as casually as possible.

"How the hell did you get here?"

"Well, I was hitchhiking along the side of the freeway and this clown just happened to pick me up—"

Esthra peeked over my shoulder and said, "Don't listen to him, he exaggerates by nature. He opened for our band, so we decided to drag him here. We're thinking of making him our mascot." She mussed up my hair as if I were a little kid.

Almost every eyeball in the room popped out of its socket upon seeing Esthra. Even the Peanut Gallery (whose sexual proclivities might have fallen anywhere in between total asexuality and forced group orgies with hairless Filipino boys—it was hard to tell which) seemed to oggle Esthra's scantily-clad body with an obvious amount of prurient interest.

"Hey, you're in that Doktor Delgado band, aren't you?" Griffin said. Esthra just nodded. "You're pretty damn good. You want a fix? On the house."

By this time TweeBoy19 had drawn another shot into the needle from a moist cotton ball perched upon a blackened spoon. He offered the needle to Esthra, who held up her hand in a gesture of refusal. TweeBoy19 seemed confused.

"She already had some with her Cocoa Puffs this morning," I said, which was meant to be an absurd non sequitur, but Twee-Boy19 actually appeared to accept this as a rational answer.

Esthra leaned toward me and whispered, "A Cocoa Puff is a mixture of PCP, coke, and marijuana."

I slapped myself on the forehead and said, "Jesus Christ, you can't say anything anymore! You mention dog food and it turns out to be code for crack cocaine."

Esthra said, "No, no, dog food is heroin. At least in Cincinnati."

I could only roll my eyes at the ceiling. In this day and age any random noun is suspect. You could get raided by the DEA just for trying to order food for your kid's poodle over the phone.

I mentioned earlier that *almost* every eyeball in the room popped out upon seeing Esthra. The only person who didn't seem to care was the burly man sitting on the toilet. His gaze hadn't left the needle since we'd entered the room, like a house bound cat watching a bird skip along a tree branch just outside the window. When Esthra refused the heroin the man said, "Shit, pass it here then, man."

I did a double take upon hearing the voice. I'm not sure why I didn't recognize him before; perhaps it was the sunglasses. Without a moment's hesitation the man unzipped his pants and whipped out a thirteen-inch dick with the circumference of a beer can. Yes, it was Chino, the strange Mexican who had molested me on the bus! I had the urge to run screaming from the room, the initial symptoms of Posttraumatic Stress

Syndrome already triggering a mental meltdown in my crumbling skull. Instead my feet remained glued to the linoleum floor as my eyes locked onto the grotesque, phantasmagoric scene before me.

Chino said, "Please excuse my manners, but all the surface veins have collapsed on my body so I, uh, kind of have to jab the needle through the veins in my dick, you see. Sorry. Please look away if you can't handle it."

I didn't look away. I was both repulsed and fascinated as I watched Chino ease the needle into a bulging blue vein that ran along the top of the penis before disappearing into a wild forest of curly black pubic hair. I glanced up at the Peanut Gallery. Judging by their stoic expressions their interest seemed far more clinical than mine. A tension-charged silence filled the air; I could sense that even the most blasé junkies in the room were holding their breath. At the exact second that Chino pressed the plunger on the syringe I released a low whistle that sounded like the descent of an incoming missile. Esthra burst out laughing. Even the Peanut Gallery cracked a smile. A mixture of a smirk and a scowl appeared on Chino's face as he attempted to keep his hand steady. After the brownish liquid had disappeared into his vein, he slipped the needle out with a doctor's care. Pure, undiluted rage flared up in his bloodshot eyes. I suspect his rage was fueled by a whole pharmacy of mind-altering substances.

Chino slammed the needle down on the counter. "What the fuck're you doing?" he screamed. "I could've missed that shot, man!"

Griffin was now staring at Chino with a bemused look on her face. "Who the hell are you anyway? We didn't invite you in here, did we?" She glanced around at her friends as if looking for an answer.

Chino opened his mouth to respond, but before he could do so I said, "Oh, that's Chino. He likes little boys." I don't know why I chose to say that. I guess I thought it was funny (but of course that's always my excuse).

Chino's anger filled eyes swivelled toward me as he rose from the toilet, his pants dropping to the floor. Then his anger turned to puzzlement. "Hey, don't I know you from somewhere?"

I began to reach into my jacket. "That's right. I'm connected to the Mexican Mafia and we don't like you mouthin' off about those two guys you killed."

Chino backed up against the counter, raising his hands until they were level with his chest. Sweat began to trickle down his forehead. "Uh, look, man, I-I didn't tell no one important. . . ."

"Only every commuter on the Rapid Transit Authority!" I poked my index finger into the inner lining of my jacket, hoping he'd think it was a gun. "Shut your pie hole, Chewey. This is your last warning. The next time we catch you mouthin' off about those corpses, we'll saw off that horse-dick of yours and feed it to you like a kielbasa. Now get the hell out of here!" Chino nodded and reached down to pull up his pants. "Forget that!" I said. "Just scoot on out of here and don't look back." To my surprise, Chino proceeded to do exactly that. When he was halfway through the door I said, "Oh, and if we catch you with your hands on the little boys again we'll tie your dick to the fender of a Jaguar and floor it, ya hear?"

Chino nodded as he scrambled out of the bathroom in an awkward, crouched position with his giant schlong swinging back and forth in the air like a clock pendulum. The spacecases lying on the bed watched Chino dash past them, then erupted into nonstop giggles, no doubt thinking they were having some kind of shared hallucination. At that moment Tom Waits's "The Piano Has Been Drinking (Not Me)" began playing on the stereo—one of those odd details that happens to stick in your brain during surreal moments such as this.

Along with the spacecases I watched him run out of the bedroom, then glanced back at my friends in the bathroom. They were all staring at me as if I possessed some sort of mystical power. Since I couldn't quite imagine being able to top that particular performance (every comedian knows the value of quitting on a high-note), and since I didn't really want to engage in further flatlining experiments with Danny's little post-mortem pals, I decided to bail out while I still could.

"Well, gotta go bust in some heads for the Santiago Boys," I said, cracking my knuckles. "See you later, Danny, Griffin, et al.!" I turned on my heel and walked right out of there, Esthra following close behind me.

"What the hell was all that about?" she said.

"Oh, I never told you about my ties to the Mexican Mafia? They call me Elliot 'The Fighting Enchilada' Greeley. I'm infamous in the Tijuana underground."

Once again we found ourselves in the hallway. This hallway was so packed full of people it took a hell of a long time just to fight our way through half of it. At one point I was looking at Esthra and not really paying attention to where I was going, so I crashed into someone coming out of the bathroom. "Oh, excuse me," both of us said at once. Since my face was smashed into his chest, the first thing I saw of the man was his tie. I thought it was pretty damn snappy; it consisted of striking, fractal-like geometric patterns that immediately caught one's eye, particularly if your eye was pressed up against it.

I took a few steps back and looked up at the man's bloody face. "Brother Lundberg?" I said.

The blond-haired, blue-eyed Mormon glanced from side to side as if searching for a convenient escape route. "Uh . . . ," he said.

I asked him exactly what Danny had asked me only a few minutes before: "How the hell did you get here?"

He said, "Uh . . . well, I was handing out copies of the *Book of Mormon* door to door when I came to this house. I deduced from the loud music that this was some kind of den of iniquity and knocked on the door. Some strange bearded man invited me in and gave me this funny cigarette." He held up a fat roach that was giving off as much smoke as a brushfire in Malibu. "I began wandering around the house, preaching the word of Joseph Smith while looking at all the weird colors on the wall." The walls, by the way, were bare and white. "Then I felt myself getting hungry all of a sudden, so I went into the kitchen to find some Oreos. As I'm opening up the refrigerator this half-naked Mexican with what looked like a thirteen inch member zipped past me and rushed out the back door. It was at this point that I began to suspect there was something odd about this cigarette. I felt myself having a panic attack, and whenever I have a panic attack I throw up, so I ran into the bathroom past a whole line of people and puked all over the toilet. If only someone hadn't been sitting on it at the time everything would've been fine. I'm not sure what happened next. All I know is that this clown leaped up off the toilet and began beating me with a leather bag packed full of heavy objects. At this point I *knew* I was hallucinating. What other explanation could there be? But I'm not quite sure I understand how a hallucination can beat you as hard as this." He touched his fingertips to the streams of blood still trickling down his face.

"What happened to the clown?" I asked.

Lundberg gestured toward the bathroom with his thumb. "He caught one whiff of my cigarette and collapsed."

Sure enough, Esthra and I peeked into the bathroom to see Ogo sprawled out on the floor, pinkish vomit staining his black and white outfit. I looked at Esthra and said, "Okay, that's it, things are getting way too weird around here."

I patted Lundberg on the shoulder and said, "Give my regards to Brother Fleetwood if you ever get home again," then made a bee-line through the living room, past the groupies surrounding Mike, who was now singing an acoustic version of Lou Reed's "I Wanna Be Black," and out the front door.

When I reached the porch I heard Esthra's voice behind me. She said, "Where are you going?"

I turned to see her standing in the doorway. I could still hear Mike singing within; he hadn't wavered for one second, not even while seeing his girlfriend chase another man out of the house.

"I'm gettin' the hell out of this nuthouse," I said. "You want to join me? I've got some vintage Marx Brothers movies back home. We can cuddle, drink hot cocoa, and watch *Duck Soup* (Paramount, 1933). What do you say?"

Esthra closed the door behind her and joined me out on the porch. She smiled. "It sounds lovely, but how are you going to get back home?"

"Well, I was thinking of stealing Ogo's van."

"Mmmm, I don't think he'd like that."

"Really? Maybe it's a bad idea then. I don't want to end up with a nose like Lundberg's."

"Who *was* that guy?"

"He's a member of the Mormon Mafia. They're fighting with the Mexican Mafia to take over the dope trade in Southern California."

Esthra laughed. "Do you ever give a serious answer?"

"What makes you think that wasn't a serious answer?"

"Okay," she said, holding up her hands, "I'll just accept anything you say as true. It'll probably be easier that way."

"So if I say that Mike's a putrid scumbag you'll accept that as true?"

She glanced back over her shoulder at the closed door, then said, "Yes, but I can't promise I'll do anything about it."

"Not even hop into a cab with me and head on back to my place for a quick screening of *Duck Soup*?"

She stared at the ground and shook her head. "Mike wouldn't like it."

"Wouldn't like *Duck Soup*? C'mon, how could you not like *Duck Soup*?"

"No, I mean he wouldn't like me going home with you."

"Why? My intentions are entirely honorable." This was true, of course, as true as the gang warfare between the Mexicans and the Mormons.

"I know that, but I don't want to give him any more ammunition than he already has."

"What was that whole scene in the bathroom for then?"

She began pouting. "I know. I feel guilty about that now. I was just so *angry*. . . ."

"You had a right to be. He was making fun of you in front of all those—" I saw her biting on her red thumbnail, looking down at the ground with worry lines creasing her brow, and realized she was beyond reason. She was hooked into Mike as much as Mike was hooked into junk. "Oh, forget it," I said, fed up with the madness, and walked away.

I got all the way to the sidewalk before I heard Esthra's voice again. "Where are you going?" she repeated, this time with an edge of desperation like a whiny little child who wants two dolls instead of one. I knew then that she was never going to make up her mind. She didn't know what she really wanted.

I turned to face her. Even in the dark, with an entire driveway separating us, you could tell she was a beautiful woman, the kind of woman you'd risk your life for just to hold in your arms for the briefest of moments. I contemplated the situation, then said, "There's a scene in *A Day at the Races* where Groucho lays his watch down on the table beside him to wash his hands. When he sees Dr. Steinberg staring at the watch, Groucho grabs it and tosses it into the water. 'I'd rather have it rusty than missing,' he says." I smiled. "I think that applies to this situation just as well. Au revoir!"

And I walked away as fast as possible before I could hear her voice again.

CHAPTER 13

Books, Baths and Blowjobs

(October 4, 2014)

The night had been such an all-around adrenalin rush that I wasn't able to go to sleep until about five in the morning. After the taxi dropped me off at my apartment I ate a dinner of left-over spaghetti from the night before, then climbed into bed and lay there staring at the ceiling. I felt both exhausted and hyper at the same time. I turned on the radio and listened to strange people talking about UFOs and Bigfoot and the coming End Times. I wasn't really paying attention. Instead I was thinking of Esthra. With a little more sweet talk I might've convinced her to come home with me. Any normal guy would've done exactly that. But I'm not normal. I have a low self-esteem, especially when it comes to women, and I give up much too easily. I tried to convince myself it was for the best. After all, who wants to be on the hit list of some paranoid punker hopped up on a speedball or some other equally nefarious illicit substance?

Nevertheless, my doubts triggered old memories, a whole laundry list of Lost Opportunities (I can't help but think of the phrase in capital letters), but one in particular always stands out because it's the earliest. Back in eighth grade, during a theatre class, I broke character on stage to do a brilliant impromptu monologue insulting the teacher who had been riding me the entire year; she was sitting in the front row and maintained an uneasy smile on her face as I confessed to the illicit affair we'd been carrying on for the past twelve weeks. I had the audience in stitches. That was the very first time I told something more complicated than fart jokes in front of a large group of people. It felt exhilarating and addictive to just let the craziness flow out of my mouth without any planning whatsoever. I got such a high from it I wanted to do it over and over again. I felt new possibilities opening up within me.

After my little performance I slunk off-stage and, for some reason I'll never be able to fathom, took a seat in the darkest shadows of the auditorium as far away from the rest of the class as I could possibly get. Why did I do that? It should've been a moment of triumph, and instead I ostracized myself from everyone I had just entertained. It was almost as if an outside force had taken over my body and forced me to be isolated from the others.

While my fellow classmates performed their scenes, a cute little brunette with mocha-colored skin and soft brown eyes approached me and told me I had done a wonderful job. "You should be a standup comedian," she said, "you're *that* good."

My heart leaped into my throat. Though I had already been performing off and on at various open mike nights for a few years, I still wasn't sure I wanted to pursue this as my life-long career. I needed some form of independent confirmation to inspire me to persevere, and how much more independent can you get than a beautiful girl you've seen only from across a classroom? Now here comes the Lost Opportunity part. It's a twisted, pitiful tale of misery and woe. Any other healthy American male with even a fraction of a brain would have recognized her compliment as an obvious opening, right? They would've engaged her in some witty repartee, kept the lines of communication flowing, maybe ask her to go catch a movie and grab a soda, whatever. I did none of that. Instead I blew her off, didn't even thank her for the compliment, just waved my hand in the air and made some snide comment. I might as well have told her to fuck off, it would've been just as polite. I'm god damn mentally deficient in so many different ways it's amazing I'm even able to cross the street in the morning. I mean, who the hell would do something as stupid as that? I wish I could blame it on some insane Imp of the Perverse that takes over my mouth at times, but I can't. I know it's entirely my fault.

And I can't blame it all on the fact that I was only in the eighth grade at the time. This is just one example of a Lost Opportunity; there are plenty more like it reflected a million times over like mirrors looking into mirrors. I never learn and I never will. Take tonight as yet another example. I tried to think of Esthra not as a Lost Opportunity, but as a Crisis Avoided. As the night wore on, however, this became rather difficult. I tossed and turned, turned and tossed, couldn't get Esthra's face out of my mind, and finally decided to masturbate into an old sock. Then I went right to sleep.

Once again I dreamed of my father, who somehow ended up at my old elementary school standing beside Mrs. Love and Mr. Taylor, watching with them as the other kids broke my finger. I also had the most vivid, realistic dream I'd ever experienced: Esthra and I were strolling the streets of the neighborhood I grew up in, having a casual conversation about the usual sorts of things, nothing dramatic at all. It was the utter mundanity of the dream that made it so eerie. I experienced every step of that walk in real time, heard every word that was spoken between us.

I awoke at around one in the afternoon. For some reason I got confused and thought it was Sunday. I bolted out of bed, wondering if Heather had gotten back from San Francisco yet. I considered calling her, then remembered that *last night* had been Friday. She probably wouldn't be home until tomorrow morning. I felt disappointed. It would've been nice to have someone to talk to at that moment. Now that Danny had descended into that extra-special corner of Hell reserved for comedians-turned-junkies, Heather was the only person in the world I could really communicate with. Just think about that: The world minus Heather equals a whole hell of a lot of people. And I couldn't communicate with even one of them.

Since Marsha didn't have any gigs lined up for me that evening, I knew I had a long wait ahead of me before I could talk to Heather. I decided to fill the hours with long overdue chores. I did my laundry, ironed some clothes, bought groceries, washed the dishes, etc. I performed all these tasks in a strange trance-like state, not thinking of Esthra or Heather or Danny or anything in particular, which was a welcome change of pace. Still, in the back of my mind I was aware of a distinct sense of foreboding floating about in the air. This much peace and quiet was far too rare in my life. I knew something weird was bound to happen before the night was through.

It happened at twenty-two minutes after eight. I remember glancing at the clock, that's how I know the exact time. I also remember the line I had just read in a book Danny had let me borrow months before, a peculiar book I hadn't had time to finish. "Evil is even, truth is an odd number, and death is a full stop," Flann O'Brien writes in his experimental novel *At Swim-Two-Birds*. The line struck a chord in me for some reason, and I was tracking backwards to read it again when this brief moment of bibliophilia was shattered by the ringing of the phone. Isn't that always the way? Books, baths and blowjobs are often interrupted in this manner; that's a universal law.

I lifted the receiver to hear a woman sobbing on the other end. At first I thought it was a prank. "Hello?" I said. "Who is this?"

"Elliot?" I had never heard Heather cry before. "Could you please come over . . . right now?" She could barely get out the words.

My grip tightened on the receiver. "Of course. Are you at home? What's wrong?"

"I-I'll tell you when I see you." She hung up.

I dropped the receiver into the cradle and shot up from the floor. What was Heather doing home a day early? Had she been attacked—raped? I flashed back to my little fantasy about the leather fetishist newspaper reporter strapping Heather down in his dungeon lair. Had I experienced a genuine moment of precognition? Had the act of fantasizing the attack actually brought it about? This seemed unlikely, of course, but when you're panicking any number of improbable scenarios will bubble forth out of your brain.

I grabbed my jacket off the back of a chair and rushed toward the door. As my fingers wrapped around the doorknob the phone rang again. Thinking it might be Heather, I ran back to the phone and lifted the receiver to my ear. "Hello?" I said.

"Oh, I'm so glad I got ahold of you," I heard Danny say.

I sighed. I didn't want to deal with his junkie woes right now. "Look, I'll have to call you back later. I was just on my way out the door."

"No, no, wait, I need to—"

"I'll call you from Heather's, okay? Later." I hung up on Danny while he was still in mid-sentence and ran out the door. On the street below I hopped on a bus and headed over to Cahuenga. I was fortunate in that nobody attempted to grab my penis this time around, but come to think of it is that really fortunate? I mean, shouldn't you just take that for granted? I believe the Constitution guarantees the right of all citizens not to be molested by mad Mexicans while riding public transport. The Founding Fathers died for that right.

Twenty minutes after climbing aboard, I leaped off the bus on Cahuenga and sprinted toward Heather's apartment building. It was well before ten p.m., so I didn't have to bother with the damn intercom. I swung open the gate and took the stairs two at a time. On the third floor I skidded to a halt outside Heather's apartment and pounded on the door. No one answered. After long, worry-filled moments I decided to open the door. It was unlocked. The apartment was dark and silent. "Heather?" I whispered. I received no response.

I brushed my hand along the wall, found the light switch and flipped it on. Three pieces of luggage lay on the floor, two of them resting on their sides as if they'd been dropped there without care. Of course, every other piece of bric-a-brac in the room looked as if it had been dropped there without care so that was nothing unusual. I shut the door behind me, picked a path through the clutter on the floor, and made my way into the bedroom. All was dark in here as well. On the bed sat a woman with her legs drawn up to her chest, her arms wrapped around her knees. Her chin rested on her right knee. She was just staring out the window, perhaps at the starry night sky above, perhaps at nothing at all.

"Heather?" I said.

She lifted her head. In a dull monotone she said, "Oh. Hi."
Beat. "I didn't see you."

"Well, no wonder, you've got all the lights out."

I reached out for the light switch, but before I could touch
it Heather snapped, "No! I want it out."

Her voice was so insistent, my hand pulled away from the
switch as if it were made of thorns. "Why?"

"I like the dark . . . I think better in the dark."

I took a few steps toward the bed. "What's wrong? Did
something happen?"

"No, nothing happened. My whole life's over with, that's
all."

"What are you talking about?" I sat down on the edge of
the bed. As my eyes adjusted to the darkness I studied Heather
closely. She was wearing a dark green silk blouse opened loosely
at the throat, a slender silver necklace, black slacks, one black
sock on her right foot, her left foot bare. Her eyes were puffy
and bloodshot; she'd been crying for a long time. She sighed
and closed her eyes, pausing for awhile, as if wanting to choose
her words carefully.

At last she opened her eyes and began speaking: "I wasn't
entirely truthful with you on the phone." As in Pavlovian condi-
tioning, these words caused me to hold my breath. I'd been told
that by women before, and those words were never followed
by good news. "I couldn't talk about it, not right then. I had
to keep up a good front or I knew I'd just . . . break down."
The second she uttered those last two words her voice broke
and she lowered her face into her hands, tears streaming into
her palms. I reached out and placed my hand on her shoulder,
stroked her forearm, tried to comfort her as best I could. She
held out her hand. I grabbed it. Her grip tightened, tightened.
"The first night in San Francisco was a disaster," she whispered.

"The moment I walked out on stage I knew there was some-thing wrong. From the second I opened my mouth to the last punchline I got exactly zero laughs. It was the longest twenty minutes of my life. Has that ever happened to you before?"

"Of course. It happens to us all, you know that. It was just a bad night for you."

"No. It happened the next night, and the next night, and the next night. It happened the entire god damn time I was there, even at that fuckin' dyke club."

"Well, dykes *are* a notoriously tough audience. I mean, how many good dyke jokes do you know?" Heather remained silent. "No, no. You're supposed to say, 'Well, Griffin for one.'" I smiled weakly, but she didn't laugh. I guess it wasn't all that funny. Moving right along. . . . "Were the other comedians getting any laughs?"

"Some, the ones who weren't funny. The rest of us were devastated, we couldn't understand it. The whole city felt dead, filled with dead people, dead cars, dead buildings, dead girders, dead molecules, everything dead. Dead to the core."

"That's definitely not the San Francisco I know."

"Tell me about it. Usually I leave there feeling vibrant and alive, wanting to leave L.A. forever. This trip left me cold, cold way down here." She pressed her hand on her stomach. "It was the worst experience of my entire life."

"The humor virus. . . ."

"After the second night a whole group of us comedians sat around at the bar and talked about that. Even the most skeptical of us were beginning to believe in it. Of course, it's the only explanation that makes sense. Some of the comedi-ans said they'd noticed the same feeling of deadness in some of the clubs in Seattle and New York and Berkeley and D.C. and New Orleans. Others hadn't noticed it at all before San

Francisco. Maybe some areas are more infected than others
. . . I don't know. It seems to be affecting everybody in San
Francisco, but they don't know it. The victims just go about
their daily routines, not even realizing that a huge chunk of
them has been sliced out and turned inside out. God, isn't
that horrible? To have your brain altered and not even be
aware of it?"

She slipped her hand out of mine and wrapped her arms
around her chest as if she were shivering deep inside. "You
can't know what it was like, you can't. I know you've bombed
at times, so have I, but this was something different. This was
totally alien to me, like being trapped in a nightmare. You know
those dreams where you're sitting in a classroom getting ready
to take a test and you suddenly realize you're naked? That's
what this was like, only a hell of a lot worse. One night . . .
one night I remember having a dream where I walked out on
stage and opened my mouth and tried to speak but I couldn't, I
couldn't remember *any* of my jokes. I woke up in a cold sweat,
one of those times when you look around the bedroom and
think, Oh, thank God it was just a dream. When I was up there
on that stage in San Francisco I kept wishing I would wake up.
Hell, I'm still wishing that."

She took a deep breath that rattled throughout her chest as
if she had a terrible cold; her arms tightened around her body,
making her look like Houdini awaiting his straitjacket. "I felt
like I was disappearing," she said. "You have to understand, I've
never done anything but make people laugh. I began working
on the stage when I was seventeen. The only other job I've had
was working behind a cash register at a Jack in the Box; it lasted
three weeks, and that's when I was sixteen. What the hell else
can I do? Nothing. I've got no fucking skills. I'm a retard off
stage. I'm nothing."

Upon uttering those last two words Heather broke down crying once again, this time erupting into heaving sobs that emerged from somewhere deep inside her gut. I'd never seen her in such a fragile state. I wasn't sure what to do, so I just did what seemed right. I slid my arms around her shoulders and drew her toward me. I felt her fingernails dig into my shoulder, her sobs muffled by my body.

"You're far from nothing," I whispered. "Don't ever say that. You're one of the most talented people I know."

"Then why didn't they laugh?"

"It wasn't your fault. It was the virus."

"But what happens . . . what happens if *everyone* comes down with it?"

I remained silent for a long time before replying, "I don't know."

"I do, I know exactly what's going to happen. I'm going to disappear. My molecules are just going to peel away from each other, drift off into nothing. My body will fade out like a ghost and I'll drift around the world telling jokes to no one at all."

I pulled away from Heather, just enough to place my hands on her cheeks. "You're not going to disappear. You're not disappearing now." I stared into her eyes . . . so soft, the color of cream and coffee . . . and leaned toward her slowly, trying to gauge her reaction. She didn't pull away. I kissed her cheek. She closed her eyes and released a little sigh. My heart began to beat fast at the sound of that brief exhalation of air. I kissed her gently on her forehead and temple, her other cheek, her neck, her chin. She began running her hands up and down my back as I pressed my lips against hers. She responded instantly; she dug her nails into my shoulder blades again, this time out of passion instead of grief. I felt the softness of her mouth with my tongue. I felt her body lowering back onto the bed; she pulled me down with her, our mouths still locked together. I was so excited I think I almost forgot to breathe. After many minutes we pulled away from each other. I found myself staring into her eyes again. At that second I was certain I'd never seen anyone more beautiful; I leaned down near her ear and told her so in a whisper. I pressed my lips against the saltiness of her tears and told her we should begin making up for lost time. At that moment I realized there was nothing sadder in the universe than lost time. Though Heather may have disappeared to the rest of the world that night, to me she seemed to be the only person who had ever existed, or ever would exist. Her eyes reflected my own words back at me: You're not going to disappear. You're not going to disappear.

CHAPTER 14

Jesus Saves

(October 4-5, 2014)

That night our love making was interwoven with whispered discussions about childhood fears and adult pleasures and past relationships gone sour and future hopes and dead dreams. We'd talk, make love, talk, make love, and talk some more. This continued until about three o'clock in the morning when Heather drifted off to sleep with her head snuggled between my neck and shoulder, her hands resting on my chest. I lay there and thought about everything that had happened in the past few days. I thought once again about all the lost opportunities in my life and realized that if I had brought Esthra home with me Friday night I might not have been there the next day to receive Heather's call. Perhaps every lost opportunity was just a better opportunity gained, I mused. About a half hour later I fell asleep while listening to Heather's gentle, rhythmic breathing.

After what seemed like only minutes, I awoke to the sound of pounding on the front door. Beams of dust-speckled sunlight streamed in through the window. I glanced at the digital alarm clock sitting on the night stand beside the bed. It was a little after eight a.m. Heather was still dead asleep, curled into a ball on the edge of the bed with all the blankets wrapped around her. How had that happened? For a moment I considered lying in bed until the pounding stopped, but I didn't want the noise to wake Heather. I got out of the bed as quietly as possible, snatched my Levis up from the floor, and dashed out into the living room. I paused to shut the bedroom door behind me. As I walked toward the door I managed to wiggle into my Levis and button them up. Still the pounding continued.

"All right, all right," I mumbled, "hold your fuckin' horses." I swung open the door to find myself staring into a pair of raging infernos within the eyes of Mr. Michael Aster.

At this point I experienced a strange moment of cognitive dissonance. It felt as if some creature from an alternate reality were intruding into the little pocket universe I had carved out here in Heather's apartment. I would've been less surprised if a UFO had flown in from the hallway and burned a crop circle into the rug.

The first words out of Mike's mouth were, "You fucked her, didn't you?"

At first I wasn't sure what he was talking about. Was he referring to Heather? Had he been peering into the bedroom from an opposite rooftop with a telescope? Did he want to congratulate me on my good fortune? Out of all of these questions the only coherent one I could formulate was, "How'd you find me here?"

He pushed me backwards into the apartment. "Shut up, you asshole. I heard about what you did to her in the bathroom!"

I held my hands in the air. "Hey, I don't know what you're talkin' about, man."

"Don't play stupid with me. Everybody knows it. Everybody who was at that party heard about what you did. The gossip spread around the house like wildfire in a couple of fuckin' minutes. I was the last to know. I'm *always* the last to fuckin' know!"

Thick, ropy veins were bulging out of his neck; the veins in his temples were pulsating like tiny blue wires in a short-circuiting computer. His head seemed to be on the verge of exploding. I knew there would be no reasoning with the man. I knew it even before his fist flew out of the fifth dimension and slammed into my jaw, sending me toppling backwards into a stack of cardboard boxes filled with who knows what—more of Heather's garbage. I heard crashing and rattling and tinkling and knew that something fragile had broken; I hoped it was nothing inside of me.

A number of thoughts raced through my mind all at once as I tried to push myself up off the floor. The only person at that party who knew where Heather lived was Danny. Had he given Mike the address during some drugged-out stupor? Is that why he'd called the previous night, to warn me about Mike? First and foremost in my thoughts, however, was the idea that I really wouldn't mind getting beat up for fucking somebody else's girlfriend if only I had had the pleasure of fucking somebody else's girlfriend. A great deal of pleasure in return for a great deal of pain is an acceptable equation in my book as long as the pleasure part isn't left out of the deal. Imagine being punished for a sin you didn't commit, but *would have* if only you'd been given the opportunity. What could be more frustrating than that?

I had risen to my hands and knees when I felt Mike's boot slam into my ribcage. Bright bluish-purple splotches appeared in front of my eyes, darting about like weird airborne paramecium. I released an animalistic grunt and keeled over onto my side. Just as I thrust my hands in the air to ward off further attacks I heard the bedroom door open behind me.

"What the fuck?" Heather said in that most concise, Heather-like way of hers.

In my peripheral vision I could see that Heather had no way to protect herself. She was wearing her fluffy white bathrobe, nothing else. I tried to open my mouth to tell her to get out of here, but all the air had been knocked out of my body. I couldn't speak.

"Who the hell is this?" Mike said, poking me in the face with the tip of his boot. "Is this your little girlfriend? Maybe she'd like to know who you were fucking Friday night, hm? Maybe she'd like to know about you and *Esthra?*" The second he uttered Esthra's name he slammed his boot into my solar plexus. What little air I had left in my body now fled south for a perpetual vacation among the Antarctic ice floes.

"Don't hurt him!" Heather shouted, her voice laced with panic. Hearing the sound of a woman pleading for my life was a pleasant sensation in some ways. I never thought a woman would care about me enough to do such a thing. If only you could edit out the life-threatening aspect of the situation, it would've been even more pleasant.

Mike backed away from me. For a second I thought that maybe Heather had somehow gotten through to him. "I'm not going to hurt him," Mike said in an emotionless drone, "I'm going to kill him." He pulled up his shirt and removed a .22 from his belt. I remember thinking, I wonder if that's the gun his dad keeps by his bed.

"I'm not takin' any more shit from her, man. No more." Both his voice and hand were shaking. "Right here and now I'm announcing Mike's new policy. You touch her, you die. Simple as that." He released the safety, then aimed the shaking gun at my head. I closed my eyes tight, waiting for the shot.

From somewhere in front of me I heard a familiar voice say, "Excuse me, we thought we'd drop by to—hey, what's going on here?"

I opened my eyes in time to see Mike spin around and fire his gun at Brothers Lundberg and Fleetwood, both of whom were standing in the open doorway holding up little blue hardcover copies of the *Book of Mormon*. The firing gun thunderclapped throughout the room. Lundberg's head snapped backward, his body toppled onto the carpet. Fleetwood's jaw dropped as he watched his companion fall; his gaze darkened with anger; he spun toward Mike and threw the *Book of Mormon* through the air like a Frisbee. It slammed into Mike's wrist, knocking the gun out of his hand. The look on Mike's face was one of stunned disbelief. Before he could have time to recover I mustered up enough energy to rise to my feet and tackle Mike about the waist. Heather jumped on top of him too, as did Fleetwood. He was such a bundle of rage it took all three of us to pin him to the floor, but I knew we couldn't hold him there forever.

"What do we do with him now?" I said.

"I don't know," Fleetwood said, "knock him unconscious?"

"With what?" I said.

"Who's Esther?" Heather said.

"What?"

"You heard me!" Her lips had tightened into a thin white line. "Who's this Esther?"

"I don't think that's very important right now!" Mike managed to get one of his hands free and almost punched me in the eye.

"I think it is. Is she pretty?"

"*Will someone get his hand?*" Fleetwood pinned the hand to the floor, but had to release the other one in order to do so. With this hand Mike tried to punch me in the jaw again. I barely swerved out of the way.

"I suppose you told her she was beautiful," Heather said, "just like you told me last night."

"I didn't do anything with her. And her name's Esthra, not Esther."

"Ooooh, exotic. Sounds phony to me. Sounds like some kind of fucking stripper name."

"Can you put a sock in it for just one second? We've got a bit of a problem here in case you haven't noticed." Mike's fist whizzed past my skull once more.

Heather sighed, grabbed for the gun (which had landed near the leg of the sofa) and clubbed Mike over the head with the butt. His body immediately went limp and his head slammed against the carpet, bouncing once before lying still. We remained on top of him for a few seconds, just in case he emerged from unconsciousness like the implacable mad man in the last reel of all those slasher movies. He didn't. We breathed a sigh of relief, then relaxed. The second we did so he shot up from the floor and tried to strangle me. Heather slammed the gun into his head again, this time drawing blood. He collapsed onto the carpet once more, then lay still. This time Fleetwood and Heather sat on him while I went to check on Lundberg.

I expected to see his head blown all over the wall, pieces of his skull scattered across the floor. Compared with this gruesome image Lundberg seemed fine. I could see no trace of blood, no wound at all. He was sprawled out on the floor like a straw-stuffed dummy, his mouth wide open, his eyelids pressed together, his consciousness lost in torpid slumber. Lying on his chest was his elephantine copy of the *Book of Mormon*. I did a double take when I spotted the bullet hole that had consumed the golden-colored "o" and "k" in the word "Book." I slipped the tome out of his hands and peeled the pages apart, discovering the bullet flattened against page 779, the last page in the book, just barely forming a slight bulge in the metallic back cover. I flipped back to the title page and found the following note written in red ink:

Elliot,

Here is your own book. Please read it, think about it, and pray to know if it is true. Please call if you have any questions and we would love to help you understand the truth.

Late!
Brother Lundberg
375-4295

P.S.: Can we please keep that whole funny cigarette incident to ourselves?

I tucked the book under my arm, then lightly slapped him on the cheeks. "Hey, Lundberg," I said, "wake up! Looks like there's something to this God stuff after all." When Lundberg's eyes began to focus, I shoved the open book in his face and showed him the flattened bullet.

"Wh-what happened?" he mumbled.

"Well, either you're blessed or god damn lucky or both."

Lundberg propped himself up on his elbows. "Uh . . . what time is it?" His eyes still weren't quite focused.

I tilted my head to look at his watch. "8:22."

"Oh good, we're not late."

"Late for what?"

"Why, for the lecture. Don't you remember? Two weeks ago you told us to drop by this morning between 7:00 and 8:30 to deliver a second lecture to you and your wife Heather. Is she home?"

I couldn't help but conclude that practical jokes actually served a utilitarian purpose in the grand scheme of things. "Yeah," I said, "she's sitting on your assailant right now."

"Huh?"

"C'mon, I'll explain everything inside. You can deliver your second lecture while we're waiting for the cops."

"What?" He began to panic. "You didn't tell them about the cigarette did you?"

"No, no, that'll remain our little secret." I patted him on the back. "Let's go, Brother. This is probably the most receptive Heather's ever going to be to the Word of God."

I helped Lundberg to his feet, wrapped my arm around his shoulders, and guided him into the apartment where a Mormon and a half-naked standup comedian sat on a comatose punk rocker to prevent him from murdering us.

Just another day in the life.

CHAPTER 15

The Necrophilia Bar
(Or) You Want Fries With That?

(October 5-November 3, 2014)

After the police had dragged Mike away in handcuffs and jotted down detailed statements from everyone involved, the Mormons wished Heather and me a happy married life (this statement seemed to puzzle Heather, but she let it go), then promised to return in a week to deliver the third lecture. Those damn Mormons certainly are determined, you have to give them that.

Emergency Medical Technicians were even called in, though I insisted I was all right. They told me I had a couple of cracked ribs. I didn't feel quite as bad as I thought two cracked ribs *should* make you feel. As the EMTs taped me up, warning me about the nasty bruises I'd probably develop over the next few days, in the background I could see Heather's neighbors peeking around the open doorway to see what all the commotion was about. I told them not to worry, the anthrax would dissipate in no time. They all went back into their apartments.

Once Heather and I were alone in the apartment again I attempted to explain the entire sordid affair to her beginning with the first time I met Mike. I told the story exactly as I had to The Brink audience on Friday night. Heather rolled around on the sofa laughing for twenty minutes. By the time I got to the part where I bumped into Lundberg staggering out of the bathroom, she almost busted a gut. She believed that nothing had happened between Esthra and me, and admitted she would've had no right to be angry even if something had. In the end she was more concerned with what was happening to Danny.

I didn't talk to Danny again for another three weeks. He stopped performing at the clubs and I couldn't reach him by phone. I'd heard from other comedians, as well as Marsha, that Griffin was going through Danny's money as if he had a printing press hidden in his bedroom. I'd also heard he was slamming a spike into his arm almost every day. It only takes about a month to get strung out on heroin if you're shooting it on a daily basis.

It wasn't much of a surprise early one Monday morning when I awoke from a wonderful dream about Heather to hear the incessant ringing of the telephone, pressed the receiver to my parched lips, mumbled something vaguely resembling the word "hello," then heard the pre-recorded voice of a mechanical woman asking me if I would accept the charges for a collect phone call from L.A. County Jail.

"If so, please press 1," she said.

I pressed 1, then heard Danny's tentative whisper greeting me through the receiver: "Uh, hello? Can you hear me?"

"Yeah, I hear you. What the hell's going on?"

"I'm in jail."

"I gathered that." In the background I could hear someone talking through what sounded like a loudspeaker and the constant mumbling drone of a crowd of people carrying on dozens of conversations at once. "What did you do? I mean, what are you charged with?"

"Nothing too bad. Just making false statements to the police, possession of a needle, and trying to break into a pharmacy."

"You tried to break into a—?" I just shook my head. "Are you out of your fuckin' mind?"

"Let's talk about that a little later, okay? Right now I need you to do me a favor."

"No, I am not baking you a cake with a file in it."

"No no, I need you to call a couple of people for me."

The first person he wanted me to contact was some woman named Diane Evans, his dealer. He'd given her name to the police as a *reference*, believe it or not. The other person was his father. He wanted me to tell them both that he was in jail under the name Matthew Fuller. The cops were planning on letting him go on his own recognizance as long as he could prove he was a legal resident of Los Angeles, which required the verification of two references. If those two references said something along the lines of "Matthew Fuller? Who the fuck is Matthew Fuller?" he was pretty much screwed.

"Uh, now Diane's kind of a wacky broad and she might yell at you for no good reason, but don't let that intimidate you," Danny said.

"Why don't you have Griffin do all this shit?"

"I can't. She left me. She left me for that punk rock bitch she met at that party in Hermosa Beach a few weeks ago. What was her name? Esther, I think. Or something like that."

I rolled my eyes. "Oh, Lord, things just keep getting stranger and stranger."

"Remember, you've got to call my dad as soon as possible 'cause the phone company might be shutting off our phone today."

"Wait a second, I just thought of something, why didn't you give *me* as a reference?"

Long pause. "I didn't think of that."

"That would've saved both you and me a lot of trouble, you know."

"Hey, if I could think clearly do you think I'd be in here?"

"No, you'd be using that fancy Neuro-Linguistic Programming of yours to hypnotize the guards into letting you go free."

"I already tried that. Ever since I started taking heroin it doesn't seem to work anymore."

I was just about to make a wisecrack about that statement when I heard a click, indicating that I had a call on the other line. I hated call-waiting. I wanted *fewer* people to reach me, not more, but the phone company refused to get rid of it no matter how much I complained to them.

"Hold on a second," I said, sighing. I tapped the disconnect button, which switched me to the other line. "Hello?"

I heard the pre-recorded voice of a mechanical woman asking me if I would accept the charges for a collect phone call from L.A. County Jail. "If so, please press 1," she said.

I found myself experiencing yet another moment of cognitive dissonance, just as I had when Mike appeared in a puff of smoke outside Heather's door. Was another Danny from a parallel universe somehow calling me at that same exact moment? God, I hoped not; it was bad enough dealing with one Danny. I guess I assumed the wires had somehow gotten crossed at the phone company, and figured I'd hear Danny's voice on the other line as well. I pressed 1.

The next voice I heard was that of a youngish fellow with a distinct Latino accent. His first words were either "Hey, this is Elliot" or "Hey, is this Elliot?"

Since I wasn't sure which I just said, "Yeah."

"You a fag?"

"Excuse me?"

"I said, you a fag?"

I suppose a normal person would've hung up at this point. Come to think of it, a normal person would never even have accepted the charges in the first place.

"Wait a second, let me get this straight," I said, "do you just randomly call people collect and accuse them of being a fag?" In the background I could hear someone talking through what sounded like a loudspeaker and the constant mumbling drone of a crowd of people carrying on dozens of conversations at once. "Where are you, anyway?" I asked, though I'm not sure why. I already knew.

"I'm in jail, motherfucker."

"Don't you think you should get in touch with an attorney instead of calling me a fag?"

"Nah, it don't matter, I'm not gettin' out of here in a long ass time, man."

"Who *is* this?"

"This is Rob. Here, talk to my friend."

The phone was passed to someone else, another youngish Latino-sounding gentleman. "Who's this?" asked said gentleman.

"This is Elliot. Who's this?"

"Billy. Where you at?"

"In my bedroom."

"No, no, what *city?*"

"Um, Los Angeles."

"You in with the Crips or the Bloods?"

I suddenly realized that Billy must have thought I was friends with the other guy. "Both. I alternate. On Mondays, Wednesdays and Fridays I'm with the Crips, and on Tuesdays, Thursdays and Saturdays I'm with the Bloods."

"Shit, they let you do that?"

"I have a special dispensation from the government."

"You a cop or something?"

"No, I just talk like one."

"How old are you, man?"

"Twenty-nine."

"Fuck, that's probably how old I'll be when I get out of this place. But that's okay, dog. I ain't gonna waste my time. I plan on usin' this as an excuse to study computer technology."

Shit, I thought, I've never been caught committing a crime and I don't even *have* a computer! In five years this jailbird will probably be the next Bill Gates and I'll be in some hovel burning my jokes for heat.

"You go to school?" Billy said.

"Yeah, I was majoring in unemployment for awhile." He seemed to like that one. I think he actually laughed.

"What do you do now?" he said.

"I work at a necrophilia bar."

"What's that?"

"It's an underground bar where they take a dead body and put it on a table in the middle of the room, then I have sex with it while everyone watches and drinks margaritas or whatever."

"Man, is that with dead girls or dead guys?"

"Hey! What do you think I am, some fuckin' weirdo? Dead *girls*, of course."

"Oh, that's good. Why do you do that shit?"

"Gotta eat, man. Better than workin' at McDonald's."

"That's where I was workin' before I was busted."

"Now I know why you're in jail. L.A. County is a picnic compared to stuffing those damn Happy Meal boxes. What're you in for anyway?"

"I didn't pay my child support."

"They threw you behind bars? Just for not paying child support?"

"Well, I committed armed robbery before, then when I didn't pay the child support they said I broke my probation or some stupid crap like that."

"That doesn't seem fair. Why can't the damn kid pay his own way?"

"Shit, that's what I said."

"So what was the reason for not paying it?"

"I didn't have the money."

"You should've just robbed someone."

"I did. But I spent it all on cocaine and shit, man."

"I see."

"Hey, do they videotape you doin' this shit?"

"What shit?"

"Having sex with dead bodies."

"Oh, of course! Through a two-way mirror."

"You get a lot of money for that?"

"A shitload."

"Who pays you?"

"My boss."

"What's his name?"

"Matthew Fuller."

"Shit, man. That's some weird shit. What's that trim feel like?"

"It's as cold as ice."

"Oh, *shit*, man. I need a girl who can *move*."

"Yeah, not like Rob."

"What about him?"

"He's not good in bed."

"How do you know?"

"I had sex with him."

I heard the sound of laughter. Billy turned to Rob and said, "Hey, he says he had sex with you."

In the background: "Shit, I don't even know him."

Billy turned back to me. "Hey, what's his asshole like?"

I didn't even hesitate. "It's like a sick donut."

"He says it looks like a sick donut!" A chorus of laughs erupted from the background—sounded like a dozen people, perhaps.

"He has a tattoo on his ass, too," I said.

"Of what?"

"A teddy bear."

"What?" He turned back to Rob. "Hey, you got a teddy bear on your ass, man?"

Rob grabbed the phone from Billy and began yelling at me. "Why you sayin' that shit, man? I don't even know you."

"Oh, c'mon. Don't you remember that romantic night out on the veranda overlooking the Pacific as we stared into each other's eyes and whispered sweet nothings?"

"Oh shit, man. What the fuck're you talkin' about?"

In the background, amidst the hooting and guffaws, I heard: "Hey, you got a teddy bear on yo' ass!" followed by a bunch of kissing sounds.

Deciding to spare him temporarily from the subject at hand, I said, "Hey, how did you get my number?"

"It's written here on the wall."

"*What?*"

"It's even got your name written under it."

"Oh, Lord. Can you do me a favor and cross it out?"

"Yeah, if you tell these assholes I'm not a fag."

In the background: "Teddy bear on yo' ass! Teddy bear on yo' ass!"

"All right, all right, you got a deal. But you gotta do something else for me. Cross out my name and number and write in this one instead." I gave him Brother Lundberg's name and number.

"Who's that?"

"Just a friend of mine."

"Does he know any bitches?"

"Sure. *Rich* bitches."

"Yeah? Can he hook me up?"

"Just call him up and ask him. He'll come through. He'll even send you money. Maybe some funny cigarettes too. He's been in stir. He's down with the whole penal scene. Uh, say, can you hold on a second?"

"Sure."

I switched over to the other line. "You still there?"

Danny yelled, "What did you do, go to the fuckin' grocery store?"

"Listen, did you by any chance write my name and number on some wall in there?"

"No."

"Are you sure?"

"Why would I do that?"

"If you did, would you remember it?"

"Well . . . maybe not, no."

In my mind's eye I had this image of Danny calling me on the pay phone while two phones down Rob and his friends were calling random numbers scrawled on the wall, hoping they'd reach someone stupid enough to accept the charges. I was just about to ask Danny to glance around and look for a group of young convicts yelling "Teddy bear on yo' ass!" at some gang-banger talking on a pay phone, but by this point Danny's time had run out and the call was terminated. Upon hearing the dial tone I switched over to the other line. I had just enough time to jot down Rob's full name and prison number. Right before the line went dead I promised to send him and Billy a money order along with a free copy of the *Book of Mormon*. I hoped Billy would remember this kind gesture when his computer company bought out Microsoft a few years from now.

I immediately tried calling Diane Evans, but the phone just rang and rang and rang. I tried his father next. Same thing. Since I could do little else, I dragged myself out of bed and took a shower. About twenty minutes later, with the towel still wrapped around my waist, I sat down on the edge of my bed and tried Diane again.

This time a deep-voiced Lurch-like fellow answered: "Yeah, what is it?"

"Hello, is Diane Evans there?"

The man sighed. "Unfortunately." I heard the receiver being set down and heavy footsteps lumbering away from the phone.

What seemed like another twenty minutes later, a middle-aged woman with a phlegmatic voice said, "What do you want?"

"Hi. Uh, are you the dealer?"

"*What?*"

"You're the drug lady, aren't you?"

"Who is this?"

"I just want to know, do you deliver? Are you offering a special on china white today?"

"What the—?"

"Aw, I'm just kiddin'. Danny wanted me to call you. He's in jail at the moment."

"*What?*"

After I'd passed along the required information she started babbling: "That Danny I told him I *told* him he came to my house last night and I walked him out to the curb I told him please go straight home and call me when you get home but when he never called I got ahold of his father and he told me Danny had stepped out for a moment to talk to the manager but apparently he *did* go out last night didn't he *didn't* he?"

"Apparently so."

She sighed in frustration, sounding quite pissed. "I'm gonna call down there right now and find out what's going on." She sounded like she knew what she was doing. I wouldn't even know where to begin, quite frankly. Baking a cake with a file in it was the most sensible idea I'd had.

After I hung up with her I tried calling Danny's father again. Instead of the incessant ringing, this time I got ahold of a now familiar-sounding mechanical female who said, "The number you are trying to reach has been disconnected. If you think you have dialed the number in error, please hang up and try again."

I cradled the receiver. Oh, well. I'd done everything I could do. Now it was up to Miss Evans and her Howling Crackhead Attack Battalion to follow through and bust Danny out of the joint. I was certain a full-frontal assault would do the trick. I could see a bunch of addicts hurling specially-made crackbombs at L.A. County, breaking down the walls with massive battering rams, firing cannons filled with hypodermic needles at the machine gun turrets. In a perfect world perhaps this would occur. Of course, in a perfect world Danny wouldn't be in jail in the first place.

At that moment, for some reason, the reality of the situation struck me like at no other point. Danny was in jail. Danny Oswald was a heroin addict and he was in jail. How the hell had that happened?

I remained on the edge of the bed, staring at the wall for a very long time as if expecting it to give me an answer. None came.

CHAPTER 16

Rain of Frogs

(November 13, 2014)

A little over a week later I read an item in the newspaper buried at the bottom of p. B-22. Someone staged a rain of frogs in the Del Amo Fashion Center in Torrance, California. How this stunt could have been accomplished was not known. All that was known for sure was that custodians spent days recapturing the leaping little amphibians. I carefully cut out the article with a pair of scissors and pasted it into a scrapbook.

I had no idea why.

CHAPTER 17

Until the Last Dog Dies

(March 26, 2015)

It's hard to pinpoint the beginning of the downhill slide. Perhaps when Danny was thrown in jail. Perhaps when I saw that press conference back in September. Perhaps when Danny freaked out on me for the first time that night at Prospero's. I don't know, I don't know. It all seems a jumble now. Sometimes I think it's a miracle I can think straight enough to remember any of it, much less minute details. All I can do is to tell it the way it happened and hope it makes sense.

Clubs began closing late in November. At first this didn't worry me. Older comedians assured me they'd lived through such busts before. When the comedy boom of the '80s—which gave birth to thousands of clubs with names like Chuckles and The Laffery—finally came to a screeching halt at some point during the first Bush administration most of the alternative comics were relieved. After all, too many clubs could only mean too many bad comics. I had a similar reaction when I first heard The Rumor, which was spreading through the back rooms of comedy clubs all over the city early in December. The Rumor was this: The humor virus had taken its toll. Five major clubs in L.A. were going to be shut down in the same week. All across the country fewer and fewer people were showing up at the clubs. Why should they? Imagine a blind man paying hard-earned money to go to a strip joint. Even the core clientele, who I think had continued to show up for the past couple of months just out of pure force of habit, had ceased coming in. Playing at the clubs, once the high point of my life, had now become a torturous ordeal that I underwent only to pay the bills. I ceased coming up with new material. Why bother? No one was listening. That was my excuse at any rate.

When I first stopped coming up with new material I told myself it was because I was on strike, protesting a God that would hook Danny on narcotics and spread a destructive new disease around the planet in His spare time just for the hell of it. Later I tried to convince myself it was Heather's fault that the jokes had stopped coming. She was my muse, always had been, even back when we were just friends; she had always been the filter through which my ideas were refined into something worthwhile. Beginning in late January, however, she began to change. She was never quite sure which of my jokes she liked and which worked better confined to the trash heap. "They're all okay, pick the ones you like," she'd say. "You're better at this stuff than I am." Then she'd wander into her bedroom and watch old television shows. The woman who had once been so egotistical and cocksure was now incapable of picking a variation of a simple one-liner over another. It was like living with Heather's reflection, a ghostly image who had escaped from a mirror and taken the real Heather's place. Ever since that

Saturday night when we first made love, we had been so happy, overjoyed that we'd found each other at last. Sometimes we spent whole days and nights just improvising new material and laughing at each other's jokes like little school kids. We laughed a lot then. Though I know it was a very short period of time,— from the beginning of October to the end of January, only about a hundred days really—in retrospect it seemed much longer.

Heather gave her last performance on January 31st at the Uncabaret. She stumbled through it like a ninety-year-old Bob Hope reading off cue cards the size of Mount Rushmore. No one in the audience seemed to notice or care. Immediately after the performance she collapsed into my arms and cried for twenty minutes straight. I took her out to her car where I held her for a long time and stroked her hair, told her not to worry. "Take a little vacation," I said. "Don't even worry about paying the bills. I'll take care of everything for awhile. I'll move into your place and pick up the slack. I'm there all the time anyway, and I'm tired of that little rathole I live in. Just rest. Forget about being funny for awhile."

"I'll never be funny again," she said. "I've lost it."

"Don't say that. You'll get it back. You've always been funny, you always will."

"I don't think so. I'm just glad I'm still sane enough to know it."

She lapsed into silence after that. Over and over again I insisted she was wrong, but I knew I was trying to convince myself more than her. Heather had changed. I still loved her, I loved her more than any other person in the entire world, but she had changed. Simple as that. She knew this full well, but I was too sick with love to acknowledge it. Unfortunately, when you're that sick love can be perverted very easily and transformed into resentment. Yes, I resented her for coming down with the virus; her condition only served to remind me of my own fragility. Every morning when I awoke and saw her face I was reminded of how easily my humor could be stripped from me. No one knew how the virus was transmitted. Was I at risk merely by touching her? This kind of thinking soon led to paranoia. That's when I began to blame her for my inability to come up with new ideas. I stopped having sex with her altogether and even avoided using the same silverware. I became distant and cold. Early in March I allowed Marsha to book me in a whole string of clubs all across the country. I hoped this time away from Heather would allow me to recover from the disease I believed I had picked up from her, the disease that was blocking my creativity.

I was so crazy at this point I didn't even want Heather to drive me to the airport for fear of further infection. Instead I took a bus to LAX. On the way there I stared at the familiar L.A. scenery, my depression broken only for a moment when the bus stopped to let off a passenger. Just outside the window was a mural that had been painted on the storefront of an Army Recruiting Center. It was a picture of Uncle Sam being anally raped by what looked like a giant frog-like humanoid wearing a skintight camouflage suit, like something a deep sea diver would wear. The expression on Sam's face was one of utter ecstasy, while the expression on the frog's face was one of infinite sadness. Judging from the style, it appeared to be the same artist who had painted the previous crazy murals I'd encountered from one end of L.A. to the other. I glanced around to see if anyone else was staring at the mural, but they weren't. They didn't even appear to see it.

At that moment an old man hobbled onto the bus and sat right next to me even though there were plenty of empty seats surrounding us. The man was thin and gaunt with grayish

stubble staining his elongated chin. He wore thrift store cloth-
ing that included a plaid button-up shirt, black suspenders, and
dark brown slacks pulled up to his belly button, and carried
a long bamboo cane with a curved head. As he stared at me
through thick Coke bottle eyeglasses, I suspected I would have
to fend off his feeble advances with a swift left hook to his jaw.
His entire body smelled like cigar smoked mixed with cheap
liquor.

"Nice day today, isn't it?" he said.

I shrugged. "S'okay."

He glanced down at the luggage tucked in between my legs.
"Goin' somewhere?"

"Yep." I prayed he'd shut the fuck up.

"Nice day for an airplane trip."

As I've already stated, the paranoia quotient in my life was
running high at that time. I squinted at him with some suspi-
cion. "How do you know I'm going on an airplane trip?"

"This bus goes to LAX, doesn't it? Mind if I smoke?" He
reached into his shirt pocket and pulled out a large black cigar,
the tip of which he held into the high flame of an ornate lighter
with the initials M.H. inscribed upon it. Thick clouds of acrid
smoke soon blew into my face.

The old woman in front of us turned around and said,
"Excuse me, sir, could you please not smoke on the bus? My
asthma—"

"Your asthma my ass!" the old man said. "Jesus H. Freakin'
Christ, it's gettin' to the point where you can't even shit where
you want to!" He slammed the burning tip of the cigar into
the sticky floor. "Smoking *cures* asthma. Don't you know that,
lady?"

The old lady seemed shocked and confused. She turned
around and tried to ignore him.

The old man rolled his eyes. "I can't stand some people. Can you stand people?"

"No. I can't."

He didn't get the hint. "We're two of a kind. When I was a kid, I desperately wanted Jesus to come back, but not so's I could go to Heaven. Fuck that. I just wanted him to take everybody else away and leave me behind so's I could live a happy life. Alone."

Since I knew the ride was long, and there was no way of getting out of the conversation, I decided to at least take command of it.

"Uh, what do they stand for?" I said, pointing at the initials on his lighter.

"Wha—? Oh, these?" He chuckled. "Manny Horowitz, that's me, all right. At least it was the last time I looked." He held up the lighter, admiring it, turning it from side to side, watching the sunlight glint off its golden surface. "This is the only memento I have from the old days. The owner of the Sunset in Vegas bought it for me after my tenth anniversary. It's real gold, through and through, at least he told me it was. I've never really bothered to check it out. I was always so flattered by the gesture, I didn't want to chance finding out that it was all just a lie."

I nodded. Even through those thick portals of glass you could detect the sadness within his eyes. I wondered what his job had been at the hotel. Had he been a night clerk, an elevator operator, a waiter? None of these jobs seemed worthy of such an expensive lighter, not after only ten years. It takes at least twenty to get a necktie.

Manny continued, "I'm not sure I want to know how much it's worth, because if I did I might try to sell it. I have to admit, I've come close plenty of times. Sometimes I've been so hungry

I think my stomach shrank to the size of a fucking peanut. The world hasn't exactly been kind to me. Lost my wife, my career, even a kidney, but through it all I held onto this little lighter. When the owner gave it to me, Al was his name, he said, 'This is for making me laugh my ass off all these years. If it hadn't been for your jokes I never would've gotten through my divorce. Hell, I probably would've offed myself a long time ago.' It's the kindest thing anybody's ever said to me. Believe you me, I know how tough a divorce can be. Eats you up inside. Makes you crazy. Can push you right over the edge if you let it. It managed to push me right off the stage and into the gutter. Sometimes I think if Dolores hadn't left me maybe I'd still be working Vegas, drawin' down a nice salary, gettin' some hot young pussy on the side. Those were the days.

"Hell, at this point I'd settle for some lukewarm *old* pussy if I could get it. Something is better than nothing. That's what my father used to say." Manny paused for a moment, as if lost in reverie. "He used to say some strange things. Imagine sittin' at the dinner table when you're eight years old, mixin' the lima beans with your mashed potatoes so you could choke that crap down quicker and get right to the strawberry shortcake, when suddenly your dad looks up at you and says, 'Son, if you only learn one thing in life let it be this: It's not the face you're fuckin'.' I'm not really sure what he intended me to do with that information. I think my dad might've been slightly retarded. Who else but a tardo would tell an eight-year-old something like that? I blame my dad's advice for my three marriages. I mean, hell, it's true it's not the face you're fuckin', but it *is* the first thing you gotta see when you wake up in the god damn morning."

Though I suppose I should've been annoyed by the man's endless monologue, I had become intrigued the second he mentioned his "jokes." What the hell jokes were those? "Excuse me," I said, interrupting him before he could continue his tirade against his father, "did you used to be a standup comedian?"

"Sure was." He sighed, staring at the view through the windshield twelve seats away, watching the brightly colored North Hollywood storefronts whizzing by. "I spent thirty-nine years on the stage. I started out when I was sixteen and built myself up from nothing, *less* than nothing. I played my first shows at a little club in New Jersey doing fart jokes and impersonations of Hirohito. This was during the war, mind you." He saw the blank expression on my face. "Hirohito was the emperor of Japan." He rolled his eyes and mumbled something about kids today not knowing anything about history. "Anyway, I've spent the majority of my career living hand to mouth, paycheck to paycheck. Most of the time I was opening for more famous comedians, always the bridesmaid etc. etc. I worked with Milton Berle and Jack Benny and even Bob Hope on radio. I don't have to tell you who they are, do I? What about radio? You've heard of radio, haven't you?" I laughed and nodded. "Okay, just checkin'. You never know these days. Sheesh. Anyway, the best gig I ever had was at the Sunset, and I blew that one big time."

"How did you blow it?"

He spread his hands in the air as if the answer was obvious. "By not being funny, of course! I was tapped out at that point. This was back in . . . oh, let's see, '84 I think? My wife had left me, I was stuck with alimony payments, I was popping four different kinds of anti-depressants mixed with alcohol. Need I go on? I'm not exactly describing a recipe for nirvana here. The booking agent had to let me go. He felt bad about it, but what can you do? That's show business."

"What did you do after that?"

"I moved down here. Calling Vegas a cesspool would be too kind. I'd had it up to here with that hole. Los Angeles is different. It's got character . . . and hot chicks. Heh! Yeah, hot chicks with big hooters!" He cackled up a storm, peering through the window at a trio of scantily clad teenage girls roller skating down the sidewalk.

I laughed and said, "You get a lot of girls down here?"

"From time to time. You'd be surprised at what a young girl likes, as long as you talk to 'em right."

From the way he said this I almost believed him. "Did you ever do any more standup after Vegas?"

His smile vanished. He grew morose and sighed. Still fondling the golden lighter he said, "No, can't say that I did. I settled down here and got a job as a PBX operator. I was lucky to get anything at all. I mean, I'd done nothing but tell jokes for thirty-nine years. Such skills aren't easily transferable from one occupation to another, in case you didn't know. During the first few weeks I was scared, real scared. I felt like I was . . . I don't know, disappearing." I must have had a strange look on my face. He had no way of knowing he was echoing Heather. He said immediately, "I know it sounds odd, but it's true. My entire reason for living had been taken away, which isn't the easiest thing to adjust to, you know. Some people don't survive a change like that at all, particularly at the age I was then. But as the weeks wore on I got used to it. Pretty soon I was just content to have a roof over my head and some food in my belly and a job to go to every morning. You learn to appreciate things like that when you get to be my age. Not because you grow any wiser; you just don't have any choice in the matter."

"Do you still make up jokes, for yourself at least?"

"Oh, you can't help not to. How about this? Pick-up line for the twenty-first century: 'So, uh . . . what medication are you on?'" There was an awkward moment of silence. I chuckled politely. "You can use that one if you like."

"Use it where?"

"The next time you're on stage."

"How . . . how do you know I—?"

"Just from the way you handle yourself, the way you walk."

"I've been sitting down the entire time!"

Manny smiled and nodded. "Trust me, an old man just knows things."

I didn't trust him. I assumed he must have seen me around town, or perhaps on a local cable talk show. I didn't really care how he knew me. I had more important things on my mind. "Why do you think you ran out of ideas in Vegas? Was it just the stress in your life or . . . ?"

Manny shrugged. "It was a combination of things. I think a man has only a certain amount of ideas in his life. Some people use up all their good ideas in their first twenty years, then spend the rest of their life coasting. Some people spread their ideas out over a long period of time, coming up with a new one every other year or so. With someone like that, it's a big occasion when they come up with a new idea. It's like a holiday. They invite friends over and cater in food just to celebrate it. It's like giving birth to a baby. Unfortunately, I think most people have all their really good ideas before they're five. Me, I happened to tap out at fifty-five." He shrugged. "That's a good long run, compared to some."

"That's a scary thought. That you could just . . . run dry like that, without warning."

Manny shrugged again.

Following a moment of silence I said, "You know, there's been talk going around lately of this humor virus—"

Before I could say anything more the old man erupted into laughter, which soon segued into a horrible coughing fit. For a second there I thought I might have to perform the Heimlich Maneuver on him, but then he began to calm down. Everyone else on the bus was looking at him warily, as if he might have a contagious disease.

"Are you all right?" I said.

"'Course I'm all right. I was just laughing at that humor virus remark. Everyone knows there's no humor virus. That's a load of crap."

"How do you explain what's happening then?"

"It's like I told you. When a person's born he's only got a certain amount of ideas available to him. The human race only has a fixed supply of ideas and we're just now hitting the bottom of the well. The first to go is always humor, next it'll be sex, then cooking, then fashion, then electrical engineering, who knows? Why do you think plagiarism's almost become its own art form? Why do you think Hollywood can only remake or re-release movies that first came out fifty years ago? Nobody has any ideas. There aren't any to have."

"That's horrifying. It's like the Apocalypse."

"It's not *like* the Apocalypse, it *is* the Apocalypse. I've always suspected that when the world finally ended no one would notice. Looks like I was right." While I was still thinking about that line Manny said, "Ah, here's my stop coming up. Got to go to the grocery store and pick up a few things. I'm gonna buy some of that cream . . . y'know that cream that numbs your penis so you don't ejaculate too soon when you're fuckin' some young chick wearing roller skates? I'm thinking of rubbing it over my whole body to numb everything, then I'll stroll into a bank and try to rob the place. If the guards shoot at me it won't matter 'cause I'll be impervious to pain. That's a pretty ingenious plan, right?"

I stared at him.

Manny burst into laughter again. "Aw, I'm just kidding with you. That's a pretty funny image though, don't you think? You can use that in your act too if you want. I've got a million of 'em, or at least I used to. Well, nice meeting you." As the bus pulled up to the curb Manny rose from his seat and held out his hand. I shook it. It felt coarse and dry like desert sand. "You know, you never told me your name," he said.

"Elliot Greeley."

"Fine, fine name. I'll look for it. I think you're going to be very successful."

"Not if I don't come up with some new ideas."

The old man smiled. "There's more to life than just trying to impress people, on or off stage. You're going to be successful. Trust me, an old man knows things. Don't give up. Keep tellin' them jokes until the last dog dies. You might as well. The Apocalypse is right around the corner."

With that he hobbled down the aisle at a sprightly pace and descended the stairs. He gave me one last wave before the doors closed behind him. I watched him dwindle into nothing as the bus drove farther and farther away.

CHAPTER 18

Holy City Asylum

(March 29, 2015)

I found irony in the fact that my first booking outside Los Angeles was San Francisco's Holy City Asylum, the very club that had so devastated Heather several months before. I was scheduled to play there for a week. The first two nights went fine. The reaction wasn't spectacular, not like the one I received at The Brink that night early in October, but it wasn't traumatic either. The atmosphere was mellow, with no hint of the Apocalypse to come.

On the third night I strode out onto stage, planted my feet on the boards, grabbed the microphone, stared out into the audience, opened my big fat mouth as I had done a million times before . . . and my brain locked. Not a single sound emerged from my throat. Even if I could have made a sound, I don't know what I would've said. My mind was blank.

At first the audience wasn't aware that anything was wrong. As I've already mentioned, I usually begin my act with silence; I then try to accentuate my fear: stuttering a bit, dropping in a few "ers" and "uhs" here and there, maintaining an open-eyed stare like a little kid caught in the headlights. Hell, I didn't know what fear was until that moment. All of a sudden I felt as if I were floating in an endless void that was empty except for me, a void that would consume what little there was of my consciousness if I remained silent even a second longer. I don't think I ever felt more alone. I could feel my body becoming numb, disappearing. After a lifetime I collapsed onto my knees and began crying. I felt as if I was crying for the entire world and every creature that walked or crawled or swam upon it. Once the tears began to flow nothing could stop them. At first I think the audience actually thought I was kidding. Some of them even laughed, hooted and hollered as if it were the funniest damn thing they'd ever seen. This made me cry even more. This caused some shock among the audience, I could tell. I didn't care. What I wanted most of all at that moment was to hold Heather in my arms again and never let her go. Never, never let her go.

They dropped me in a little dressing room somewhere backstage and asked me if I needed a doctor. I told them just to go away. They left me there in total darkness. I liked it that way; somehow the darkness in that room was nowhere near as frightening as the void I'd experienced out there on the stage. All I remember is the owner himself entering the room some time later and ordering me to get the hell out.

"I don't know what fuckin' drugs you're on," he said, "but you blew it, man. You're never workin' this club again."

I said nothing. I didn't even laugh. I didn't have to. I rose from the couch and strolled out of that room as casually as I'd strolled out on stage and into the void. I made a conscious decision to leave the club through the front door and not the back. I had to walk past the entire audience. I could feel their eyes on me. For some reason they found me more fascinating than the teenager who was now telling tit jokes on stage. Pain is always more fascinating than comedy. Pain wins respect, comedy takes it away. Tragedy is what wins awards.

I strode through the swinging doors and out onto the sidewalk, breathing in the fog-laden San Francisco air as I headed back to the hotel, knowing I had just delivered my swan song performance. I would never enter a comedy club again. They held no interest for me, not anymore. I don't think I'd ever felt more content, as if I'd somehow returned to childhood. For the first time since I could remember I felt . . . I don't know how to describe it. . . .

I guess I felt free.

CHAPTER 19

No Jokes, Please

(March 29-30, 2015)

Upon arriving at the hotel I booked myself on the first flight back to Los Angeles. I felt no need to inform Marsha about this, as I would no longer be needing her services. Free people don't need agents. I called Heather and told her I loved her and that I'd be coming back home tomorrow. I didn't even need to tell her what had happened. She knew.

The next morning I saw something very odd at the airport. Perhaps such things were at all airports and I had simply never noticed them before. Above the metal detector was a large sign that read "No Jokes, Please." Perhaps the airport wished to discourage off-hand remarks about thermonuclear warheads tucked away in purses, but I interpreted it very differently. I saw it as a summation of all the craziness that had occurred over the course of the past seven months; I saw it as an encouraging portent, a reminder from the universe that I was at long last on the right track.

CHAPTER 20

How I Learned To Stop Worrying and Love the Rat Race

(March 30-April 18, 2015)

Within the month I landed a job as a stockboy in a bookstore. Heather became a cashier at a little grocery market. We made just enough to pay the rent and buy food and see a movie once in awhile. We were happy.

Our agent continued to call us every other day, pleading with us to go back to work.

We are working, I would tell her over and over again, we *are* working.

CHAPTER 21

Two Opposing Seas

(April 19, 2015)

Meanwhile, I continued to cut out obscure articles from the paper. Someone hung flyers all over Los Angeles announcing a Ku Klux Klan rally on the steps of the Federal Building at twelve noon on April 19th. Simultaneously, someone else hung flyers announcing a Nation of Islam rally on the steps of the Federal Building at twelve noon on April 19th. Two opposing seas of protestors showed up at the same place, at the same time.

I pasted this into my scrapbook. Perhaps out of pure instinct, like a conditioned muscular reflex.

CHAPTER 22

Not Fit to Survive

(May 27, 2015)

I decided to pay a visit to Danny's father on his birthday. I had learned through the grapevine that Danny had been given a three-year prison term. The state of California had been doling out tougher and tougher sentences for drug-related crimes and Danny just happened to be caught in the flood of offenders who were going to be held up by the Governor as "examples." Danny had picked the wrong century to be an addict. It was possible that he wouldn't be released until the next millennium. I knew his father was probably taking it pretty hard.

When I showed up outside his apartment door I was surprised to hear Bone Thugs-N-Harmony blaring from within.

"Uh, Mr. Oswald?" I said, knocking on the door with one hand while balancing a plate with the other. The plate was wrapped in clear plastic and held only a fraction of the delicious birthday meal Heather had cooked earlier in the day. She thought Danny's father might appreciate the gesture, since he was no doubt spending the day alone. Or so we assumed.

"C'mon in!" I heard the old man yell.

I pushed open the door to see Mr. Oswald and Karen Griffin dancing in the middle of the room, grinding their hips together to the beat of the music. Griffin's clothes were completely rumpled as if she'd rolled around on the carpet one too many times. One of her breasts had popped out of her tube top and was jiggling around with great enthusiasm but no one seemed to care, particularly not Mr. Oswald. His clothes were just as dishevelled as Griffin's and despite the fact that he was nearing eighty his eyes sparkled like crystals and his grin was as wide as a church door. Sitting cross-legged around the coffee table were the Neo-Gothic Hipster Peanut Gallery accompanied by a gaggle of other strangers. They were all snorting white powdery lines off the table's glass surface.

"You here for the party?" Mr. Oswald said. He didn't seem to recognize me, which was hard to believe. At one time I had been visiting Danny almost every day.

"Uh, I just dropped by to say hello. I brought some food."

"Set it down in the kitchen. Maybe we'll get to it later." The old man did a little Irish jig, then reached out for Griffin's exposed breast. She allowed him to stroke her nipple for a couple of seconds, then danced away to the opposite side of the room. He pursued her, laughing the entire time.

I entered the kitchen and set the meal down on the counter. The place was a mess. The garbage bag was stuffed with so many empty beer cans that they had spilled over onto the floor. I considered placing some of the cans back into the trash when I heard a phone ringing; it seemed to be nearby. I pushed aside a pile of crushed Heineken cans on the counter to find a light blue phone lying there waiting to be answered.

I picked up the receiver and said, "Hello? Oswald residence." A mechanical woman asked me if I would accept a collect phone call from L.A. County Jail. I said yes, then pressed 1.

A couple of seconds later I heard a Latino-sounding voice say, "You a fag?"

I paused for a moment before I said, "Rob?" (Or was it some other felon entirely?)

I suddenly realized I had never mailed the money order or the free copy of the *Book of Mormon* I had promised Rob.

"Hey, you a fag?" the voice repeated.

Had Danny scrawled his own number on the wall of the jail? In the past I might have engaged Rob (or whoever the hell it was) in a conversation just to learn the answer to that question, but now it didn't seem worth it somehow. I hung up and left the kitchen.

Danny's father was dry humping Griffin on the couch. He seemed to be enjoying it. So was she. The Peanut Gallery couldn't have cared less. In the past I would've stuck around just to find out how this situation had arisen. Now I didn't even have the energy. I don't think anyone even noticed me leave.

I closed the door behind me and started to head back down the stairs. Something stopped me, however, drew me upwards to the roof.

I was amazed at how peaceful it was up there. I stood three stories above the street, one foot resting on the ledge, staring down at all the people walking back and forth on the trash-strewn sidewalk below. Pigeons surrounded me, cooing and pecking at the tiny pebbles that littered the rooftop. Perhaps they were searching for something to eat. Hell, I thought, I should've brought *them* the birthday meal.

I glanced around me, trying to view the place as Danny had viewed it on those nights so long ago when he used to sneak up here and practice his routines for the stars. At the moment, of course, it was the middle of the afternoon, but nevertheless I could imagine the full moon and the stars and the cool night wind blowing against Danny's back. Behind me was a small bungalow that housed two washing machines and a dryer. Through the open doorway I noticed cigarette butts littering the bare concrete floor. I could almost see Danny sitting there in front of the washing machine at midnight, watching his clothes spin around and around, biting his fingernails as he nervously whispered the new routine he'd try out at Prospero's the following night.

I turned to the pigeons and told them some of my old standard jokes, the ones that used to draw big laughs. I could no longer remember why I'd been so fond of them. I felt like a ninety year old man flipping through a tattered photo album of old girlfriends, wondering why he'd wasted so much of his lifetime chasing after so many worthless women. I tried out three of the jokes, but the pigeons simply looked at me with blank stares and said, "Coo?" I knew exactly how they felt.

I took one last look around, scoping out the taller buildings that surrounded me, spotting one or two unfamiliar faces staring down at yours truly with idle curiosity, then headed back toward the stairs.

Part of me missed Danny so much it hurt, burned deep down inside me, while another part of me never wanted to see him again. The sole personality trait we'd ever shared was a sick sense of humor that the rest of the universe didn't understand. Somehow the situation had reversed; Danny and I had been left out of the loop while the rest of the universe seemed privy to an esoteric punchline neither of us could ever comprehend. If given the choice, I think I would've elected to remain out of the loop.

May 27th was a day of coincidences. Seeing Griffin made me think of Esthra. As I climbed back into Heather's car I wondered what she and the rest of the band were doing now that Mike was in jail. I'd read in the *L.A. Record* that the prison had granted Mike the right to record a CD behind bars, but I'd heard nothing more about it for a couple of months.

Imagine my shock when I turned on the car radio to hear the DJ announcing a brand new song by Doktor Delgado's All-American Genocidal Warfare Against The Sick And The Stupid live from within the hallowed halls of some local prison. I turned up the volume to hear Mike say, "This is a song I wrote a few weeks ago. It's called 'Not Fit to Survive.' It's a song about . . . well, I don't know . . . just being alive, I guess. You know, it's kind of like about . . . well . . . aw, fuck it. Just listen." Feedback rolled out of the speakers like waves of pure anger, followed immediately by Mike's voice, a voice that came across as tortured and serious and yet sarcastic and playful at the same exact time.

> I'm not a Catholic priest with my cock up some boy's hole
> I'm not a Hollywood whore with my lips around a Senator's pole
> I'm not a cop with a baton and a burning cross
> I'm not a journalist with the Pentagon for a boss
> I'm not fit to survive
> Not fit to survive
> I'm not fit to survive
> Not fit to survive
> I'm not a President with a fat Swiss bank account
> I'm not a white serial killer with human heads to mount
> I'm not a Gulf War vet with a medal and a melting face
> I'm not a scientist trying to destroy the human race
> I'm not a school teacher with a ruler and a gun

I'm not a comedian with another idiotic pun
I'm not a CIA agent selling crack to teens
I'm not a writer with a bestseller on the screen
I'm not fit to survive
Not fit to survive
I'm not fit to survive
Not fit to survive
I'm not a psychiatrist shoving Prozac Pez down kids' throats
I'm not a politician rigging all your damn votes
I'm not a doctor handing out toxic pills
I'm not a pharmacist with a prescription to kill
I'm not a librarian who doesn't read books
I'm not a sedated wife who puts out and cooks
I'm not a rock star who can snort and sing
I'm not a coked-up pilot in a flying wing
I'm not fit to survive
Not fit to survive
I'm not fit to survive
Not fit to survive
I'm not a poet with a pretty little rhyme
I'm not a machine that can tell the exact time
I'm not a landlord who spits in your food
I'm not a colonel on Paxil and ludes
I'm not a terrorist planning a revolution
I'm not a biologist into human evolution
I'm not a televangelist with a tainted soul
I'm not a chemist into population control
I'm not fit to survive
Not fit to survive
I'm not fit to survive
Not fit to survive
I'm not fit to survive

Not fit to survive
I'm not fit to survive
Not fit to survive

As Mike's mind-warping guitar solo drew the song to a close I wondered if that line about "a comedian with an idiotic pun" was about me. If so I found it rather strange. After all, I was never a big fan of puns and I was no longer a comedian. Perhaps I wasn't fit to survive either then.

Perhaps.

I switched off the radio before the next song could begin. Right then a line from an old Lou Reed song floated up out of the recesses of my memory. How did it go exactly? Oh, yeah. "Some people are like human Tuinals."

I drove the rest of the way home without music. Sometimes silence is better.

CHAPTER 23

The Only Known Cure
for Premature Ejaculation

(May 30, 2015)

Heather and I were cuddled up in bed watching television. This was Saturday, our day off. The news happened to be on. We saw stories about the latest terrorist alert in Los Angeles, troop movements in Afghanistan, nuclear weapons in North Korea, the gang-related murders of innocent children in South Central, hate crimes inspired by religious demagogues in expensive suits. It all seemed rather familiar to me. One story stood out above the rest. It was a local story about an old naked man who had hobbled into a bank in North Hollywood in an attempt to rob it, armed only with a bamboo cane and a cigarette lighter. Believing the lighter to be a gun, the security guards shot him twice in the head. He died before he even hit the ground. Strangely, his entire body had been covered in a clear viscous liquid that remained unidentified.

The old man's name was not known.

CHAPTER 24

Page 69

(June 7, 2015)

A brief article in the *L.A. Weekly* reported that someone in Los Feliz had been sneaking into bookstores at night and tearing out page 69 of almost every book in stock.

CHAPTER 25

The End of the World

(July 1, 2015)

On the way to work I happened to see a homeless man standing on a street corner. He had a long gray beard and a tattered robe, giving him the appearance of a down and out Moses. In his dirt-caked hands was a large cardboard sign that read "The Apocalypse Is Nigh!" I just stood there staring at him for a second, wondering if the man would recognize The End when it really came.

That night, this is what I wrote in my journal:

Nothing seems funny to me anymore. It's hard for my old fans and colleagues to accept this. Many of them actually think I'm playing some kind of elaborate Andy Kaufman trick on them, that I'm still performing comedy in disguise, planning a future comeback that will somehow propel me into fame and fortune. The harder I try to convince them this isn't true the more they believe it. As you might imag-ine, this can grow rather annoying. After hours of contem-plation I've decided there's only one solution to this prob-lem: stop talking to my old fans and colleagues. Of course, this might fuel the myth even more but I don't care. I don't need their attention. If they want to accept me for what I've become, fine. If not, they can just leave me alone. As a very wise man once said, "There's more important things in life than trying to impress people, on or off a stage."

I haven't laughed in a very long time. Occasionally I feel as if I should regret this, though I'm not sure why. Most of the time . . . most of the time I don't think I would have it any other way.

Looking back on it, the Apocalypse might've been the best thing that ever happened to me.

To all of us.

CHAPTER 26

A Clown at Midnight

(August 23, 2015)

My scrapbook continued to grow. In Pasadena, CA someone had been dressing up like a clown—a colorful, happy happy Bozo-type clown, not like Ogo at all—and peeping into people's bedroom windows at midnight, then running away in a pair of floppy crimson shoes. The culprit was still at large.

What kind of disturbed mind would dream up such an unnerving prank?

This question bothered me for months.

CHAPTER 27

A Peaceful Day

(December 26, 2015)

It was the day after Christmas, around four in the afternoon. I'd just heard the news about Karen. Marsha called and told me. I didn't know what to do, didn't know what to say. Heather hugged me and started crying, real heaving sobs. Jesus, she'd hated Karen more than anyone else. Nonetheless, she was another piece of our past now dead. A suicide. Apparently the jokes wouldn't come anymore. She was left alone with her own reflection, and probably didn't like what she saw.

I had to be alone. I just had to be. It wasn't that I didn't want to be with Heather at that moment, it was just . . . I really don't know how to explain it.

I decided to take a walk, to clear my head. The air was crisp and fresh, unusual for Los Angeles. Winds from the ocean had blown the smog farther north, removing the grayish curtain that obscured the distant mountain peaks for most of the year. There were few cars on the road. Everything was quiet. One of those rare, peaceful moments. The only other person on the sidewalk was a little boy crouched behind a nicely clipped hedge, playing with a brand new toy rifle. With one eye closed he was aiming it at invisible enemies, yelling "Pow! Pow!" Probably got it for Christmas, I thought. I glanced to my left to stare at an elaborate Christmas display someone had constructed on their lawn out of scrap wood and metal: a stylized sculpture of Santa Claus riding the back of a dolphin. I recalled walking by here the previous year, thinking, Only in California. At the time the decoration had struck me as . . . odd. Noteworthy somehow. Why?

I faced forward once again. I was almost upon the boy. He was only a few feet away now, staring down the barrel of the toy rifle while his finger idly caressed the trigger. I wondered if the thing shot bee-bees. He might poke his eye out if he wasn't careful. Then there was an explosion. A fountain of wet redness sprayed out of the back of his head, which shattered into shapeless fragments. The rest of the body crumpled onto the sidewalk. The rifle dropped onto the manicured lawn with barely a sound.

I stood there staring at the madness for what must have been only a few seconds. No one came out of the surrounding houses. The neighborhood was still very quiet. The boy and I were alone. I kept walking, skirting a wide arc around the body. I shoved my hands deep into my jacket pockets and kept my eyes locked on the ground.

When I got home I crawled into bed with Heather. Tears still stained her eyes. I snuggled against her back. I gripped her tightly around the waist. She wanted to talk about the virus. I insisted on changing the subject. In the distance, I could hear sirens.

"I wonder what happened," Heather said.

"I don't know," I said, almost believing my own deception. "Maybe some kind of an accident. I hope nobody's gotten hurt.

"It's hard to imagine," I said after a few moments of silence, "anything going wrong on a peaceful day like this."

I never told her what had happened. Never told her what I had witnessed.

CHAPTER 28

Radiation

(January 7, 2016)

Someone wearing a faux radiation suit slowly walked the perimeter of a Mobil Oil Refinery one morning with a Geiger counter in hand, causing panic to spread throughout a four-mile radius of the refinery. Neither the impostor nor the radiation suit were ever found.

CHAPTER 29

Insect Eyes

(January 18, 2016)

I was walking down the street on my way home from work late one night when I saw someone spray painting the outside of a Coffee Bean & Tea Leaf.

I think I saw the mural before I saw the person spray painting the mural. Your eyes could do nothing but linger on that expertly rendered image. Though half-finished, it was impressive. It depicted a cockroach with the head of Uncle Sam crucified to a cross that had been planted into a dirt mound. Safety pins held his tiny wiggling legs in place. Next to the mound was an unfinished black sneaker, oversized, perhaps added to indicate how small the insect really was. In the circle on the side of the sneaker, where the company logo would normally go, was a sloppy black anarchist symbol.

I overcame my initial surprise pretty quickly and managed to shout, "Hey, listen, you can't just deface pri—!"

The painter spun around. It was some young girl, maybe sixteen, dressed in a wine-colored corduroy jacket, a black tank top, torn blue jeans, black sneakers with the laces flapping loose. Her face went white, but not as white as the fresh spray paint making up the rim of the giant sneaker; it looked like *her* sneaker. Her skin was naturally dark. She could've been Arabic, though I wasn't certain. Details. I needed to remember details. She tore off down the street at a fast clip. The clattering sound of a metal spray can hitting the cement echoed between the buildings.

"Hey, wait!" I said, but she just kept running. She disappeared around a corner within seconds.

"Hey," I said to the darkness and the silence, "somebody needs to clean up this mess . . . right?"

I walked over to the fallen spray can. For a moment I had an urge to pick it up, grip the curved metal in the palm of my hand. . . .

I thought better of it. No. No, better let it lie there, Elliot. The police may need to dust it for fingerprints. This is official evidence.

Then I realized I didn't even know the girl's name. How much help could I be? Not much.

Nonetheless, I jogged over to a pay phone across the street (perhaps the last pay phone left in the city), plunked in a few dimes, and asked the police to come right away.

"It's horrible," I said, "what some people will do to other people's property. You know how long it takes to open up a business like this? These bums who aren't willing to work for a living, why don't they just keep to themselves instead of ruining everybody else's lives?"

I glanced over my shoulder at the cockroach. So finely detailed. Such craftsmanship. Why couldn't a talented person like that find a real job somewhere?

"Why do *you* think?" said the gravelly voice on the other line. An older woman with a smoker's cough. "'cause they're sick in the head. There're as bad as terrorists."

"Sick?" I said. "Yeah, that's it. I think you're right. They're ill. *Mentally* ill."

"No use worrying about it," the woman said. "There's nothing you can do . . . except give me your exact location."

I gave it to her slow, so she wouldn't miss a syllable. I was so happy, so pleased to be of service. All the while I couldn't stop looking at that cockroach. It seemed to be staring right through me.

I was glad the thing would be gone soon, so I wouldn't have to see its eyes anymore on the way to work or coming back home.

Those tiny insect eyes. . . .

CHAPTER 30

Kill Your Kids

(January 24, 2016)

In the middle of the night someone began putting stickers on the pristine bumpers of very expensive cars in very expensive neighborhoods. These were highly adhesive stickers imprinted with enigmatic slogans such as, "No U.S. President Should Ever Have AIDS," "I Never Touched Her," "Help Stop Youth Violence—Kill Your Kids," and "I Support War, Just Not *This* War."

CHAPTER 31

The Day after the President's Speech

(January 27, 2016)

The day after the President's speech—I remember the speech annoyed me because it cut into my favorite show—I was at work unpacking a shipment of a popular new E.L. James novel about bondage when one of my co-workers said, "Hey, did you catch that clown on the news last night?" He was a lanky teenager with severe acne distorting his pale skin into a craggy landscape of bright red scars. His name was Bill.

"Yeah," I said. "I used to imitate him. In my act. Everybody loved it. All my fans."

"*Fans*?" Bill released a nervous little laugh. "Of what? Your advanced stock boy skills?"

I laughed too, mimicking his actions. Of course, I thought, how could he know? I had never told him about my previous life. "No," I said, "I was just jokin' with you."

Bill nodded, not smiling anymore. "That clown has some good ideas, you know. I think I could get behind some of what he was saying, except I've heard he's secretly soft on them Muslims. He takes credit for bumping off Bin Laden, but that's ridiculous. He'd never go out of his way to jack up a Muslim. Know why? 'cause he *is* one." He laughed again, much louder than necessary. "I mean, listen, how're we gonna know if these fuckheads in Iran want to kill us unless we torture 'em and find out, y'know?" He went back to stocking the E.L. James book. A novel about sadomasochism. Part of a series.

"Some of his ideas were good," I said. "Some of them weren't. I heard a guy on the radio say he's crazy."

"Aw, he's not crazy. He's just way too politically correct is all. What we need is to get someone in the White House who could have a sense of humor about these things."

"Yeah," I said.

CHAPTER 32

Heart

(February 18, 2016)

Someone parked a pickup truck on the sidewalk in front of L.A. International Airport that contained a gigantic papier-mâché representation of a heart. Not a Valentine's Day heart. A real one, aorta and all. Hung around the heart on a thin chain was a large, sloppily painted sign that read "Ceci n'est pas une bombe."

CHAPTER 33

Dr. Mary's Monkey

(July 4, 2016)

I was standing behind the information desk, on a slow shift, wishing someone would ask for help just so that I could have something to do, when I spotted a young couple arguing quietly in the political science section. They seemed frustrated, like people who've been looking for a particular book for a while and can't find it. The young girl was pointing toward me, but the boyfriend seemed reluctant. I tried to ignore the argument, but couldn't. They fascinated me.

They were dressed strangely. The girl wore a green bomber jacket with orange lining on the inside. One side of her head, just above the left ear, was shaved. That spot was now taken up by what looked like a tattoo of a Maurice Sendak illustration. The rest of her hair was a raven-deep black. She had silver piercings in her eyebrows, lips, cheeks, and nostrils. She wore a green and black plaid mini-skirt, torn fishnet stockings, and combat boots imprinted with details from what might have been a Hieronymus Bosch painting. The boyfriend wore a black bomber jacket with military patches sewn haphazardly all over them. Unlike her, his entire head was shaved. He had piercings, too, even more than she did, and colorful tattoos that covered his massive arms. I couldn't make out what they were exactly . . . just abstract shapes, perhaps.

She was so much smaller than him, but she seemed to have a savage temper that made up for this discrepancy. The boyfriend finally gave in, and they approached my desk, holding hands.

As they drew nearer, I realized the boyfriend was much older than I had expected. He was at least twenty years older than her, maybe even more. The girl had to be in her late teens. Certainly no older than twenty.

When she spoke, when she was close enough for me to study the hazel specks in her eyes, I realized I had seen her before.

The tagger outside the Coffee Bean & Tea Leaf.

Sweat beads began to trickle down my forehead. I now had her within reach. Should I call security? Even if I did, would they arrive in time to make the difference?

The girl said, "We're looking for a couple of books."

"Which two?" I said. Just remain prim and business-like, I told myself. Don't let on that you know their true identities.

"Two?" she said.

"Yes. The titles. Of the two books."

The boyfriend was staring down at the floor. He wanted to be elsewhere, no doubt about that.

"Well," she said, "I guess I meant more than a couple. One book is called *The Turner Diaries*."

The Turner Diaries. I had read an article about that book in the *L.A. Times* many years before. It was a flagged book. Timothy

McVeigh had used it as a blueprint to destroy the Murrah Federal Building in Oklahoma City. If you tried to check that book out of a library, the librarian had to turn your name in to the FBI. I knew that for a fact.

I'd seen it in a movie.

I punched in the title on the keyboard in front of me. I was relieved to see we didn't have it.

"Sorry," I said, "we don't have that one."

"I *told* you," the boyfriend said, under his breath.

The girl nudged him in the ribs with her elbow. "Shh," she said.

"The second title?" I said.

"*The Anarchist Cookbook*," she said.

Now I knew they were criminals. *The Anarchist Cookbook* was on the American Library Association's Top 100 Challenged Books. It taught you how to make bombs and LSD at home and even worse things. What were these people up to?

I punched in the title. "We used to have this title in stock," I said, "but not anymore. Would you like me to order it?"

"No," the boyfriend said quickly. "That's okay."

The girl sighed in frustration—at him, I think, not me. "The third title," she said, "is *The Big Brother Game*." That title seemed vaguely familiar. I remembered seeing it in the stacks, but I couldn't remember where.

"There's a revised edition out," I said, reading the information off the screen. "It says we have a copy in the store."

"We *know* that," the boyfriend said. "We looked it up on the computer, but when we went to the section it was supposed to be in, it wasn't there."

"Political science," the girl said, pointing at the shelf where I had first seen them arguing.

"Let's go take a look," I said, leading them back over to that section. I tried not to think about the fact that I was standing within the proximity of suspected terrorists, no doubt wanted by the anti-terrorist division of the FBI. I tried to focus. Do your job, Elliot, I urged myself, just do your job and everything will be fine.

I scanned every single title in that section, but couldn't see it. "Perhaps it's been misshelved," I said.

The boyfriend said, "Let's just *go*."

Then it hit me. Of course. I had shelved the book myself, just a couple of weeks ago. The cover was white and showed an eye peering through a keyhole. It was a guide to protecting yourself from electronic surveillance and other forms of government scrutiny. When I saw it, I assumed it belonged in the conspiracy section, which was lumped in with the paranormal books: all the UFO nonsense and the memoirs of demonic possession and reincarnation and ghostly visitations.

"I remember where it is now," I said. "Come over here."

What're you doing? I thought. You're leading them right to the tools they'll use to destroy innocents.

And yet I couldn't help myself. I had a very strong work ethic. I had to do my job.

I guided them right to the book. I pointed at it. "Is that what you're looking for?"

The girl pulled it out of the shelf. It was stuck between a book called *The 80 Greatest Conspiracies of All Time* and another one called *Dr. Mary's Monkey* which (according to the cover) somehow connected the creation of the AIDS virus to the assassination of JFK.

"Hey, that's it," the girl said, all smiles, "thanks a lot, man."

"Thank you," I said, genuinely happy that I had managed to please her.

"Let me *see* that," the boyfriend said, yanking it out of her hand. He flipped through the pages. "Yeah . . . yeah, this should do okay. How come it's stuck in here with all these weird books?" He gestured toward a recent book about Atlantis, and another one about pet spirit guides.

"I shelved it wrong," I said. "From the cover, I thought it belonged in the conspiracy section, which we keep right next to the paranormal section. Both genres seem to attract the same audience. According to the computer, though, it's supposed to be in political science. Sorry about that."

"It's okay," he said, "forget it." He grabbed the girl's elbow and began to walk away.

"No," I said, "it's not okay. It's my fault. I should've done my job more efficiently than that. I sincerely apologize. Allow me to ring you up, and I'll give you a ten percent discount for your troubles."

"That's nice," the girl said, "but you don't have to do that."

"No, it's okay," the boyfriend said. "That sounds good to me. Lead the way." He laughed.

I led them over to the cash register. As I said, it was a pretty slow shift, so there were only two registers being used. I walked over to a third register and began ringing them up. I hoped they would use a credit card. Then I would have the information I needed to bring them to justice.

"This would normally be $22.95," I said, "but you can just give me $20.65."

The boyfriend was looking the other way, at some anorexic Goth chick passing through the horror section, when the girl pulled a man's wallet out of her purse. She laid the black leather wallet (decorated with a skeleton wearing a sombrero) on the counter, then pulled out a gold credit card from a small flap inside. I took it from her and read the information on the card.

I wanted to memorize it right then and there, just in case. Her name, it said, was Gretchen Malone.

"May I see some I.D.?" I said.

The boyfriend's head snapped back toward me at that moment.

"Oh, hey, listen, that's okay, man," he said, "we'll pay cash. I'll take care of it. Don't worry about it."

I said nothing. I just nodded and gave the card back to Gretchen. More suspicious behavior. I was checking these behaviors off on a list unscrolling rapidly in my mind. I had to remember *everything*. The FBI would need it for their investigation.

"Uh . . . hey," the boyfriend said to Gretchen, "you got some extra cash? All I've got's a ten and. . . ."

Gretchen sighed and rolled her eyes. She dug out a couple of crumpled bills from deep inside her jacket pockets and handed them to me. I gave Gretchen a plastic bag and wished them both a nice evening.

"Thank you," Gretchen said. The boyfriend said nothing.

They left the store.

That's when I noticed her skeleton-wallet was still sitting on the counter.

I didn't turn it in to lost and found. I kept it. During my break, I went into the back room and sat at a Formica table covered with sticky spots of Coca-Cola. When I knew no one was watching, I riffled through the wallet. I found photos of friends, dressed just as strangely as her and her boyfriend. Also, I discovered tiny photos of murals spray painted on private property in the dead of night—all of them anti-American propaganda.

It scared me. It scared me that such a talented person could piss away all her creativity on such negative nonsense. What must have happened to her in her childhood to make her this way? Had she been sexually abused?

Suddenly, I felt sorry for her. I didn't want to turn her into the authorities, not if I didn't have to. That would be a last resort.

The second my shift was over, around eight, I grabbed my jacket from the back room and started walking toward the address printed on her I.D. I knew that street. I wasn't far. Only about twelve blocks away. Besides, it was a nice night for a stroll.

It was a relatively upscale area just off Melrose. Not chichi, but nowhere near being poor either. It didn't surprise me that a girl like that would live in such a neighborhood. I remember commenting once, on stage, that I had never seen an anarchy symbol spray painted in the ghetto—only in the suburbs. "Poor people don't give a shit about anarchy," I said. "They'd just be happy if we tried democracy for a change. Oh . . . hey, now there's a crazy concept. Don't spread it around. These days we might get arrested for even joking about it." That had been at Prospero's, not so long ago. I couldn't comprehend a mind that could think that way, and yet I could remember it. All of it. The words. The delivery. The intonation. It seemed like another life-time, like watching myself in someone else's movie.

I approached the house. A duplex. From the upper window I could hear loud music blaring. The Ramones? *"There's no law, no law anymore/I want to steal from the rich and give to the poor/Winter turns to summer/Sadness turns to fun/Keep the faith, baby/You broke the rules and won/Sha-la-la-la/Sha-la-la-la-la-la/Sha-la-la-la/Sha-la-la-la. . . ."*

The door was white, and had a decorative stained glass window in the middle. It was cracked, as if somebody had thrown something hard at it. I knocked on the door. A tired-looking woman in her mid-forties answered the door. She had dark rings under her bloodshot eyes, too much flesh on her gut. She was wearing a rumpled nightgown with cigarette holes in it. She stared at me, puzzled.

"Who're you?" she said.

"Is Gretchen here?" I said.

"*I'm* Gretchen."

I was thrown off balance for a second. But just for a second. It kind of made sense.

I held out my hand. "Hi. Is your daughter home?"

She ignored the hand. "I thought so," she said. "Jesus, another one. How many of you are there?"

"I'm sorry?" I said.

She closed the door in my face. I didn't know what to do. I stepped away from the porch, thinking I should just leave. Then I heard the sound of The Ramones shutting off abruptly.

A few seconds later the door opened again. It was her, dressed exactly as before.

"Hi again," I said. She stared at me, confused. "Uh . . . I just came by to give you this." I held out the wallet.

She looked at the wallet, then back at me. "Oh, you're the dude from the bookstore! I was wondering what happened to that. I didn't even notice it was gone until a few minutes ago." She came down off the porch and took the wallet from me. "This is kinda special. My first boyfriend gave it to me years ago, back in the eighth grade. He didn't know it was a man's wallet. He didn't know much of anything. He was kinda sweet, though."

She paused for a moment. "Hey . . . how'd you know where I live?" she asked.

"From your driver's license," I said. "I mean . . . your mother's name on the credit card."

Her eyes narrowed. "Okaaaay. Well, that's kinda creepy."

"Just trying to do a good deed."

"Jesus, that's even creepier. I guess you're a real Boy Scout, aren't you?"

"Um . . . no," I said. "I've never been in the Boy Scouts at all."

She paused for a moment. "Riiiight," she said. "Well . . . thanks for the assist." She started to back away.

"Hey, wait a second . . . can I ask you something?"

She just stopped and stared at me, waiting.

"Why do you *do* it?" I said.

"Do what?"

"Spray paint those . . . *murals* . . . all around town."

She glanced down at the wallet, as if remembering the photos. Then she smiled. "What, you a fan?"

"You're extremely talented."

"I know."

"Why do you waste it?"

A wave of anger flashed across her face. "What the fuck're you talkin' about?"

"Why don't you use your talent to paint positive images?"

She laughed. "Because I paint what I *see*. There's not a lot of positive things going on in the world, in case you hadn't noticed."

"I see a lot of positive things. Every day. The world's filled with a whole lot of nice people, selfless people."

"Who? You mean *you*?"

I shrugged. "Well, I'd like to think so. . . ."

"A lot of people would like to think so. And it's usually the bastards, rapists, and serial killers who think they're the most 'selfless.' Which category do you fall into?"

"None of them. Honestly. Listen, I'm just saying. . . ."

"Where the fuck do you get off commenting on my art? What're you, some fuckin' critic? You write for *Juxtapoz*? *ART-news*?"

How could I make her understand? "No, no. I'm not a journalist." I was growing more and more frustrated. "Try to see it from another perspective. Don't you know you're defacing private property?"

She laughed. "Are you for *real*? I'm sorry, man, I don't believe in private property."

"Belief has nothing to do with it. How would you like it if someone destroyed something that was precious to you? What if they spray painted *your* house?"

She shrugged. "I'd probably help 'em out."

"Okay, well . . . what if they spray painted over one of your *murals* then?"

"That's what it's there for. To be destroyed. That's what everything's here for, as far as I'm concerned. You'll find that out if you stick around any longer. Till November, let's say. That's gonna be a good month for everybody."

"I'm just asking you to *think* a little bit about what you're doing."

"Believe me, I've thought about it a lot. Too much. I already decided I need to leave all that stuff behind me. It's too childish. I realize that now . . . really."

I smiled. "That's encouraging." Maybe there was some hope for this girl.

"Sure is . . . now it's time to get serious. My murals don't seem to be doing the trick. People like you need to be shocked out of their comas."

"Comas?"

"You don't even know, do you? You've got the disease big time, with a capital 'B.' I can tell. All the usual symptoms are there. A complete inability to comprehend sarcasm's at the top of the list. And it's a long one, believe me. A real long one. I've been compiling it for months."

I furrowed my brow and just stared at her. "Disease? I don't have any dis . . . diseases. . . ." I could feel myself sweating again.

"Denial. That's another symptom." She started backing away, slowly. "I might burn the wallet. Who knows how it's spread? I don't believe anything the CDC says."

"It's not a disease," I said. "That's the wrong way of looking at it. It's just a. . . ."

"God, I hope I never become like you," she said. Her face had drained of color. "I bet you used to have it, didn't you? Before the disease took it away? The ones with the most to lose seem to get hit the worst for some damn reason. Maybe it's God's sense of humor. Or lack of it?" She chuckled. "Wouldn't it be funny if he had it too? Hell, maybe he's *always* had it. That would explain so damn much."

"I haven't . . . *lost* anything. I've gained *so* much. We all have. My girlfriend and I, we. . . ."

"What you need is a condensed intravenous dose of Situationist Theory. Right through the top of the noggin."

"Situ . . . situationist . . . ?"

"Guy Debord. Look him up, asshole."

"I'm sorry, I don't know what you're talking about."

"Keep the faith, baby. A cure's comin' down the pike. And if not. . . ." She shrugged. "Well, we might just have to shit-can the whole kit-'n-kaboodle and start all over again. Let the cockroaches take a shot at it. Hell, maybe they'll do better. At least they haven't lost their sense of humor. I'll probably see you around, mister. Don't eat any wooden snakes. Oh, and wipe my address from your memory banks, or I'm gonna have my boyfriend—all twelve of 'em—wait outside that lame ass, corporate-controlled, caffeine-peddling, hippie-infested hellpit of a bookstore of yours and beat the living crap out of you and your girlfriend on your way to the parking lot. You got that, four eyes? Oh, and thanks for the discount." She slammed the door behind her.

I stood on the sidewalk for a moment, just staring at the crack in the window, until I heard The Ramones blaring once more into the night. I took two steps toward the porch, to make one last effort to force the girl to see reason.

Then the door opened, and I saw the mother peering out at me with a cell phone in her hand. I turned my back on her, and started walking away at a fast pace.

Everything the girl said swirled around in my brain. November, she had said. Wait until November. What was going to happen in November? What was so special that. . . .

The election. The Presidential election.

My God, what were they going to do, her and her boyfriends?

The Turner Diaries. *The Anarchist Cookbook*. *The Big Brother Game*.

It was all so clear. I had stumbled upon a vast conspiracy of disastrous proportions. The failure to report such a plot would be the same as being in league with the terrorists.

Who would I call first?

I reached into my inside jacket pocket and pulled out the cell phone Heather had recently bought me. She was concerned about the health effects of the phone, so insisted I only use it during emergencies.

This was definitely an emergency.

I dialed 411, and asked the operator for the number to the local FBI office. They needed to send someone over to her house and interrogate her right away, I thought. Even a simple visit might scare her and her co-conspirators away from this horrible scheme. . . .

The operator gave me the number and offered to connect me for an extra charge. I said yes.

When at last the woman at the FBI headquarters identified herself, when I opened my mouth to speak . . . nothing came out. She said, "Hello? Hello?" I hung up.

I suddenly felt dizzy.

I was back in the void, right there on the stage in Holy City Asylum, the set-up for a joke teetering precariously on the tip of my tongue. So close . . . and yet so far away. . . .

Why?

I grew angry all of a sudden. I yelled at the sky, nothing but unintelligible screams, then tossed the cell phone in a trash can and started walking away. Toward nowhere.

I hated myself and didn't know why. Something the girl had said still echoed in my memory.

I bet you used to have it, didn't you? Before the disease took it away? The ones with the most to lose seem to get hit the worst for some damn reason.

What was it? What was it that I used to have? What was *it*?

I shoved my hands deep into my jacket pockets, stared at the trash littering the sidewalk, and never looked up once, not even as the first fireworks of the evening began to shoot off into the cloudless night sky.

CHAPTER 34

Life Begins

(August 28, 2016)

Someone hacked into an anti-abortion group's website and sent out emails to thousands of people that read, "Life Begins At Laughter." Few of the anti-abortion crowd thought this was funny. In fact, they were very angry and immediately sent out follow-up emails explaining exactly *why* they didn't think it was funny in language as stern and volatile as the fire and brimstone I used to read about as a child.

CHAPTER 35

Bang

(September 4, 2016)

The Secretary of Defense died today.

I saw it happen. Right there on live television in the middle of the Democratic Convention.

Bang. Bang. Bang.

And that was all.

I saw the man who did it. They showed his photograph on the news. I recognized him. He was Miss Malone's boyfriend.

Shaved head. Tattoos. Military patches.

It was him, no doubt about it.

They shot the skinhead down the moment the third bullet entered the Secretary's head. The assassin is dead now.

Fox News has reported minute details about his background (they've been doing it all day, in fact), but they haven't mentioned Miss Malone at all.

Heather and I were watching the news coverage of the Convention when it happened. *Bang. Bang. Bang.*

Neither of us could believe it. It was so sudden.

During a commercial break I finally told her about my encounter with the man in the bookstore. I mentioned Miss Malone, but only briefly. I said nothing about following the girl to her home.

"Do you think I should call somebody?" I said. "What if this girl's involved somehow?"

She hugged me tightly, there on our new sofa. She thought about it for a moment.

"I would say yes," she said after a while, "if it was something serious."

"But . . . the Secretary of Defense is dead."

Heather looked up at me, confused.

"So? There'll be another one. Isn't there always another one?"

"I guess I hadn't thought about it that way."

"Why bother thinking about it at all? Just sit here with me. Hold me, and be still."

CHAPTER 36

Spiral Jetty

(September 22, 2016)

Someone, late at night, recreated Robert Smithson's Spiral Jetty out of Top Ramen in the middle of Dodger Stadium.

CHAPTER 37

Why Did the Chicken Cross the Road?

(October 2, 2016)

Heather said something strange the other day, just as I was leaving for work.

She said, "Why did the chicken cross the road?"

I said, "I don't know."

Her brow wrinkled. She began snapping her fingers in the air. "God, almost had it."

"Had what?"

She sighed. Her shoulders slumped. "I don't know, but it seemed real important a moment ago."

"Well, maybe it'll come back to you later on, hon." I slipped on my coat, kissed her on the cheek, then went outside to deal with the world. Just as I did every day.

But for some reason, unlike the countless days that had preceded it, my mind was now wracked with frustration. Heather's question went round and round and round in my head. Why *had* the chicken crossed the road? Whose chicken was it? What was it doing by the side of the road?

Why did I care?

CHAPTER 38

Blue Kool-Aid

(October 2, 2016)

Someone filled the L.A. River with blue Kool-Aid.

CHAPTER 39

Scrapbook

(October 3, 2016)

From time to time I would think about Miss Malone. She made herself known to me not through her presence but through her absence, like the ripples that appear in the ocean in the wake of a submarine sailing just beneath the surface. Strange stories continued to crop up in the local newspaper, and now I knew their source. I continued to cut them out, behind Heather's back, and secretly taped them into my scrapbook (along with photographs I would take from time to time of the various murals I'd spot around town, the ones I suspected of being Miss Malone's handiwork). Of course, not one of the newspapers ever indicated that these stories were connected in any way. Perhaps they weren't.

CHAPTER 40

A Ten-foot-high Teddy Bear

(October 7, 2016)

Mr. Little, the manager, tore into me again near the beginning of my shift. He said I'd been slacking off more and more lately. He said my head had been in the clouds for the past couple of days. He said this in front of the whole store. Out of the corner of my eye I could see Bill snickering into his collar. Mr. Little asked me if I wanted to lose my job.

"No," I said.

"Can you *afford* to lose your job?"

"No," I said. I tried to be calm. I knew Mr. Little had some self-esteem problems. I tried to take that into account. He was 5'3" and his name was Mr. Little. I felt sad for him. It must've been a strange sight for the customers: this bald little man in a suit and tie pointing his finger up at me as I towered over him nodding docilely.

"Do you have more important things to think about than your duties here?" he said.

"No," I said.

"Well, you're certainly thinking about *something,* and I know it's not your job. Maybe you'd like to share it with the rest of us, hm? I'm sure we'd all like to hear the existential quandaries you're contemplating on company time, Greeley."

"Okay," I said.

Mr. Little planted his hands on his hips, gestured for me to proceed.

"Why did the chicken cross the road?" I said.

Everybody in the store burst out laughing. Mr. Little quickly turned bright red. I could see him shrinking into himself. He began to bluster, then at last managed to choke out the words: "Get back to work, Greeley, and do your job from now on!"

I nodded. I was confused.

Why was everybody laughing?

Later I was in the stockroom unpacking a shipment of the new E.L. James novel (not the same one as before, a new one, also about bondage) when Bill came up behind me and slapped me on the back.

"Hey, that was great how you embarrassed The Midget like that. I didn't know you were so good with a comeback." He snapped his fingers three times in row.

I smiled. "Oh, thank you." I wasn't sure what he was talking about.

"Man, I wouldn't have the balls to say something like that. I can't risk losing this job. I'm saving up money for college. You think I want to stay here all my life? I want to open a business someday, maybe a bookstore of my own. Then I'll have my *own* employees to push around. Yeah."

At that moment Little stuck his head into the room and said, "Greeley! I'd like to see you in my office. Now."

Bill almost jumped out of his pants. When Little had disappeared Bill patted me on the shoulder. "Good luck," he said and continued unpacking the E.L. James novels for me.

I entered Little's office. He was sitting behind his desk with his hands folded in front of him. I noticed he had a lot of hangnails. His fingernails were bitten to the quick. He told me to close the door. I did so.

He just stared at me for a few seconds, then said, "Do you think you're funny?"

I shook my head. "No."

"Do you think you're funny?"

I stared at him silently. I had already answered the question.

"Well, maybe you'll think this is funny." He picked up a black felt-tip marker and scrawled two words on a blank sheet of typing paper. He held up the sheet of paper for me to read, his pinkies sticking out primly.

"What does that say?" he said.

"'You're fired,'" I read.

"Do you think that's funny?"

"No."

"It doesn't feel good to be made fun of, does it?"

I shrugged. "I wouldn't know."

His face began to redden again. "*Aren't you going to get angry?*"

"Why?"

"Because I'm firing you!"

"Well, what can I do about it?"

"Nothing! That's exactly the point, isn't it?"

"The point of what?"

He crumpled the paper into a ball and tossed it toward the trashcan. It missed and landed on the floor. He shot up from his chair and said, "Get out of here! *Now!*"

I nodded.

I left.

I had about two hours to kill before I went home, so I just wandered around for a while, sometimes stopping to peer through the store windows and look at all the pretty things I couldn't buy.

I've got a few hundred dollars in the bank, I told myself as I stared at a giant teddy bear in a toy store. It was ten feet high. Why would anyone want a ten-foot-high teddy bear? I thought, then realized I was getting off-track. Focus, focus. The money I've got in the bank will last me a few weeks at least. By then you'll have found a new job. Heather doesn't have to know. Why worry her? She worries too much already. God, it used to be so much easier just walking onto a stage and talking. A ten-foot-high teddy bear. What the fuck?

I wandered around in a daze for the next hour or so, then caught a bus for home. I wandered around the block twice before I entered the apartment building.

"Just in time for the debates," Heather said as I came in the door. She was sitting on the sofa, hugging a throw pillow to her chest. "Too bad you had to work late last night. You missed the next President mopping up the floor with that idiot. Who's Audrey?"

"Audrey? What're you talking about?"

"Some girl called. Said she met you at a club. She was going through these phone numbers she'd written on the backs of old receipts and wondered what you were up to now. That's what she said. Oh, yes, and she said she thought you were *hilarious*."

I remembered the girl. I'd met her at Prospero's several years earlier, right after one of my best performances. My fellow comedians assured me my monologue had been a masterpiece, divinely inspired stream-of-consciousness. Audrey had been a sexy teenage groupie flashing doe-eyes at me all during my set. She'd had a mean-looking, monstrous golem of a boyfriend, but he hadn't been paying much attention to her that evening. With just a little sweet talk I probably could've convinced her to come back home with me. As with Esthra, however, I barely even tried. Why? Who knows? I recalled getting her phone number, but I'd lost it long ago. Around the time that every-thing changed.

"What . . . what did you tell her?" I said.

"I said you were at work. Then she asked me who I was, and I told her. I told her to fuck off, that's what I told her."

"Oh, Heather. There was no need to do that."

"Did you *fuck* this girl?"

"No . . . I-I think I know who she is. She came up to me after one of my gigs." Sweat began to pour down my cheeks. My head hurt. I felt a migraine coming on. "I don't even remember giving her my phone number. I must have, though. I mean, she probably *asked* for it."

"I'm sure she did."

"I can't imagine being brave enough to just give it to her."

"Did you kiss her?"

"No."

"Did she kiss you?"

"We never kissed each other."

"Well, what *did* you do? It must've been something special. Why call you after all this time? Everyone knows you're not . . . *hilarious* anymore." Sweat was pouring down Heather's brow too. "Neither am I. Neither is Danny. Neither is. . . ."

"We didn't do anything. We hugged each other."

"What? She let you hug her, but she didn't let you *kiss* her? C'mon."

"I wasn't trying to kiss her."

"But would you have, if she'd let you?"

I sat down beside her and closed my eyes. I knew she was just being playful, in her own way, but I wasn't in the mood.

CHAPTER 41

Fetus

(October 8, 2016)

Someone left a giant ceramic red fetus on the roof of an abortion clinic in San Francisco with a sloppily printed note hanging around its neck that read: "A major university has just released the results of a five-year-long scientific study; the scientists involved have come to the conclusion that the deterioration of the ozone is due not to the burning of fossil fuels, but to the methane in cow farts." It was as if Miss Malone were plugged into my mind . . . but not my mind *now*. My mind *then*.

CHAPTER 42

Memories of the Future

(October 8, 2016)

Hearing Heather utter Audrey's name made me feel so odd; it's hard to describe in words. I felt sad. As if someone had died. That single name, those six letters, made me feel nostalgic for something I had never experienced before. Memories of a past I could barely remember. Memories of a future I would never experience. . . .

The next morning I awoke when I normally did, just so Heather wouldn't be suspicious. But instead of going to the bookstore, I hopped on a bus and visited one of my old stomping grounds: Prospero's in West Hollywood. I always remembered liking Prospero's better than any other club. Why?

C'mon, think, I told myself, *just think about it . . . because . . . because?*

You could do what you wanted there. You just didn't have to tell the same jokes about . . . about . . . ?

Airplane food? Parking meters? The weather? Traffic school?

Yes . . . I remembered always hating material like that. I was into something else . . . something more . . . but what? I couldn't remember exactly. Just . . . something *more*. Whatever that was, Prospero's would let me and Heather do it.

What *was* it?

I was afraid to enter the club. I just stood in the alley staring at the back entrance where me and the other performers used to enter. I remembered talking about my only suicide attempt on stage. I closed my eyes and concentrated, trying to resurrect the feeling of standing there on the stage with a crowd of people listening intently to my every word, trying to recall what the hell it was I found so amusing about a failed suicide attempt.

Like most things in my life, it didn't work. I resurrected nothing. I felt such an overwhelming sensation of loss and yet . . . and yet I didn't know why. Do you ever feel as if something has been stolen from you, something unquantifiable, something you never even knew you had in the first place?

God, I felt so dejected, so lost.

I was just about to leave when the back door opened and a familiar figure came walking out with a Hefty trash bag in his hand. It was Ivan. He looked the same: long gray hair pulled back into a pony tail, bushy moustache, beard, unkempt sideburns, paisley shirt . . . as if he'd stepped out of a PBS documentary about that place in San Francisco . . . what's it called?

He just stopped and stared at me for a second. "Elliot?" he said. He looked as if he'd seen a ghost. I guess that ghost was called Elliot Greeley.

I stared down at the concrete like a guilty man. I felt embarrassed for even being there.

Ivan dropped the trash bag on the ground and said, "God damn, it's been such a long time!" He placed his hand on my shoulder and guided me toward the back door. "C'mon in! I hope you're lookin' for a job. I could put you on stage tonight if you'd like—you and Heather. The people I've got working for me these days are all second-raters. The last time they had a dangerous thought was the first time. It'll be nice to have someone who actually has some fresh ideas—"

I pulled away from him. I wanted to remain in the alley. "No," I said. "I'm not looking for a job."

"Oh?" Ivan slipped his hands into his pockets, shrugged his thick shoulders. "That's too bad. We really need you, particularly right now. Your political routines were always your best."

I nodded. "So I've heard." There was an uncomfortable moment of silence. "So . . . what did you think of the debates last night?" I said, just to be saying something.

Ivan laughed. "The asshole's got my vote." He pulled his hand out of his pocket and showed me a small pinback button that read: "Are You Tired Of Voting For The *Lesser* Of Two Evils?" "Can you believe it? This was made by some *anti*-asshole group. Makes me want to vote for the asshole even more—not because I agree with everything he says. Sometimes I don't know *what* he's talking about. Nah, I'm gonna vote for him just because it would be pretty god damn fucked-up if he won. How about you? Who're you voting for?"

"Heather and I aren't very interested in politics," I said. "Not anymore."

"Hell, that's all you used to talk about. Remember the '96 campaign? That's when you first started out. You were just some prepubescent kid. Remember? You said that Bob Dole and Jack Kemp should change their names to Bob Dope and Jack Hemp if they wanted to win votes in California." Ivan chuckled. "That's the first joke I ever heard you tell."

"Then it must've been funny, I guess."

"Is everything okay with you?"

"I don't know. I feel as if I'm coming down with a cold. Have you ever had memories of the future?"

"Uh . . . no, can't say that I have. Why?"

"I don't know," I whispered, "I don't know."

CHAPTER 43

Vipers

(October 10, 2016)

Someone snuck into the Viper Room on Sunset Blvd. on a busy Saturday night and dumped vipers onto the dance floor.

Real ones.

Live ones.

CHAPTER 44

The Society of the Spectacle

(October 18, 2016)

One afternoon I looked up the name Guy Debord in the central library downtown. I found a book by him, or at least by someone with that same name. It was called *The Society of the Spectacle*. I opened the book randomly and found this passage staring up at me:

> In a society where no one is any longer recognizable by anyone else, each individual is necessarily unable to recognize his own reality. Here ideology is at home; here separation has built its world.

I felt another migraine coming on. I put the book back on the shelf and returned to the apartment to watch television with Heather.

The new *Hoarders* was on tonight.

CHAPTER 45

Xenu

(October 26, 2016)

Someone broke into the Scientology Celebrity Center in Los Feliz and spray painted the words XENU WAS A GAY PSYCHOLOGIST on the twenty-foot-high bronze bust of L. Ron Hubbard. The letters were so large they covered Hubbard's entire forehead.

CHAPTER 46

Ghosting

(October 30, 2016)

On the way home from work, while waiting for the train, I heard two men talking to each other. One man was white and dressed in an expensive black business suit. The other man was Japanese and dressed in an equally respectable manner. Both had briefcases sitting by their polished leather shoes like motionless, trained pets.

"But you're throwing your vote away," the Japanese man said. "If you want to make a difference you've got to vote for someone who can win."

"I'm tired of that excuse," the white man said. "Is that the big difference between us and . . . and . . . and Stalinist Russia? In a dictatorship you get one choice. In a democracy you get *two* choices. C'mon, man. Wake up. Sometimes I think the terrorists are right. I mean, sometimes I feel like picking up a bomb and—"

The Japanese man sniffed the liquid inside his flask. I could hear it sloshing around inside. "Careful now. I'm just saying, voting for that nutcase—"

The white man cut him off with a wave of his hand. "I've made up my mind. I'd rather throw my vote away than give it to the lesser of two evils."

"Whatever. People like you are going to push some right-wing crackpot into the White House."

The white man shrugged. "Might be nice for a change. Been years since we had someone in The White House we could really *hate*."

The Japanese man laughed. "I'll drink to that," he said.

And did.

I didn't go straight home that night. I wandered around the neighborhood again until I found myself standing outside the Coffee Bean & Tea Leaf.

Miss Malone's Uncle Sam mural was now a massive block of anonymous white paint surrounded by gray ghosting around the edges—a fruitless effort to make the image blend in with its surroundings. Whoever they'd hired to eradicate the image had failed. Though you couldn't see the cockroach anymore, you could see where it had once been pinned, its insect spore staining the otherwise perfect wall.

I glanced from left to right and behind me. I was alone.

I don't know what made me do it.

I walked across the empty street and bought a can of spray paint from Rite Aid. It was on sale for $2.99. The generic Rite Aid brand was much cheaper than the name brand. I remember feeling proud that I had saved eighty-nine cents. My initial urge was to tell Heather about it, but of course I could never do that.

I wasn't sure I was going to do it, not even as I stood there staring at those vague, gray edges.

I lifted my arm and pressed my index finger on the button, sending the black paint shooting out onto the wall.

I didn't even bother to glance from side to side anymore. I kept going, all my attention focused on trying to create the clearest image possible.

I wanted to make a man, a stick figure chopping off the top of his own one-dimensional skull with a pitifully crude representation of a pair of immense scissors.

It took all my strength to do what a five-year-old could accomplish in less than three minutes. Sweat poured down my forehead and pooled into the crook of my neck and shoulder.

I once saw an interview on TV with Charles Schulz, the creator of Charlie Brown, right before he died of a heart attack. A few years before the interview he had suffered a stroke that left his drawing hand a twitching, spastic mess of flesh that could barely pick up a pen much less draw. But Charlie didn't retire. No . . . instead he would thrust a pen into his fist every morning and use his other hand to guide the fist as steadily as possible, resulting in a Charlie Brown with an imperfect circle for a head, wavy and out of focus . . . and yet still recognizably Charlie Brown. The amount of concentration it took to do this appeared to be enormous.

It took far more concentration for me to draw that one stick figure.

My fist shook, ached, as if it were clawing its way up a jagged, rocky slope instead of just defacing a stranger's private property.

Once the stick figure was done I added six jittery words arcing above his head like a substandard proscenium arch.

YOU BROKE THE RULES AND DIED, read the message.

I wasn't even sure why I wrote the words, or what they meant.

I was an amanuensis (a word I had learned from Ivan on the first night I met him). I was just taking dictation. From whom, I didn't know.

Maybe a ghost.

Maybe *my* ghost.

CHAPTER 47

All Hallow's Eve

(October 31, 2016)

Someone broke into a mosque and left behind a herd of cows wearing pink yarmulkes.

Someone broke into a Catholic church and replaced the bell in the generations-old tower with a giant squid. When the priests found it, the poor thing was gasping its last.

Someone broke into a Jewish temple and spray painted a crude, black and white drawing on the ceiling. According to all reports the drawing was composed of six square panels, almost like a comic book. In the first panel an angry group of cats were spray painting swastikas on the outside of little houses populated by frightened mice wearing yarmulkes; over the course of these six panels both the cats and mice morphed gradually until by the sixth panel an angry group of mice were spray painting Stars of David on the outside of little houses populated by frightened cats wearing turbans.

Someone replaced the fifteen-foot-high stone owl in Bohemian Grove, a private getaway for elite politicians located just outside San Francisco, with a 22-foot-high ceramic statue of a frog dressed in a skintight camouflage suit, like something a deep sea diver would wear.

Someone mailed the sixty-ninth page of several hundred different novels to Joshua Sutler at the Twonky Literary Agency in New York and asked him to rearrange the words into "a transcendent message of spiritual liberation."

Someone mailed a book of dirty jokes to Elliot Greeley's apartment on the 31st of October. Elliot Greeley threw it in the trash without reading it.

CHAPTER 48

Who Cares Who's President?

(November 8, 2016)

By the time the night of Nov. 8th rolled around everyone knew who was going to win. Heather and I began watching the coverage at around six. I couldn't concentrate on it, though. My savings had dwindled to a couple of dollars and I still hadn't found a job. I hadn't yet told Heather. Every morning I left the apartment for some imaginary purpose. I felt like a phantom as I wandered the streets looking for nothing. For memories of the future.

I knew I would have to tell Heather the truth the next morning, and I wasn't looking forward to it at all.

At around 7:30, as we lay in bed staring at the TV, I grabbed the remote and said, "Who cares who's President?" I pressed the OFF button. Heather and I buried ourselves beneath the covers, lost ourselves within each other's bodies.

We didn't hear the news until the next morning.

CHAPTER 49

Acceptance Speech

(November 8, 2016)

On the night of Nov. 8th, just before Miss Malone pushed her way through the cheering crowd during a crucial moment of the President-elect's acceptance speech and ripped open her trench coat revealing a belt filled with six-inch-long gray metal canisters, at the exact second that the bullets from the standard military issue revolvers of the Secret Service shattered the girl's skull into a thousand jagged bloody fragments, I ejaculated inside Heather. It wasn't often that we came simultaneously, but this time we did. She idly slid her hands down my back, from my shoulder blades to my tailbone. Then her eyelids fluttered open. She looked up at me and grinned, that old puckish twinkle in her eyes.

Something I hadn't seen in years.

CHAPTER 50

To Get to the Other Side

(November 9, 2016)

After examining Miss Malone's corpse, the authorities discovered that the suspicious looking metal canisters strapped to her waist did not appear to be plastique or any other form of explosives. X-rays of the canisters revealed a dozen or more coiled plastic snakes, ready to strike. Talk was the Secret Service agents would receive a reward. Maybe several of them.

The next morning, after seeing the gory image played and replayed endlessly on the news, Heather sank into a depression over the girl's needless murder. When I saw her tears—I hadn't seen such a reaction from her in over two years, not even when Marsha called us with the bad news the day after Christmas—I made my decision.

I removed the scrapbook from its hiding place.

I told her everything I could remember about the girl. I told her, all over again, about how I met her, this time in exacting detail. And for the first time I told her about the conversation we had outside her mother's home. Heather listened intently while studying each page of the book. After I was done she said, "It's good you didn't report her."

"But . . . why?" I said. "I mean, if I'd turned her in that night she might still be alive. There's so much more she could've accomplished. I mean, fuck, to end up like *this*? It's just stupid. What a god damn waste." Heather didn't respond. She just kept flipping through the scrapbook and staring—particularly at the photographs I'd taken of all those murals.

"Listen," I said, "I don't really know if she was responsible for every news story in there. I mean, how is that even possible?"

Heather nodded solemnly while pointing her index finger at me (a gesture she knew I hated): "How deep is Miss Malone's Axis of Evil buried in the fragile loam of our Republic?"

I cocked my head to one side, confused. I had the faint notion that Heather didn't mean exactly what she was saying. There was a word for that, but I couldn't quite think of it, not right now. I chose to ignore her question and countered with one of my own: "Why the fuck did she *do* it?"

Heather eyes widened as she said softly, "To get to the other side?"

For a moment we just stared at each other.

Then we began to laugh.

After the sun had set, as the news broadcasts aired specials about the peculiar psychology of the deceased would-be-terrorist, Heather and I visited the Rite Aid across from the Coffee Bean & Tea Leaf where I first saw Miss Malone.

We strolled through the antiseptic, brightly-lit aisles, hand-in-hand, and with great calmness approached the shelf where the spray paint cans were stacked in precise, grid-like fashion. We bought the generic kind. Nothing fancy.

We walked the night streets, which were oddly humid for November—it felt more like summer, or what summer used to be like before all that bovine methane started eating away at the ozone layer—and found a spot that we liked.

We worked all night, worked like we haven't worked in years.

By the time the sun was rising over the city, a primitive new mural had arrived to beautify the front of Prospero's. Those infamously gaudy, green velvet-lined double doors were now unrecognizable.

Ivan had asked us to go back to work for him, so we had . . . just not in the way he would've wanted.

Our new routine didn't require a stage or a microphone. Comedy isn't just words, syllables, phonemes. It's not just parking meters and airplane food and bad weather and tired punchlines. It's seeing what no one else sees and saying what no one else wants to say.

It's the crude picture of a dozen or more plastic snakes erupting out of a dead girl's chest.

THE END

ACKNOWLEDGEMENTS

I'd like to take a moment to acknowledge the assistance of the following co-conspirators:

Andrew Long, for helping me give birth to a coke whore; Suzanne Greenberg, for her thorough critiques of the initial chapters; Ray Zepeda, for publishing Chapter One in *The Chiron Review*; Phillip Sipiora, for publishing Chapter Eight in *The Mailer Review*; Eric A. Johnson, for his invaluable critique of an early version of the manuscript; Chris Doyle, for his much needed legal advice and *Prisoner*-related percepts; Eric Blair, for last minute proofreading; Jeremy Lassen, for a fine editing job; Cory Allyn, for being a mensch; Catherine Bottolfson McCallum, for reading several different versions of the novel as it evolved sideways over time; the late Mike Webber, for "In This Room" and the strange, impromptu bedroom tour; Damien Watts, for the unforgettable, indispensable jabberwocky; Gary D. Rhodes, for being a constant source of inspiration; all my fellow inmates of CW96; Jack Womack, for going above and beyond the call of duty; Pat Cadigan, for being Pat Cadigan; everyone enrolled in the CSULB MFA Program (2001 to 2003); Steve Cooper, for general bouts of encouragement; Eileen Klink, for staving off Homeland Security agents when necessary; Melissa Guffey, for nearly everything; and Olivia Guffey, for everything else.

Robert Guffey is a lecturer in the Department of English at California State University, Long Beach. His previous book is *Chameleo: A Strange but True Story of Invisible Spies, Heroin Addiction, and Homeland Security* (OR Books, 2015), which *Flavorwire* has called, "By many miles, the weirdest and funniest book of 2015." A graduate of the famed Clarion Writers Workshop in Seattle, he has also written a collection of novellas entitled *Spies & Saucers* (PS Publishing, 2014). His first book of nonfiction, *Cryptoscatology: Conspiracy Theory as Art Form*, was published in 2012. He's written stories for numerous magazines and anthologies, among them *Catastrophia, The Chiron Review, The Mailer Review, Pearl, Phantom Drift, Postscripts,* and *The Third Alternative. Until the Last Dog Dies* is his first novel.